Richard Westmacott

Handbook of Sculpture

SALZWASSER
VERLAG

Richard Westmacott

Handbook of Sculpture

Reprint of the original, first published in 1864.

1st Edition 2022 | ISBN: 978-3-75259-209-2

Verlag (Publisher): Salzwasser Verlag GmbH, Zeilweg 44, 60439 Frankfurt, Deutschland
Vertretungsberechtigt (Authorized to represent): E. Roepke, Zeilweg 44, 60439 Frankfurt, Deutschland
Druck (Print): Books on Demand GmbH, In de Tarpen 42, 22848 Norderstedt, Deutschland

HANDBOOK

OF

SCULPTURE

ANCIENT AND MODERN

BY

RICHARD WESTMACOTT, R.A., F.R.S.

ADAPTED FROM THE ESSAY CONTRIBUTED TO
THE ENCYCLOPÆDIA BRITANNICA

EDINBURGH

1864.

PREFACE.

THE chief object in reprinting the following pages is to supply a want that has been felt by students in sculpture who have desired to know something more of their art than the merely technical processes to be learnt in academies, schools, or the workshops of sculptors. The writer remembers when he would have been glad to know where to find some elementary work that would afford information upon the history of the art, and give a greater interest to its practice, by shewing its rise and condition in ancient times, and especially pointing out the steps by which it reached the eminence it attained among the Greeks. No such work in English was in existence. Though there are numerous publications relating to art, there is no work in our language that supplies, in a compact form, useful information upon the history, the principles, and the practice of sculpture. The greater part of the treatises in which this art is referred to are of large size, and are too costly for beginners commencing their studies to be able to possess them; and although there are some few descriptive works in English, by far the majority, and the most valuable, are in foreign languages. It happens, too, that such works usually relate to subjects of archæological rather than artistic interest. They are for the most part by learned antiquaries and scholars, who refer to sculpture incidentally rather than directly, and who, it may be said without disrespect or disparagement, are not usually conversant with such particulars of practice as are useful to students, or that the professed sculptor desires and requires to see authoritatively discussed.

Another circumstance that must affect the general usefulness of such works to students, is, that they are confined to the ancient sculpture of the Greeks and Romans. They take no account of modern practice; while the few separate publications which refer to the sculpture of the revival and later schools, give no adequate account of ancient art.

The present publication only professes to be a compilation from more extensive works. It is therefore, necessarily little more than a sketch, though it is made as comprehensive as is compatible with its purpose.

In the hope of giving further value to the work, the writer has occasionally added critical and practical remarks upon the characteristics of the various schools, in order to assist students in estimating the monuments left by the great masters of sculpture; and to show them, on one hand, the source of the excellence of the Greeks, and on the other, the causes of the decline and decay of sculpture, when the true principles upon which art should be practised were neglected and ignored.

It would have been easy to multiply the quotations from and references to various works, ancient and modern, which have been consulted while preparing this essay. But the accumulation of passages from the works referred to would have greatly increased the size of the volume, and this would have defeated the main purpose of its publication. The authorities have therefore only been given when it has appeared absolutely necessary; and here they are only briefly noted, chiefly for the convenience of the more curious and learned reader, who may desire to refer to the original sources to verify the statements, or to acquire a still further acquaintance with the subjects under review. The writer gratefully acknowledges his own obligations to the numerous authors he has had access to. To state the names of all these, and the titles of their works, is scarcely necessary; but it is just to them, and may be useful to students, to point out to the latter the advantages they may derive from carefully reading some of the essays especially referred to, relating to particular objects which have engaged the attention of the respective authors. Many of these are of recent date, and are well worthy the attention of artists. Where so large a portion of the sculptor's time must be devoted to the practice of his art, it will be sufficient to suggest to him, as has been done in the foot-notes, the most easily accessible and most useful works which treat of sculpture throughout its long and eventful history.

In rendering this essay, originally written for the Encyclopædia Britannica, fitted for separate reading, it has been found desirable to add to some portions of the article published in that work. Many passages required fuller illustration than could be given them in a treatise so compressed; and the opportunity has now been seized to explain many details of ancient practice that could only there be referred to in a general way. The subject of Polychromy has been considered at some length; and as the writer differs entirely from the few admirers of that practice, and especially in their wish to see it introduced in modern English sculpture, he has thought it but fair to give, succinctly, all the authorities and arguments he could find for and against so novel a proposition. Admiring or disapproving the addition of colour to sculpture may be a mere matter of fancy, or perhaps taste, in the present day; and he wishes it to be understood, that a difference of opinion on this point is quite compatible with the highest respect for the talents and preferences of those who may entertain views with which he cannot sympathize. His own objections are not confined to the mere technical question. Recognising the moral influence art is capable of exercising, he cannot but feel that if so meretricious an accompaniment to sculpture as flesh tints should become popular, it must inevitably lead to a preference of a class of *subjects* that would tend to lower the character of this art; easily rendering it an instrument of corruption, rather than the means of refining and elevating the taste of a people.

In conclusion, the writer will only say, he has not undertaken this work in a spirit of presumption or conceit. His object is to be useful to students; and as he has had leisure, since retiring from the practice of art, to collect and arrange the notes made during many years, abroad and at home, it has been a pleasing occupation to him to endeavour to assist in pioneering the way for others, more competent than himself, to complete the design which is here only partially attempted.

LONDON, 1864.

PART I.

SECTION I.

SCULPTURE is the art of cutting or carving any substance into a proposed form. In its strict sense it is confined to carving, from the Latin *sculpto*, to cut or carve out; but in the fine arts it is generally applied to the art itself and its products, where the imitation of objects is effected by giving their real appearance by *form*, and not, as in drawing and painting, by lines and colour. The various processes by which this is produced are—carving proper; modelling or the plastic art; ordinary casting and moulding; founding or metal-casting; and gem-engraving. The Greeks, the greatest masters of this art, employed various terms to distinguish the operations of the sculptor. The above Latin derivative, though used in so general a sense, expresses but one of these. It is called the glyptic art, from *γλύφω*, to carve or excavate; the plastic art, from *πλάσσω*, to represent or simulate; and toreutic art (*cælatura*, Lat.), from *τορεύω*, to scrape or chase, or, as some have thought, to turn, as in a lathe. Toreutic appears to have been exclusively applied to works in which the

1. *Definitions.*

employment of metal entered. A distinction appears to have been made by Roman writers between the artist who produced carved works, in whatever material, and the artist in metal works. The first was called *sculptor* or *scalptor*, one who used the chisel; the latter *statuarius.*

Carving, it need scarcely be said, is simply the art of cutting any comparatively hard material by means of the best adapted instruments, as chisels, gouges, files, etc., into the form required.

Modelling is practised upon soft and yielding substances, as clay or wax, which are formed into the desired shape by the hand and different kinds of modelling tools, generally made of boxwood or ivory.

Casting is the art of reproducing form out of a *matrix* or mould. It is effected by pouring any material capable of being dissolved and of again becoming consistent and hardened, into a shape or mould adapted for the purpose, and then withdrawing the substance after it has taken the form contained in the mould. The ductility of the material may be produced by mixture with liquids, as plaster of Paris with water; or by the action of heat, as in the case of wax, and especially of all kinds of metals. The latter is usually designated *founding,* to distinguish it from the simpler process.

Another mode of executing works that come under the general denomination of sculpture is *hammer-work* (σφυρήλατον, from σφῦρα, a hammer). Here the representation of the object was effected by beating the metal into the desired form. There were peculiarities in the manner of doing this in ancient times, which will be more fully described hereafter.

2. Materials.

The materials which have been employed at all times in the various branches of this art are infinite. For modelling, clay, stucco, plaster, and wax were used. Works of great antiquity formed of these substances are still preserved in the different museums of art. Models in clay were dried and then baked in an oven, by which they became as hard as stone, and were very durable, as they were unaffected by atmospheric changes. Moulds were then made, by a similar process, into which soft clay could be pressed, and objects were thus multiplied with facility. Clay thus treated is called *terra-cotta.* The ancients must have used it extensively, as may be seen from the countless number of figures and reliefs, lamps, architectural ornaments, vases, domestic utensils, stamps, and other objects, which are preserved in museums and similar collections. Usually such works are of small size; but there are some statues in the museum at Naples which prove it was also used for statues of large dimensions. There are two figures there, especially deserving attention, of Jupiter and of Juno, full life-size; also two others about four feet high, with masks, representing an actor and an actress, which probably formed the decoration of a theatre. The specimens in England of ancient *terra-cottas* are for the most part of small size. They are chiefly reliefs. Some of those in the British Museum are, however, extremely interesting, both for subject and execution. As such works were usually, if not always designed for architectural decoration, it is probable they were more or less painted. From the numerous examples that exist, where colour is found, they seem in the first place to have been washed with a thin coating of white stucco, and the colour was then laid on with a brush, the preservation of the original surface evidently not being considered of any great importance. The employment of wax for modelling and casting is very ancient. It is recorded that many Roman families of distinction preserved the statues and busts of their ancestors, which, on particular occasions, as at certain festivals or ceremonies, were carried in procession. Being so portable, it is probable they were made of comparatively light materials. Pliny* alludes to this employment of figures of wax, and says they were sometimes dressed in real drapery. Plaster or stucco is constantly found in the ornamental parts of ancient buildings. In the ruins of Pompeii there were, some few years ago, two stucco *bassi-rilievi* of considerable size and of elegant design, in panels on the outer

* Hist. Nat. xxxv. 2.

walls of a small temple in the court of the temple of Isis. The material was extremely hard, and the colour a creamy white. In the British Museum are several specimens of the *stucco*-work of the ancients, both in figures and ornament. They exhibit great delicacy and sharpness of execution.

Every substance that could by possibility be used for carved works has been employed by sculptors. Among the Egyptians especially the hardest were preferred, as basalt, porphyry, and granite, though they also worked extensively in other materials. Marble, various kinds of alabaster, stone, ivory, bone, and wood of all kinds, were used according to circumstances. The variety of marbles both found and recorded is almost infinite. Pliny* supplies an interesting catalogue of those most generally employed in ancient times. The chief Greek marbles were the Parian and the Pentelic. The former was found in the island of Paros, whence its general name; but it is also alluded to as the marble of Marpessus, from the particular mountain where it abounded. Its colour is a warm or creamy white; and it is remarkable for a sparkling quality in its crystals, from which it is supposed it received its epithet of *lychneum*. The Pentelic marble came from Mount Pentelicus, in the neighbourhood of Athens. Its colour also is white,

* Hist. Nat. xxxvi. 7; and see also the authorities collected by Fr. Junius, "De Pict. Vet." lib. iii., c. 11.

but it often has blue or gray, and even light green streaks running through it, which give it a cold tone compared with the Parian marble. The ancients also much esteemed a marble procured from Mount Hymettus in Attica. It bore in many respects a close resemblance to the Pentelic. A great quantity of this marble was imported into Italy after the conquest of Greece by the Romans. A marble of Thasos was also much used, but more for architecture than for sculpture. It was in this way employed for baths, fish-ponds, and for encasing buildings.

Italy produces marble of a very fine quality. That spoken of as the marble of Luni* was procured from the range of mountains near which are situated the modern towns of Massa and Carrara. It does not appear that it was known, or its quarries worked, before the time of Julius Cæsar, in the century before the birth of Christ. Remains of the former working in the quarries of Luni may still be traced; and it is thought the material found here was of a somewhat finer texture than the more modern produce. In many respects the Italian is superior to the Parian and Pentelic marbles. The grain of the Carrara marble is much closer and finer than that of Greece, and its general colour is a rich white. It must, however, be admitted that the Carrara marble, now so generally used by sculptors, is not often found quite

* Marmor Lunense. See Pliny, Hist. Nat. xxxv. 5, 6.

pure in very large blocks. Veins and spots of gray and blue-black, and red and yellow streaks (the latter probably oxides of iron), occur in it, and the quality or texture of the material varies also in different parts of the quarries. Occasionally large crystals are found which resist the chisel. The Romans formerly procured a white marble from some quarries they worked in Africa. Marble is no longer procured, as a rule, from Greece, though occasionally blocks of it are used. This, however, is exceptional, and the only supply for general purposes of sculpture, in modern times, is from the above-named source, the mountain quarries in the former duchy of Massa and Carrara on the west coast of Italy. Though the subject is by no means exhausted, enough has been said to give a general idea of the extensive use of marble by the sculptors of antiquity.

Among the varieties of wood used by the ancients for sculpture, the oak, cypress, cedar, box, sycamore, pine, fig, the vine, and ebony occur. Pausanias mentions, in his Travels in Greece, numerous statues made of wood (ξόανα). This to us apparently humble material seems to have been employed for statues of the most elevated personages. The above writer mentions, among several, those of Apollo Archegetes and of Diana Limnitis, which were of ebony. The statues of Castor and Pollux, with those of their children and of their mothers, in the temple dedicated to Castor and Pollux at Argos, were also made of this material. At Lacedæmon was a statue of Venus of cedar. In the treasury of the Sirgonians, at Altis, was a statue of Apollo made of box. Pliny* especially mentions cypress, cedar, ebony, and box, for their capability of resisting the effects of time; and he says cedar was on this account preferred for images of the gods. Yet all these works have perished, notwithstanding the anticipation of their everlasting durability, in the bold expression of Pliny, "*materiæ ipsæ æternitas.*" Figures of the kind, usually of small dimensions, have constantly been found in Egypt, preserved in the most ancient tombs; but there also are examples of Egyptian statues on a larger scale, and even of life-size, made of wood. In the Egyptian gallery of the British Museum are some interesting specimens of great antiquity, showing that this material was thus employed in very early times. The wood of which they are made is usually sycamore.

All materials that could be applied to the purpose were employed for casting. For the common kind, wax, plaster, and stucco, were extensively used, and for metal-work (founding), gold, silver, copper, tin, and their various compounds. The composition which was so extensively used by the ancients for statues—called by the Greeks *chalcos* (χαλκός), the Romans *æs*, and the moderns *bronze*, from the Italian *bronzo*, a name derived from its colour,

* Hist. Nat. xvi. 40.

a rich brown—is a mixture of copper and tin, with, sometimes, small portions of other metals. The composition of this material, so extensively used by the artists of antiquity, appears to have been a subject of the greatest care. The mere list of titles of the different kinds of bronze known to and used by the ancients is astonishing from its extent, and the refinements it suggests in their practice. A few of the most important only need be mentioned to show the student how profoundly all subjects connected with their art were considered by the great masters of sculpture. There were even rival schools for its preparation. Pliny especially records those of Ægina and Delos; and says* the highest honour was given to the Delian and the next to the Æginetan bronze. It has been supposed from a passage in Plutarch that this famous bronze of Delos was of a pale colour; but it appears that in the time of this writer the secret of its composition was unknown. Pliny† says there was rivalry between two of the greatest sculptors of the best period of the art in the material each employed.‡ Myron used the bronze of Delos, Polycletus that of Ægina. Besides these more especially celebrated bronzes of Delos and Ægina, there were at least three, if not more varieties of the Corinthian. That which was called *æs candidum* is supposed to have had a por-

* Hist. Nat. xxxiv. † *Ibid*, xxxiv. 2.

‡ Emulatio autem et in materia fuit.

tion of silver mixed with it, which gave it a white or light tint. There was also the famous *æs Corinthium*, which, it was pretended, was accidentally produced by the melting and running together of various metals (especially gold and bronze), at the burning of Corinth by L. Mummius, about 146 B.C. The mention of works in this highly valued material, by artists who lived prior to this catastrophe, shews, however, that there is some error in this account. It is clear that the bronzes of Corinth enjoyed a very high celebrity, and that they possessed some remarkable excellence. Pliny refers to the Corinthian alloys, and particularizes one which had a peculiar yellow tint, from the introduction of a considerable quantity of gold. Another, he says, was composed of an equal quantity of different metals, but he does not state what metals. Another bronze that is recorded is called *æs Demonnesium;* another *æs nigrum*, or black. What the Demonnesian mixture was, there are now no means of learning. Pausanius* mentions *Tartessian bronze* (Ταρτήσσιος χαλκός), as being very celebrated, but gives no particulars as to its colour or composition. There can be no doubt, from all this testimony, that the ancients had bronzes, or metal alloys, of a great variety of ingredients, and especially of colour. There is one called *æs Hepatizon*, supposed to be derived from the Greek word signifying the liver. It probably resembled the brown or true

* Lib. vi.

bronze colour of the *cinque cento* works. This epithet, and the terms *candidum* (white) and *nigrum* (black), place this fact beyond question. It is, however, very remarkable, that no monuments have reached us which throw any light upon this curious subject. The composition of what is now known as bronze, an alloy of tin with copper, gives, on analysis, very nearly the same results in all the examples which have been subjected to examination. From 10 to 12 parts of tin occur in 100 parts,* the remainder being copper. Sometimes very minute portions of other metals, as silver, have been discovered, but in so small a quantity that their occurrence, not being sufficient to produce any appreciable effect, has been considered purely accidental.

Bronze has been found of such extremely ancient date, that its composition must have been known at a period long prior to the existence of any certain history of the arts of metallurgy. Tin, so necessary in the composition of bronze, is not found in all countries. The great traders in this material, at a very early date, were the Phœnicians, and it is recorded that they procured it in considerable quantities from the *Cassiterides*, now

* It may not be altogether needless to observe here that writers on art often confuse the terms *bronze* and *brass* in speaking of metal statues. The former, as has been shewn, is quite a conventional term, derived from a modern Italian word having no reference to the material; but they are distinct compositions. The essential difference consists in one, the bronze, being a mixture of copper and tin; the other, brass, of copper and zinc.

generally understood to indicate the Scilly Islands and coast of Cornwall. The intercourse of the Phœnicians with this country for commercial purposes, at so remote a date, is a very curious fact, especially when it is remembered how little knowledge the ancients had of Britain even in periods much later and much more civilized. It has been inferred from this, that in order to secure a monopoly of this trade, the Phœnicians studiously concealed their discovery of, and their commercial dealings with, the coast of Britain. Tin is found in some parts of India. Bronze was used by the ancient Greeks for offensive and defensive weapons and armour, till, in subsequent times, the processes of tempering steel and of making iron malleable were understood.

Before entirely quitting the subject of materials used for metal-casting among the ancients, it may be well to allude to a composition mentioned by Pliny as *aurichalcum*, written also *orichalcum*. Some writers have supposed this to have been a mixture of gold and bronze, or of gold and copper. The latter, alone, is not probable. It is possible that there may have been a mixture so called, but it is much more likely that the true meaning of the word is *mountain-metal*,* and that some particular locality produced a favourite or peculiar quality of metal. The passage alluded to in Pliny suggests this solution, for he says distinctly it (that is, this metal) was not met

* From ὄρος, *a mountain*.

with in his time, the mines which produced it being exhausted. One other mixture may be mentioned before the subject of materials for *casting* is altogether dismissed. It was called *electrum*, and was composed of gold and silver in certain proportions. Helen is said to have dedicated, in the temple of Minerva at Lindus, a cup made of *electrum*, of the exact size and form of one of her own breasts—"*Mammæ suæ mensura.*" *

Iron, though rare in comparison with other metals—and deriving from this a character of value—was known to and used by the ancients, as is seen in the very oldest writings; but its employment is not referred to in a way to render its consideration of importance in this general sketch of materials used for casting or founding. The rapidity with which this metal is destroyed by oxidation is sufficient to account for the scarcity of examples of works of sculpture executed in it in very remote times; but where it has been possible to exclude the moisture of the atmosphere, iron has been found preserved, as pins and plugs, in many extremely ancient monuments.

3. Mixed Materials and Colours.

The ancients, from what has been said, appear to have had the means of giving a variety of colour to their bronzes. This, of course, must have been in the mass of the metal, and the tint so given must have been uniform over the surface.

* Pliny, Hist. Nat. xxxiii. 23.

Ancient authors allude, however, to some very remarkable effects produced by what they describe as the mixture or fusion of metals on portions only of the figure, by which the complexion of the countenance, under emotion or passion, could be given. In some, it is said, the mantling blush of modesty or of shame was expressed, in others the pallor of approaching death and similar delicate changes of colour. These accounts, so far as they assert that these expressive and *partial* local tints were produced by any possible *fusion* of metals in the furnace or melting-pot, are not deserving of credit; but as indirect testimony to the ancient practice of colouring sculpture, they are of great interest. The Egyptians, according to Pliny, coloured their bronze statues after they were cast: a very likely practice and an extremely easy process; and the Greeks may have done, and no doubt did the same. Among primitive and barbarous nations the introduction of varied materials and of gay and brilliant colours is universally met with in their idol sculpture. It might cause surprise to find the same custom prevailing among the more refined Greeks, in particular cases, even after their art had reached its highest perfection, if it were not known that anciently certain forms of art were prescriptive; and that especially in all works connected with religion (and it may be said almost all early sculpture was, directly or indirectly, so applied) the artists were bound by established regulations, strictly enforced by the priests, and submitted to, from long usage and devotional feeling, by the community. The subject of *Polychromy,* or of colouring sculpture, will, however, necessarily require careful consideration at a more advanced stage of the history of the art, when the whole subject will receive the attention it deserves.

It will be sufficient to state generally, that the enrichment or decoration of statues by the employment of a variety of materials in the same work, was by no means unusual. Many examples occur of the introduction of foreign substances, either metal, precious stones, glass, or paste, in statues and busts of the best period of Greek sculpture. The practice is not limited to the eyes, but instances occur of the lips being thus inlaid. There are examples of it in the fine collection of bronzes in the Museo Borbonico at Naples, and instances may also be seen of it in the national collection in the British Museum. A small silver statue of an Egyptian king or deity has the dress ornamented with gold; and a bronze faun bears a leopard skin marked with silver spots; another has silver appendages. There are instances of inscriptions, in a different metal from the statue, being inserted into the figure itself. Cicero* speaks of an Apollo inscribed thus, with the name of its author, Myron, in very small silver letters. There is a bronze statue in the Musée in Paris of a youth, on the

* Or. in Ver. iv.

left foot of which are the remains of two Greek words (ΑΘΑΝΑΙΑ. ΔΕΚΑΤΑΝ.) in silver letters.

Before quitting this branch of the subject, referring to combinations and mixtures of materials, it may be right to notice that, when different kinds of stone or marble were used in the same work, it was called *polylithic* sculpture; to distinguish it from sculpture in one kind of marble, which was called *monolithic.** Marble and bronze and wood were occasionally used in these combinations; the heads, and hands, and other portions of the figures being given in the nobler materials, and the drapery and accessories in the less costly. Pausanias mentions several of these as existing in his time.

Statues were not only made of the above-named materials, but occasionally of others which would seem to be but little adapted to the purpose. There was a statue of Augustus of amber. Statues were also sometimes made of gum and aromatic substances, as well as of others of a combustible nature, to be used on particular occasions. Even hay is mentioned. At the celebration of *Funeralia,* as at those in honour of Sylla, statues of this material were used, no doubt to be burnt on the funeral pile. Sometimes strange and childish conceits were illustrated in these performances. There is mention, by the same authority, of a statue of Venus,

* From πολύς *many,* and λίθος *a stone,* and μόνος *only* or *single,* with the noun.

the fascinating goddess of beauty and love, made of loadstone, which attracted to it a figure of Mars made of iron. These are only alluded to here in illustration of the great variety and extent of the materials which were, of old, employed for figure-making. As works of art these performances were in all probability of a very inferior quality, being produced only for a temporary purpose.

It may now be proper to describe briefly the different modes of practice employed by sculptors, and the terms used to express them. *First*, there is the representation of insulated objects, whether in single figures or groups. As these may be seen entire, or all round, like the statue of the Belvedere Apollo, or the well-known statues of the Fighting and Dying Gladiators, or the group of the Hæmon and Antigone, or of Laocoon and his sons, such works are technically called "in the round." *Secondly*, when objects or figures are attached to a background; and they are then called "in relief." The different degrees of relief are defined by modern writers and artists by the expressions *alto* or high relief, and *basso* or low relief; and the Italians have introduced the term, *mezzo-rilievo*, which is intended to describe something between the two extremes. But nothing very definite is expressed by this middle term, and it is sufficient to remark that, however slightly a figure may be attached to a plane behind it,

4. *Modes of Representation.*

the mere fact of its touching it in any part constitutes it a work in *relief*. There is a peculiar mode of working in relief, which is chiefly met with in Egyptian sculpture. The design is sunk or hollowed slightly into or below the surface of the ground, and the figure is then formed and rounded on the principle of a very flat relief. Of course, in this mode of execution there is no projecting part above the original plane of the material. It is, in fact, a kind of relieved *intaglio;* but, unlike works in legitimate *intaglio,* the forms are correctly raised or rounded within the limits described. In *intaglio* all the sinkings are inwards, as is seen in seal engraving, and have not their true appearance till an impression of them is taken. The work described is simply an extremely low *rilievo* within, or surrounded by a plane, no part of which is higher than the most rounded portions of the sunk sculpture. This style of execution lends itself very advantageously to internal decoration, its effect being extremely delicate, from the harmonious distribution of light and shadow which is insured by such a mode of treating the parts, while the sharp outline satisfactorily defines the design. Another variety to be noticed, of a peculiarly low or flat style of relief, is that called *stiacciato* by the Italians. It was chiefly employed by Donatello and his imitators. Here the object represented is above or upon a ground, but the raised portion is much pressed or flattened, and the parts or drapery that are intended to show as projections have, in fact, little more real relief than a drawing.

The Greeks appear to have used the word *anaglypta* as a general term to denote sculpture in relief, though, according to Pliny, *ectypa sculptura* also means relieved work. Some writers have supposed that the *toreutic* art, before alluded to, meant relieved sculpture, but this may be questioned, for though toreutic art may be relieved, the technical term corresponds to the *cœlatura* of the Romans, and it signifies *chasing*, which is an operation, and not strictly a class of art.

As it is proposed here only to supply a concise and general history of sculpture, any extended remarks upon particular branches of execution would scarcely be considered as coming strictly within the prescribed limits. At the same time, some excuse may be found for dwelling upon this peculiar exercise of the art, for among the remains that time has spared us of Greek sculpture there are none, if any, of greater value, as examples of art-excellence, or of more interest in subject and in their applicability as architectural accessories, than the ancient *rilievi*. The great masters have here exercised their genius and skill upon every variety of treatment that site and circumstance required; and modern sculptors can have no surer guides, as canons of art, for their own practice, than are afforded by the ancient monuments of this class that have been preserved. In describing the sculptures of the Parthenon at Athens, of the temples of Ægina and Phigaleia, of the Mausoleum at Halicarnassus, as well as other remarkable works, of which, fortunately, we have the originals in England, especial notice will be taken of the peculiar excellence which each of these exhibits. In this place, it is only desirable clearly to point out, for the instruction and direction of those who really desire to comprehend the beauty of the highest styles of sculpture, the general principles upon which the ancients appear to have conducted this especial and popular class of design.

The condition necessary, then, for a work in sculpture being considered in relief, or in *rilievo*, is, that it should have, and be attached to, a ground behind it. Whether the relief be so bold as, like the Metopes of the Parthenon, to make the figures almost entire, or whether it be as flat in treatment and close to the background as it is in the Frieze of the same series of sculptures, the fact of the attachment, in any part or degree, to this ground, constitutes its character.

It is evident that the ancient sculptors considered this background only in the light of a wall, against which the sculpture was to be placed as enrichment, and in no wise as the representation of the open air, as if it were a picture. This mode of treating the subject is founded on perfectly rational and intelligible grounds. As relieved figures must of necessity throw their shadows on the plane immediately behind them, the *solidity* of this surface is at once betrayed, and therefore no fair exercise of the imagination can avail to invest the ground with the character of space. For the same reason, and the consequent absence of air-tint for distance, foreshortening, and attempts at giving perspective effects, landscape, clouds, sunsets, and similar accessories, are never found in relieved sculpture of a fine period or of a high school of art. The limitations by which the ancient sculptors were confined in these respects are consistent with strict common sense, inasmuch as they are regulated by the special possibilities of their art. The fatal consequences of a departure from the rule thus established by these great masters, in the extravagancies exhibited in the fanciful, picturesque sculpture of later schools, especially in the seventeenth century, will be more clearly seen when the works of that time are under consideration. These few observations seem to be necessary here, when the practice of *rilievo* is being referred to, because, in the early as well as in the best periods of the history of sculpture, all the works executed in this mode or manner will be found to be carried out on the sound and intelligible principle above described.

Reference has been made, while speaking of casting, to another mode of working in metal among the ancients, which requires particular notice. This is the hammer-work (σφυρηλατον) and *holosphyraton* (ὁλοσφυρητον),* described by Pliny and others. It was effected by beating lumps of metal, either solidly or in plates, into the proposed form, and fastening the pieces together with pins or keys. Pausanias † alludes to a very ancient Greek work produced in this manner, a statue of Jupiter at Sparta, by Learchus of Rhegium; also another by Onassimedes,‡ of solid metal, as existing at Thebes in his time. Pliny§ mentions a statue of Diana Anaïtis which was worked in the same way; and that there may be no doubt that it was of *solid* hammer-work, he uses two expressions to give emphasis to his statement. The statue was made of gold; and he says it was of greater antiquity than any bronze work executed in the same manner.|| Pliny relates the following anecdote in connection with this remarkable statue: "A veteran of the army that had made spoil of this valuable work was present at a royal banquet, when the emperor happened to ask whether it was true that the person who first dared to commit violence on this figure was deprived of sight, and struck dead? The soldier replied, 'he was that individual, and that Augustus was then feasting off one of the legs of the goddess,' alluding to the gold plate on which the repast was served." The

* From ὅλος, *solid* or *entire*.

† iii. 17, sec. 6.

‡ ix. 12, sec. 3.

§ Hist. Nat. xxxiii. c. 4.

|| "Aurea statua prima nullâ inanitate, et antequam ex ære aliqua illo modo fieret quam (*quem?*) vocant holosphyratum, in templo Anaïtidis posita."

statements of Pliny and of Pausanias, as to the extreme and even primitive antiquity of metal works produced in this way, must be received with some qualification. They can only mean that these particular works were extremely ancient, and probably of the most archaic *style* or type of Greek art. One mode, above alluded to, of executing hammer-work statues was by beating out the metal in thin plates over a core or *nucleus* of wood; and the terms *holosphyraton* and *sphyraton* may have been used to distinguish the solid and the plating processes. There is an interesting specimen of Egyptian work of the kind, bronze on wood, in the British Museum. It is a small head of Osiris, and a portion of the wood is still remaining within the metal.

In the accounts of metal-working in connection with art, almost all the references are made to the practice of the Greeks. It must be obvious, however, that, if so limited, a very inadequate knowledge would thus be gained of the real history of founding. It is well known that long before any authentic notices occur of any acquaintance with this subject among the Greeks, other nations had made great progress in some of the most advanced processes of the art. It will be sufficient to refer to the most ancient parts of the Scriptures, to the poems of Homer and Hesiod, to the accounts of the works carried on by Solomon, and to the discoveries of travellers in Assyria, Egypt, and elsewhere, to prove that a very considerable practice in metallurgy existed from a very remote period. That there may be much truth in the statements respecting the first employment of metal by the Greeks, whether in sculpture or in the manufacture of arms and armour and other works, need not be disputed; but it is scarcely necessary to add that the comparatively late Greek traditions cannot comprehend the whole history of the practice of art; and it is therefore important to point out that the statements of Pliny and Pausanias upon these particular matters must be received with some modification.

In attempting to supply a history of sculpture, it must at once be admitted that the earlier accounts of

5. *Early History.* the practice of the art are so vague and indistinct that but a qualified reliance can be placed on them. The obscurity in which its origin is enveloped throws doubts upon the statements that have reached us, both as to the dates of some of the most archaic monuments, and the sources from which various nations of antiquity derived their art-inspiration. It will be necessary to notice here such particulars as have usually been accepted by historians of art; but as modern discovery and inquiry are constantly opening up new information and *data*, by which usually received opinions are acquiring correction, it will be obvious that many assertions of the older critics and antiquaries must now be taken with considerable qualification. This ap-

plies especially to the origin of schools, than which nothing can be more vague and uncertain. It is not till the history of sculpture is connected with its progress in Greece and Asia Minor that it can be said to have any really reliable foundation; or that sculpture can excite any very great interest as a refined or fine art, however important its existence and practice elsewhere may be upon other grounds. This latter claim to attention is not, of course, to be underrated; but it is to be referred to other considerations, rather than to that interest which attaches to it in connection with the progress and development of a particular branch of æsthetic study which, only by degrees and after long practice, reached the highest perfection of which it was capable. A cursory review of such traditions as exist of the employment of sculpture among the more remote nations, must, however, form a part of a general history of the art.

Various speculations have been offered with respect to the comparative antiquity of sculpture and painting. The story related by Pliny * of the daughter of Dibutades having traced the outline of her lover's profile cast by shadow on the wall, and this outline having been afterwards filled in with clay by her father, would give the priority to drawing; and it seems obvious that drawing must be antecedent to modelling or to carving in *relief*. But it is probable that *insulated* models or

* Hist. Nat. xxxv. 43.

figures were made in the first attempts at imitative art. The above may fairly be considered as simply a Greek poetical invention; and, referring as it does to an artist of comparatively late date, it cannot be taken as authority for the origin of sculpture. There can be little doubt that rude attempts at forming clay or any other plastic substance into defined shapes were amongst the first exercises of the natural imitative faculty of man. The comparatively easy task of copying the real form of an object to representing its partial appearance by lines on a flat surface, suggests the inference that sculpture or modelling in the "round" must have been the earliest mode of imitation.

The attempts of almost all writers on art to trace the origin of sculpture to a common or single source have not led to any satisfactory conclusions. The great antiquity of the art renders it a matter of the utmost difficulty, in the first place, to trace its backward history through the obscurity of ages; but the difficulty is further increased when the question arises whether it is quite reasonable to attribute its origin to any one particular nation or people from which all others must necessarily have derived its practice. The faculty or desire to imitate is instinctive in man; and the earliest nation, therefore, would probably have first exercised this natural tendency. When we come to consider sculpture in the category of fine art, we must seek further for the principles which gave it a distinctive character than in the mere bald fact of a people having imitated objects by form. There can be no doubt that the intercourse of nations had its influence on the, so called, *style* of any existing art: or, where it was not previously known, that its practice may have been introduced; but the discovery, constantly occurring, of specimens of rude imitative art, of a totally different style and character, in countries that cannot by any apparent possibility have had communication with other nations, proves that primitive forms may have been quite independent of any such intercourse. There is very much to interest and incite scholars and antiquaries in this inquiry; but when the very late date of the oldest ancient writers who refer to sculpture—late, that is, compared with the undoubted remote antiquity of the art—is taken into consideration, there is enough to account for the difficulties they had in collecting any evidence to be relied on upon so intricate a subject; and in the case of modern inquirers who have depended upon these insufficient authorities, this difficulty of course becomes still greater. Where again the ancient writers are Greeks, the strong bias in favour of their country has no doubt led them to lay stress upon every little tradition that could flatter their patriotism. Of this the numerous inventions and works of art attributed to a single Dædalus afford an instance, and shew the limited knowledge that existed of the first artist who is noticed in the annals of Greek sculpture. There can be no question that the progress and improvement of the various useful arts must have been gradual, and due, not to one, but to a series of ingenious inventors. These, however, have all been attributed by the older historians to one individual, who bore a name which, in all probability, was but a general appellation given in early times to any workman or artificer who was remarkable for his skill. In the same manner, the introduction into Italy of the simple art of modelling has been attributed to one Demaratus, a fugitive from Corinth about 600 B.C. He was accompanied, it is said, by two artists, Eucheir and Eugrammus; whose names, it must be confessed, appear to be epithets of skill rather than the simple names of persons.* Again, some ancient images are spoken of as having fallen directly from heaven; shewing, unless this is to be treated in the same way as some similar modern instances of superstitious credulity —intentional frauds to deceive and impose upon the ignorant—how little real historical knowledge existed of the origin of the earliest sculpture. This, however, is not the case at a later period, when the art held a more defined position, and when, fortunately, epochs in its history were clearly marked by those changes in style which enable

* The derivatives εὖ (*well*) and χεὶρ (*a hand*), and εὖ and γράμμα (*writing* or *drawing*), are plainly suggestive of this interpretation.

the archæologist both to classify the various schools and to fix important dates. After noticing cursorily the first rude attempts at mere mechanical and rude imitation, the inquiry into the history of sculpture, as an art having a wider range and nobler purpose, will be found to be a subject of great interest.

The desire to record in some palpable form the memory of extraordinary events and persons, and to hand down to posterity some enduring monument of the great prowess or useful deeds of benefactors, was doubtless the earliest impulse which led to the use of sculpture. The first works applied to these objects were probably of the rudest description, and therefore would scarcely come under the conditions of fine art. Still, from these simple beginnings may probably be traced the development of great results. The oldest histories make mention of what may truly be called *monuments* erected to mark the scene of any remarkable incident. They were composed simply of heaps of stones, and sometimes of blocks of large size; but even these rude forms indicated at a later time ideas of pregnant meaning. A heap of stones was set up at Bethel by Jacob, to mark the spot where he had seen the vision of angels ascending to heaven.* The agreement or covenant entered into between Jacob and Laban was recorded in the same simple way, by a pillar and heap of stones.† A similar monument was built over

* Gen. xxviii. 18.

† Gen. xxxi. 44.

the grave of Rachel; and other instances of the kind might easily be quoted.

It has been said that the history of sculpture is almost the history of idolatry. It is true in part. Religious feeling, no doubt, had much to do with the progress of the art in its more advanced condition; but it is probable that the first defined images or statues were of men and not of abstractions, such as deities or gods; and that human idols, so to speak, preceded those of divinities. As far as can be ascertained, the heavenly bodies were among the earliest objects of worship among the ancient nations; and the symbols that represented them, when palpable images were required, were most likely merely pillars of a conical or pyramidal shape, and not imitations of the human figure. It has been ingeniously supposed* that when such objects or images are referred to in the oldest records as "graven," it is in allusion to the signs (or hieroglyphics) that were inscribed or cut upon them; and some extremely ancient Assyrian monuments, of which there are examples in the British Museum, give strength to this notion. The Sun was worshipped at Emessa under the form of a black conical stone, with marks on it to represent or symbolize that luminary; and Pausanias† mentions that, as late as A.D. 170, certain of the divinities of Greece, which he specifies, were still worshipped

* Landseer, *Sabæan Researches.*

† vii. 22.

under the archaïc symbolic form of mere columns or blocks of stone set upright.

The tradition handed down from generation to generation of feats of arms, of the prowess of a *6. Origin.* warrior, or of the founder of a nation, led, in all probability, to the first attempt at individualizing in some way the hero whose fame was thus repeated from mouth to mouth. Profound respect and the desire to show gratitude for real or supposed benefits, would, in the course of time, lead to the payment of extraordinary honours to the memory of persons so esteemed; and the elevation, in the imagination of the people, of these heroes or public benefactors to a grade above the ordinary class of mortals became the natural course: a promotion the more easy, it must be remembered, when the real existence and individuality of the person so honoured had become somewhat obscured by the lapse of time, and long ages of unchallenged belief in the actions attributed to him had loaded the earlier traditions with fabulous and exaggerated additions.

When to this was added the belief that the subject of this honour, though no longer in this world, could still exercise an influence on the fate of men—could confer benefits or avert evils—the passage to direct worship would easily be made. Thus the admiration of great and noble achievements led, first, to hero-worship; and hero-worship easily led to investing the mortal with the attributes of a supernatural being, and at length to considering him and addressing him as a god. This, there can be little doubt, was the process which occasioned, in the course of time, the vast polytheistic imagery of the ancients, exhibited in the fanciful, and often beautiful, poetical myths of some nations, and, in all, the physical or palpable representations of their divinities.

It is to be noticed that it is not only in the history of the most archaïc peoples that this occurs. There are parallel instances of the proneness of the human mind, at all times, to take much the same course, and to indulge, when under strongly excited religious feeling, in similar superstitions. Gratitude and veneration have here equally expanded into worship and into prayer-offering to deceased fellow-mortals; and here, again, the simple types and representations, probably at first innocently intended only to refresh the memory or to realize to the sense the subject of grateful and affectionate remembrance, have insensibly become the recognised and established objects of a material idolatry.

It would be vain to speculate upon the age or character of art of the earliest sculptured attempts at personal representation alluded to in ancient history. The people were taught to believe that some of these were not even the work of human hands, but had been sent by divine favour direct from heaven—a stretch of credulity that could only have been evoked long after the rude and no doubt hideous images, so strangely accounted for, had been placed in the temples, and had received the homage and the offerings of a simple and imaginative population. It might never occur to an uncultivated people to question the fact of the miracle of a wooden or other image falling from the skies, or the possibility of forms of such monstrous ugliness as is always exhibited in these "heaven-sent" productions, being the performance of the divine ruler of the universe, the author of all that is most beautiful and perfect in creation. A confiding submission to those who exercised the functions of the priesthood, and who directed the devotions and the belief of the community, would therefore effectually restrain any bold inquiry that would seem to suggest doubts as to the truth of the fables so taught. It is sufficient here to know that images were produced as objects claiming the most implicit devotion; and, as images, their existence is to be recognised in the history of sculpture. However inadequately, at first, the purpose was effected, the attempt to produce a personal resemblance at once gives such works a place in imitative art; and from this opening the various phases of the progress of sculpture are to be traced, from the most rude and mechanical experiments of primitive times to the noble position the art subsequently attained when fully developed and exercised under circumstances favourable to its perfection.

SECTION II.

THE oldest record of the existence of objects which it may be assumed were imitative of the human form, is in the sacred writings; and, limited and concise as are these notices, they still afford some curious and valuable information on the earliest practice of *iconic* art. The first intimation found of the existence of sculpture, in connection with idolatrous worship, is among the Chaldeans. Some early Christian writers have stated that Terah, the father of Abraham, made images; but Scripture gives no authority for this assertion. It is, however, recorded that when Rachel, in company with Jacob and Leah, quitted her father's dwelling, she carried away with her certain images upon which Laban appears to have set so much value that he immediately followed her in order to recover them. It is to be regretted that no particulars are furnished as to what these images were like, or of what material they were made. That they must have been small and light is evident from the facility with which Rachel contrived to carry them away unobserved; and also from the way in which she concealed them, when Laban is said to have "searched all the tent, and found them not." Images are also similarly referred to in other places; and especially where Jacob is described as taking the "strange gods" and hiding them under an oak which was by Shechem.* In the book of Joshua,† also, allusion is made to the corruption of the Israelites by the superstitions of the people among whom they had so long dwelt; and after the Exodus they are most solemnly warned against this influence, and exhorted to return to a more pure and simple form of worship.

It may be observed here that the earliest known names of sculptors are found in the Old Testament. They are of the artists employed to make the ornamental works for the Tabernacle. One of them was Bezaleel, the son of Uri, who was of the tribe of Judah; the other, Aholiab, the son of Ahisamach, of the tribe of Dan. Their date, therefore, is about fifteen hundred years before the Christian era. No remains of the sculpture of this nation are known to exist; so that no useful speculations can be offered upon the character of their art, nor upon the original sources of their knowledge. That they were considerably advanced in the various branches of practice must be assumed from the accounts handed down to us of some of their performances; and it is plain they must have been acquainted with some of the

* Gen. xxxv. 4.

† Joshua xxiv.

more difficult processes of metallurgy to be able to set up the image of the "molten calf," and to make the "brazen" serpent. No doubt much of their later improvement may be attributed to their intercourse with the Egyptians, but it was improvement upon pre-existing practice.

The influence of this people—the Egyptians—in the more advanced periods of their history, and when they extended their conquests to the north-east of their own country, was, of course, considerable, and will be referred to presently. They introduced important changes of all kinds in the arts and habits of the nations with whom they came in contact, and, no doubt, the intelligence attributed to them made itself felt wherever they penetrated. But they cannot be considered the original teachers of art to the people here referred to, for it seems clear that "image-making" had been practised among the Hebrews prior to any account that exists of their intercourse with Egypt.

The important and interesting discoveries that have been made of late years of remains of some of the most ancient cities of Assyria have opened a wide field of observation to the antiquary, while they have also afforded most valuable examples of the character of Assyrian sculpture. The light these may throw upon the early history of this remarkable nation can scarcely be over-estimated. Hitherto, though the Assyrians—and especially the inhabitants of Babylon and of Nineveh—have been associated in name with some of the most interesting subjects of sacred history, little or nothing was accurately known of them. It is true that certain ancient Greek writers have described the almost fabulous riches and luxury of this people, and the splendour of Babylon itself; but for the most part they supply but vague general assertions, and but few remains of authentic Assyrian art have, till lately, reached modern times to confirm any of their seemingly marvellous statements. The enterprise and intelligence of European travellers have now, however, restored, as it were, this long-lost nation to our knowledge, by bringing to light the well-preserved authentic monuments of their mythological and religious sculpture; while the labours of scholars and philologists give promise of eventually being able to decipher and understand the inscribed language which so thickly covers many of the sculptures that have been recovered.

Herodotus (about 450 B.C.) had an opportunity of personally inspecting some of the wonders of Babylon. He speaks in admiration of the objects that everywhere arrested his attention: of the hundred gates in the walls "all of bronze," and of the temple of Belus, which, he also notices, had bronze gates. He describes a statue of gold which was placed in this temple. The god, he says, was represented seated; and a golden table stood near, and the step or footstool and the throne itself were made of gold. He alludes also to the existence of another statue of *solid* gold, twelve cubits high; but with his usual conscientious reserve, he admits he did not himself see this, but only repeats what he was told. The distinction made in referring to the latter statue as made of *solid* gold, is so far curious as it suggests the probability of the other works which he did see being worked or laid on in plates, as has been described in the process of "hammer-work." Notwithstanding the confidence that generally may be placed in what Herodotus describes from his own experience, considerable allowance must be made for some of the statements founded on what he learnt by hearsay. The vanity of the Babylonians would be excited to astonish a traveller who had come from so great a distance to see their wondrous city; and there can be little doubt that the story he was told of the latter statue (measuring no less than twelve cubits in height), being made entirely of solid gold, was an exaggeration intended to incite his admiration of the riches and grandeur of the nation he was visiting.

It is recorded that Darius, the son of Hystaspes, wished to possess this valuable statue, but, out of respect to the public feeling, did not venture to remove it. His son Xerxes, however, equally rapacious and less scrupulous, boldly seized it, and, it is said, even slew, with his own hand, the priest who attempted to prevent this act of spoliation. Diodorus Siculus refers also to numerous works, shewing the scale of magnificence of the Babylonians in their public monuments, and he pretends to give the names of the various sovereigns of the earliest dynasties under whom the respective works were said to be produced. These details are not, it must be admitted, received by scholars as entirely worthy of confidence; but although much exaggeration may have crept into the account given by Ctesias,* from whom Diodorus professes to have derived his information, there can be no doubt that the most astonishing splendour and luxury prevailed, especially in the gorgeous decoration of their palaces and other public buildings; and from which it may be inferred that the arts of design had been practised by this people for a very long period. From whence the Babylonians derived their first knowledge of art, if it was not indigenous, there are at present no means of judging; and any speculation upon so difficult a subject would exceed the limits to which this history is necessarily confined. But without insisting upon attributing the works mentioned by Diodorus to such a remote date as the earlier Semiramis of Ctesias, or to that still more mythical personage Ninus, there can be no question that

* Ctesias was a physician of Cnidos (about 400 B.C.), who wrote a History of Assyria in twenty-three books. He began with the reign of Ninus, and continued the record to his own time. Diodorus Siculus lived about 40 B.C.

the arts must have existed in Assyria for a long series of years before they could have reached the high condition described by the various writers referred to, and which is now fully attested by the numerous monuments that are extant.

Some curious particulars respecting the practice of the Babylonians in connection with their sculpture, at a later period of their history than that immediately referred to, are furnished in the book of the prophet Baruch. He notices not only the various materials of which their statues were composed, but also the manner in which they were dressed; namely, with real drapery, a custom by no means unusual in very early times. The following extracts are interesting, and throw light on the state of art in that remote part of the world so far back as the seventh century before our era. "Now shall ye see in Babylon *gods of silver*, and of *gold*, and of *wood*, borne upon men's shoulders, which cause the nations to fear;" "they are *gilded* and *laid over with gold;* yet cannot these gods save themselves from rust and moths, though they *be covered with purple raiment;* neither when they were *molten* did they feel it."*

The most remarkable results of the researches of travellers in Assyria are the extensive sculptured monuments, in a species of *gypsum*-marble or alabaster, that have been found in the ruins of the ancient Nineveh

* Baruch, ch. v. vi.

and neighbouring places.* They seem to have been intended to serve the double purpose of dividing and decorating rooms, and as records either of remarkable incidents in the history of the nation, or of the prowess or the personal habits of the sovereign. The most striking objects to be noticed, from their size and character, are some colossal figures in which the human form is represented combined with the animal or brute type. These are evidently mythological personations, in which the union of intelligence with force is intended to be characterised. The grand effect of these gigantic figures is very remarkable ; and standing, as they appear to have done, at the entrance to sacred or royal buildings, they must have produced an awful impression on the spectator. It is to be remarked that, although they are of a peculiarly conventional style of art, they generally exhibit an intimate knowledge of the brute character, both in action and expression. Whether the imitation be of the lion or the bull—the animals which chiefly occur in these larger works—the individuality of each is admirably portrayed. There is also a technical peculiarity which deserves especial remark in the execution or composition of these portal or gate sculptures, which has not hitherto been found in

* The object here being to refer to this sculpture generally, it is unnecessary to particularize the different localities in which various monuments have been fonnd. For these the reader may consult the interesting works by Botta, Layard, and others.

the monuments of any other nation: namely, that the lions and the bulls, as the case may be, have five legs. Each animal is represented with his two fore-legs firmly planted under him. In the front view these are clearly defined, but in the profile, from their parallel position, one is, of course, entirely concealed by the other. To obviate the appearance, in this view, of the animal having but three legs (for of the hind-legs one is slightly advanced before the other), a supplementary fore-leg is added, which can only be seen when the spectator looks at the sculpture sideways or in profile; when all the four legs are clearly defined. These colossal figures are all attached to backgrounds; but the relief is so high, that they have the effect of entire statues. Those that decorated the walls of the apartments represent battles, sieges, armed men scaling walls, figures crossing rivers, lion-hunting, and endless details of the ordinary occupations of the people. In these the most minute circumstances are noticed; and the obvious care bestowed upon the representation gives a value to these records of the past which cannot be too highly appreciated. The vegetation of the country in trees and shrubs is shewn, as well as the various animals in common use; sometimes persons are represented passing through rivers, supported on skins filled with air, while, in the water, fish of different kinds are seen swimming about. In other slabs buildings are being erected, showing all the appliances and implements then used by the artificers. These commonplace objects, with the ornaments on the dresses of people, as well as the rich decoration on the accoutrements of the horses, are all copied with the most marvellous care and accuracy. The finished execution of these works is in itself evidence of most skilful practice in the workmen, and affords convincing proof of long experience.

The mode of treating or representing the human figure in all the works referred to, shews that here, as well as elsewhere, there was a prescribed form established for the guidance of the artist. There is neither variety nor

HEAD.—ASSYRIAN SCULPTURE.

ideality, but all the figures are treated according to a fixed standard. However busy and multitudinous the

composition—whether the actors are engaged in the battle-field, or are seen scaling the enemy's walls, or are employed in the hunting-field, or in the ordinary pursuits of life—the same outline, as of one family or even of one individual, is met with in all the faces. They also have a peculiar expression which, it will be seen, is preserved in all early representations of historical and mythological subjects; namely, that of a complacent smile which lights up the countenance, however seriously or even savagely the person is supposed to be occupied: a curious characteristic of all very ancient sculpture, which will be further exhibited as our history proceeds.

Besides the numerous *rilievi* referred to, other objects procured from these excavations are deposited in the British Museum, which afford the most valuable illustration of the arts and habits of a nation whose history is connected with some of our most interesting reflections. Nineveh, it is well known, was utterly destroyed so early as 606 B.C.; so that in many of these works, allowing for the time necessary for the execution of the latest, we contemplate productions certainly of nearly three thousand years' antiquity, while others are doubtless of a very much older date. Some of the sculptures appear to have been executed at no very long period before the fall of this great city. From the inscriptions which have been deciphered they are thought to represent the history and actions of Esarhaddon, who succeeded his father

Sennacherib (710 B.C.) The latter, the record says, was murdered by Adrammelech and Sharezer, two of his sons, "as he was worshipping in the house of Nisroch, his god." They effected their escape, and "Esarhaddon his son reigned in his stead." Nearly all the slabs bearing reliefs are inscribed with arrow-headed letters or characters in close horizontal lines, which often pass entirely over the figures. The engraving does not, however, materially affect the sculpture in its general effect; and it is obvious that the greatest advantage may be derived from this double mode of recording events, as each may mutually throw light upon the other, and, in time, enable scholars to define the meaning of, and give dates to, the whole series of illustrations.

Among the remains of art brought away from these excavations are many of undoubted Egyptian character. These, as has before been observed, may be considered as quite distinct from the pure or true Babylonian and Nineveh type. That the sculpture and art generally of each people was influenced by their mutual intercourse may be accepted as a very probable and natural consequence; but a careful comparison of the character of form in the earlier works of both these nations seems to exhibit peculiarities which indicate a distinct originality, although, in a certain quaintness or simplicity in the composition of the figures, there may be considerable resemblance between them.

The Assyrian sculptures cannot be put forward as successful works of fine art. They are obviously of a prescribed style and type; and, though some exhibit greater excellence in their execution than others, they belong to a fixed and not a progressive school of art, and any superiority observable in them is entirely of a practical kind. Thus there is little feeling for beauty, no knowledge in the anatomical construction of the figures, nor taste in the arrangement and flow of drapery, or in the composition of extensive groups of figures. Still, with all their deficiencies, it must be admitted they are works of immense interest; and their recovery, after so many ages, is an event of great importance on every account short of art-excellence. Chiefly they claim the attention of the scholar and the antiquary for the light they may throw upon the long-lost history of one of the greatest nations of the earth; but these curious works also suggest some interesting subjects of speculation in connection with art, and especially as regards the indirect influence they may have exercised on the practice of that remarkable people who, long after Babylon and Nineveh had ceased to exist, carried sculpture to its highest perfection.

It is much to be regretted that no ancient works of Phœnician art remain. It may be assumed, however, from their position on an extended sea-coast, and the constant intercourse that existed between the several nations which were located between the two great rivers of Assyria and the sea, that whatever sculpture the Phœnicians had must have partaken of the general character of the art above described. The enterprise and skill of this people gained for them especial notice at a very early period. Homer speaks of the Sidonians as remarkable for their skill and ingenuity, and calls them Σιδόνες πολυδαίδαλοι.* It is a remarkable fact that a Phœnician artist (of Tyre) was selected to execute some of the most important works required for the temple proposed to be built by Solomon. This king, it is recorded,† applied to Hiram, King of Tyre, for competent workmen to carry out his magnificent design, and he sent him "a cunning man, skilful to work in gold, silver, brass, iron, stone, and timber." This was about one thousand years before the Christian era.

The geographical position of the Phœnicians gave them the command of almost all the commerce of the ancient nations, and they appear to have extended their dealings to the most remote known boundaries of the earth. It has already been shewn that they traded with the British Isles, procuring tin from Cornwall, the supposed Cassiterides of the ancients; while the

* Iliad, xxiii. 743. The application of the term Δαίδαλος (Dædalus) in this place strengthens the opinion before expressed of the character and large meaning of this word among the ancients.

† 2 Chronicles, and 1 Kings vii.

coast trade of all the nations of the Ægean and Mediterranean seas must have been entirely in their hands. Besides the ample ancient classical testimony to their extensive enterprise, there is frequent allusion in the sacred writings to the greatness and fame of this people. Thus Tyre is finely apostrophized by the prophet Ezekiel with reference to its commercial importance. He calls it "the merchant of the people for many isles:" "the ships of Tarshish," he says, "did sing of thee in thy market; and thou wast replenished and made very glorious in the midst of the seas."

Carthage was a colony of Phœnicia; but although there are coins existing of this settlement, they are of too late a date to throw any light upon the early art of their ancestors.

The history of sculpture receives little assistance from the remains of art found in Persia. There is no trace of any original design among them, and the earliest monuments bear, in many respects, so close a resemblance to those of Assyria, both in the character of the forms and in the peculiar types, in the arrangement of the *rilievi* against the walls, and in the entrances flanked by gigantic winged animals with human heads, as to leave no doubt of their derivation. It is thought that the earliest existing remains of Persian art are in the buildings of Persepolis, and that these are to be attributed to the date of Darius, or about that time. The art of the Persians has, however, some peculiarities that, so far, give it a definite character. The processions of warriors, captives, tribute-bearers, and others, are, as has been observed, in many respects similar to those found at Nimroud and Khorsabad; but while the Assyrian dresses shew no movement or folds, the Persian work exhibits these accidents in the draperies.

BASSO-RILIEVO.—PERSIA.

The conquests of the Persians over the Egyptians, and their intercourse with different parts of Asia Minor, would account for some slight changes in their art, but sculpture was never developed by the Persians into an art of beauty. Strong national prejudices, of a religious character, prevented this, and even led at one time to the systematic destruction of the works of art they met with. Xerxes was thus instigated, in his invasion of the country, to destroy the temples in Greece, because it was considered impious to pretend to inclose within walls the immortal gods, whose appropriate temple or dwelling-place is the entire universe; and their statues were also defaced under the same impulse of religious prejudice. Under these circumstances, notwithstanding the great interest that must attach to the history of this nation in its influence upon those countries with which it became associated, Persia cannot take any position as a school of sculpture, in the sense in which that term may, with more or less propriety, be applied to Assyria, Egypt, and parts of Asia Minor, where the art, even when it had little or no beauty, at least possessed a distinctive character of its own.

There is no temptation to dwell at any length upon the sculpture of Hindùstan. It affords no assistance in tracing the history of the art, and its debased quality deprives it of all interest as a phase of fine art, the point of view from which it would here be considered. It must be admitted, however, that the works existing have sufficient character to stamp their nationality; and although they possess no properties that can make them valuable as useful examples for the student, they offer very curious subjects of inquiry to the scholar and archæologist. The sculptures found in various parts of India, at Ellora, Elephanta, and other places, are of a strictly symbolical or mythological character. They usually consist of monstrous combinations of human and brute forms, repulsive from their ugliness and the outrageous defiance of rule and even possibility. They are remarkable for their dimensions, many of the works being colossal; and they often are elaborately ornamented, the carving being very careful and minute. The highly-wrought execution of many of these monuments is in itself a proof of the works not belonging to primitive times; and it is indeed now generally believed that there are no very ancient productions of the kind in India. Although architectural remains of supposed great antiquity are found in different parts of the country, the native sculptured representations now known of the human figure are considered to be of comparatively modern date; not anterior, indeed, to the first Christian century. The conquests of Alexander the Great do not appear to have exercised any important influence on the art of India, by introducing new forms or improved principles of beauty. At a somewhat later period, the coins of the successors of that prince were circulated in some of the more northern provinces, as Bactria, but the normal type of Hindù symbolical sculpture was not affected by it.

Indeed, after a short time—about one hundred years—even the better design of the money of the Satraps was so debased that what it had of the Greek character was lost. The legends and names, also, instead of being in Greek, were again inscribed in the native character. Many examples of Hindù imitative art are in baked clay. These are for the most part of small size, and exhibit some curious varieties and even improved character in their forms. It must be remarked, however, that since the study of Indian antiquities has been seriously undertaken, there is reason to believe that many of these smaller works have been forged, to meet the demand for examples of Hindù art.

There is much that is very curious in Chinese art, and it is evident, that many very refined processes were known to this people at a very remote period. It also appears, from objects that have been found in distant localities, that the productions of Chinese artists penetrated into countries usually supposed to have been beyond the reach of any intercourse with so jealously insulated a people. Some of the ornamental designs, in scrolls, leaves, and flowers, on their most ancient porcelain are almost identical with those found on some of the oldest Greek vases; suggesting that the latter nation may have received these through the traders travelling from the far east to the sea; and it is known that their wares were also distributed by the Phœnician navigators, who were the great carriers of the world. The painted figures on their vases and dishes occasionally exhibit a feeling for grace and beauty, which causes surprise that much greater progress in the higher department of fine art has not been made among a people so sensitive and ingenious, and especially so accomplished as copyists. In the arrangement of colour they also show a refined sense of harmony. The treatment of sculpture by the Chinese is generally of a much more grotesque character than their painted subjects ; and it offers nothing worthy the attention of the student, or that can interest the historian of art.

The art of the Japanese exhibits some interesting points of difference from the Chinese. There is much more boldness in foreshortening and freedom in the drawing, and infinitely greater variety of action, of character and expression in the figures ; but even here, with this superior power and feeling for the picturesque, nothing is found which deserves the title of fine art, and their sculpture seems never to have aspired to represent anything beyond the native types, with increased grotesqueness both in form and attitude.

What has been observed above of Hindù and Chinese sculpture, in its relation to the history of the art, is equally applicable to the quaint specimens that have been met with by modern travellers in some parts of South America. There is sufficient in their design and execution to make them objects of great interest to the inquirer into the early history of the people and of the localities in which these monuments have been found, but they afford no reliable indications to guide the archæologist in connecting them with the progress of sculpture. They exhibit proofs of considerable facility in execution in the artists who produced them, affording, so far, an argument for long practice; but they possess no qualities whatever that can connect them with fine art. Their subjects and types seem to refer to a people long passed away, but of their date and their origin it is impossible, in the present unsatisfactory state of our knowledge, to offer any acceptable conjecture.

The sculpture of the Egyptians, already referred to incidentally, though it never reached the perfection the art attained in Greece, has great claims to attention. The extent of their works in architecture, painting, and sculpture, of an antiquity so remote that it seems to defy research, and exhibiting at the same time all the characteristics of long practice, shew that this remarkable people had made themselves a considerable nation at a very early period in the world's history. The most ancient sacred writings speak of the "wisdom of the Egyptians." When Abraham visited Egypt he found there established institutions, royal, hierarchical, and social, and a regularly organized form of government. But although these old traditions of the learning, the prowess, and the greatness of this people, are daily receiving confirmation from the discoveries of modern travellers and scholars; and notwithstanding the testimony thus afforded to the value of the most ancient and sacred records, it seems impossible to penetrate the darkness which obscures their earliest history. The dates of the foundation of some of their most celebrated cities, as Thebes and Memphis, can only now be conjectured. The sculpture and other remains found at Karnak, a portion of Thebes lying on the Arabian or eastern side of the Nile, bear inscriptions in which is said to occur the name of Osirtasen, the Pharaoh or ruler who is supposed to have been contemporary with Joseph, at above 1700 B.C.; while some of the ruins in the neighbourhood are believed to be of a date even long antecedent to that king. The pyramids to the north of Memphis are considered to be the most ancient monuments existing in Egypt, and it may therefore be assumed they are the oldest in the world. One of the most competent authorities on Egyptian antiquities refers them to about 2120 before our era.*

But if the evidence of the monuments themselves cannot always be adduced in support of the remote ancient practice of the Egyptians in sculpture, there still is other proof, in the opinions of scholars and antiquaries, that in extremely early times certain laws and rules had

* Wilkinson, *Ancient Egyptians*, vol. i.

been organized, by superior authority, by which artists were bound in the execution of all religious sculptures and paintings. A most curious and interesting confirmation of this belief may be seen in the British Museum. A tablet, said to date about 1250 B.C., is there preserved, which exhibits on its face an engraved diagram shewing the proportions in squares, which were applied to the human figure. If this monument be really of the date attributed to it, it affords not only the most satisfactory testimony to the great antiquity of the arts in Egypt, but it attests also the very remote foundation of a scientific principle or system by which their practice was regulated. It is affirmed that instances of similar lines or diagrams have been found under the colours painted on statues as well as under paintings on walls, and that unfinished works have also shown traces of the same kind.*

With respect to the origin of the religious sculpture of Egypt, it is useless to offer any conjecture. The most important settlement of the Egyptians seems to have been in the Thebaid or Upper Egypt; and it is supposed that civilization advanced northwards from thence. To the south was the country called in the Scriptures and in the Egyptian language the "foreign land of Cush;" and its natives, with whom the Egyptians

* Bonomi, *Proportions of the Human Figure*; Lepsius, *Letters from Egypt*, etc.; Sharpe, *Chronology of Egypt*, etc. etc.

were constantly waging war, are generally represented in the monuments as captives or as bearers of tribute to the Pharaohs. They were a black people, and of distinct physical character from the Egyptians; and, as is proved by the difference in the form of the skull of the two nations, of a totally different race. Without venturing to speculate upon the origin of the more civilized and intelligent people by whom the inhabitants of Upper Egypt were eventually subdued, the above simple facts are sufficient to establish the belief in the colonization of the Thebaid by a foreign, and therefore, in all probability, an Asiatic race. Such authority as can be derived from a careful examination of the peculiarities of their monuments would strengthen the belief that the grand and simple scheme of their art, as it is exhibited in the massive architecture of their temples and other public works, and in the colossal scale and severe tranquillity of their statues, claimed kindred with the early Asiatic nations.

Antiquaries have attempted to define marked epochs in the history of Egyptian sculpture; but though it is very possible that some slight peculiarities and changes may be detected in monuments attributed to different early dynasties, they do not afford sufficient authority for anything like a strict chronological classification of what is understood by schools. The only great leading divisions that are suggested in the practice of Egyptian art are those marked, in the *first* instance, by the Egyptian types, in their representation of the human figure, in the remote ages before the country was invested by foreign invaders. The *second* division may be referred to the occupation of Egypt by the Persians under Cambyses, in the sixth century B.C. At the same time it is not clear that any important changes in the art of the country followed this revolution; and it is probable, also, that the Persians had no art which they could substitute for that which they found already established. The strong national prejudice of that people against all religious sculpture has already been referred to. It is said that Darius shewed the Egyptians some indulgence, by permitting them to return to many of their old usages which had been forbidden by his predecessor Cambyses; but this probably had little reference to art. From this time, however, the star of Egypt's glory had begun to set; and though the Persian rule was overthrown the country never recovered its ancient renown, nor held again its old proud position in the history of the nations. The next or *third* epoch, marked by innovations in the arts of design in Egypt, is that which has been called the Greco-Egyptian period, when Greek influence is clearly discerned. This dates from 324 B.C., when, after the death of Alexander the Great, Ptolemy Soter assumed the sovereignty of Egypt. The *fourth* and last is distinguished by the effects of the Roman rule in Egypt, after the capture of Alexandria by Augustus, 30 B.C. These seem to comprehend the only large divisions into which Egyptian sculpture need be distributed for a general understanding of its varieties; and even here it must be borne in mind that throughout these changes the national peculiarity of style still maintained its defined character. From the high finish and more careful execution of the works of the time, it is thought that the national prosperity, and therefore the condition of art, were highest in what archæologists have called the fifteenth dynasty, that is, during the reign of Rameses—who seems to be the same as the Sesostris of the Greeks—about 1350 B.C.; and, judging from other remains, that the country and its art were most depressed from the date of the Persian conquest, that is, from 525 to about 414 B.C.; when, no doubt, the national spirit had been broken, and the energies of the people were irretrievably paralyzed.

In the wall paintings and similar coloured works found in temples and tombs in various parts of Egypt, there is evidence of considerable power of design. Battles, processions, festive meetings, agricultural and domestic employments, manufacturing occupations—all exhibit varied action, busy composition, and considerable dramatic effect in illustrating the subjects chosen; shewing that, although in certain respects they were limited by prescribed regulations, and were bound to preserve the established national types in their figures, the artists who *painted* their designs were allowed to exercise considerable freedom. This seems not to have been the case with the more staid and solemn sister art. Sculpture was in the special service of religion, and here, as a general rule, there is little if any deviation from old and established usage.

The characteristic of Egyptian sculpture is everywhere the same. It consists in extreme simplicity of design, with great breadth of treatment, to the exclusion of minute details, and a solid largeness of form. There is little or no variety of expression in the heads, especially of the superior personages represented who, generally, are characterised by a calm, unimpassioned, and lofty bearing, as though ordinary worldly incidents could not disturb their divine composure. The only indication of sensibility that is allowed to interfere with this solemn equanimity is a benignant, placid smile, that appears on all the countenances. Where dress is introduced, there is no composition of drapery in the way of action or movement; no volume or thickness of mass, nor any indication of folds. The action of the figures, however important or exciting may be their occupation, is limited by the most severe conventionalism. If sitting, they have the legs parallel; if standing, one leg is sometimes slightly advanced before the other. The arms usually are close to the sides, with the hands, whether holding anything or not, firmly clenched ; or, if open, the fingers are never free or detached, but are closed against each other. It is also a characteristic of Egyptian figure-sculpture that the heads uniformly look directly in front. It may be observed that the proportions of the figures in the Egyptian monuments are always agreeable. This is accounted for by the curious discoveries before alluded to, by which the fact is established that, even in the most remote times of which there are any records, the artists executed their works according to a prescribed uniform canon or standard of proportions.

It is not necessary to dwell more minutely on the peculiarities of the Egyptian style. Original monuments now abound in all the various museums of art, and these will afford a much clearer view of the design of Egyptian sculpture than can be given by any mere verbal description. This country is rich in such illustrations, and our national collection in the British Museum now boasts some of the most valuable examples of Egyptian antiquities, and of sculpture especially, extant. The student may easily here consult original specimens, from which he will much sooner than by any other means acquire a competent knowledge of the style of art of this extraordinary people.

There is one fact to be observed in connection with art in Egypt, which is both curious and significant. When the undisputed antiquity of the Egyptians, and their long duration as a powerful and independent nation, are considered—taking into account, too, the various fortunes of the country, both from their own conquests, and, later, from the invasion of foreigners—it is remarkable how little change occurred in the leading characteristics of their art. Whether the monuments be of the most remote archaïc period, or of the period of the Persian occupation, or of the more recent ante-Roman time, no sufficient alterations were introduced to destroy that peculiar and distinctive character which stamps all Egyptian art with its national individuality. This may, in a great measure, be accounted for, but still the fact remains, as a very curious proof of a nation's immobility.

The attachment of the Egyptians to that peculiar style which has made their art so remarkable, may be traced primarily to the same influence that was exercised on all the earlier nations where sculpture was employed for religious purposes. Art was a means of direct appeal to the commonest apprehension, and, at the same time, to the most cherished prejudices of the people, and, as such, was used and controlled by the ruling class. This power was exercised in Egypt by the hierarchy; and as the kings or Pharaohs were also priests, in virtue of their royal dignity, the acts of the sovereign were associated in the public mind with sacred influences. Thus the conquests of the king in battle, the submission of foreign nations, the receipt of tribute, the execution of prisoners and captives, were all represented in their sculpture and painting with the accompaniments of well-known overruling divinities, either expressed in form or implied in familiar emblems. The decorations of their tombs were also equally associated with these feelings; and the solemn, colossal statues of lines of kings, attended by the most sacred personages and symbols of their mythology, must have made the most profound impression upon a population which, from its earliest infancy, had been educated to believe in the divine appointment and attributes of its rulers. In art, then, the priests permitted no innovations; and the division of the population into castes or callings secured among the artists, who no doubt were especially attached to the sacerdotal institutions, a strict conformity to established types. This indeed seems to have been carefully provided for, for not only were the canons of art fixed and engraved for reference, as has already been shewn, but, according to a passage in Synnesius, the profession of an artist was only allowed to be exercised by persons properly qualified, lest they should, in ignorance, transgress against the old laws which regulated the representation of the gods and sacred subjects. Plato also says the artists were not allowed to innovate; "hence the art remains the same, the rule of it the same." This, then, may be taken as the real cause of the long duration of Egyptian art under its own peculiar form or style.

Some stress has been laid on the recorded fact, that the Egyptians were ill-favoured in point of personal attractions. Ælian observes that, in his time, it was rare to find a well-made or beautiful woman.* It is well known that they had no public games, like the Greeks and Romans, for the exercise of their bodies, by which their artists could have the opportunity of studying the actions and variety of the figure; causes sufficiently powerful to prevent their imitative works possessing much excellence of form. The artists too, it must be remembered, were altogether precluded from studying anatomy, so essential to the perfection of the fine arts, by the extreme respect, approaching to veneration, that was paid to the dead.

But even if the statements of the absence of beauty among the general population are trustworthy, and if the check to the development of and acquaintance with the human form, from their not having the advantages enjoyed by the Greeks, be admitted, these causes are scarcely in themselves sufficient to account for the stationary condition and very peculiar character of their sculpture. The true ground of the unprogressive character of their art, as regards its style, is with much more

* Another writer says of them, "Homines autem Ægyptis plerique subfusculi sunt et atrati, magisque mæstiores, gracilenti et aridi," etc.

probability to be sought in the nature of their institutions. That the Egyptians were not incapable of conceiving an *ideal* of beauty is shewn in some of the heads of colossal and other statues that have reached us, where, within the limits to which we have adverted, a very decided character of beauty of expression, and even of form, is met with. No better example of this can be

HEAD, SUPPOSED OF RAMESES.

found than in the colossal head, in the British Museum, of the (so-called) young Memnon; but which, more probably, is a portrait of Rameses II.

From the comparative skill which they have evinced in executing animals, it seems more than probable that it was in these inferior objects alone that they were permitted to exercise their own natural judgment and talent; while statues or pictures of men and women, appropriated to purposes of religion and employed in the representation of divinities, kings, and priests, were not to be elevated at the will of the artist beyond the character left by the ancients, and therefore established by law. We must also notice another influential cause—the division of the people into castes or professions—which obliged a son to follow the trade or calling of his father, whatever it might be; and by the same rule it was prohibited for any person, however decided his disposition for them might be, to practise the arts of design, unless he had an hereditary right so to apply his talents. One more cause for the slow progress of the arts in Egypt—more influential perhaps than any other in a profession which requires for its consummation and perfection much nursing and protection—was the little esteem in which artists were held in the country; they were classed in the lowest rank, and neither had opportunity nor permission to rise above it. Thus their practice was merely mechanical, unaided and unenlightened by the mind or sentiment which a student, who feels he may arrive at distinction by excelling in the higher branches of his art, would endeavour to throw into his works.

The statues and *bassi-rilievi* remaining, even at the present day, are almost without number; and wherever ruins have been discovered—whether of temples, tombs, or obelisks—there also have sculptures and paintings been found. The continual practice, therefore, which such a vast quantity of work afforded must, under any other circumstances than those adverted to, have occasioned improvement; and were it not for the paralyzing influence of these causes we should be utterly at a loss to comprehend how it was possible, in a country where art was so extensively cultivated, that it could have remained so stationary in point of style.

The remarkably clean and finished execution observable in Egyptian sculpture in the hardest materials—basalt, granite, or other substances most difficult to deal with—has always excited the attention of the curious, as a proof of the wonderful proficiency of this people, even at a very remote date, in some of the processes of handicraft, and especially in the hardening of the metals of which their tools were made.

SECTION III.

THE next school of sculpture which demands notice in the history of the art is the Etruscan. It cannot, indeed, claim a place in the series of practice which culminated in the perfection of sculpture, for no original works of these people shew that their art was progressive. It was exercised in different ways and under different influences, but it never appears to have been followed as an art of beauty; at any rate till it became associated with that of a mixed or foreign people. Of the earliest inhabitants of this portion of Italy nothing is certainly known, though the subject has occupied the attention of the learned of all times. The architectural remains which are found scattered about that which was considered Etrurian territory, are evidence of a very remote antiquity; but no examples of imitative art can be assigned to the earlier period of the existence of this people. Whether the first colonization was from the east or from the south—from Phœnicia, from Asia Minor, or from Egypt—it is at present impossible to determine. The colossal character of construction, observable in their buildings, and especially of the so-called Cyclopæan walls still remaining, is equally met with in the earlier erections of all these nations. In the greater part of the works in sculpture that have reached us there is, in their subjects, undoubted evidence of Greek influence, though in the style there is an exclusive and individual character; but it must be admitted that there are also examples of sculpture as well as of painting in tombs, evidently of a very remote antiquity, and that appear to be quite original in their subjects, and, as far as we can judge, totally independent of Greek fable and mythology. It has been a common error to suppose, because the earlier works of different countries shew considerable resemblance in their forms, that it is an indication of their derivation from a common source. The more archaïc sculptures of Greece and Etruria have thus been frequently confounded, from the supposed similarity of style; when, as has before been observed, this is only the common characteristic of all art in its first stage. This fancied resemblance to some of the Egyptian figures led at one time to the belief that the Etruscans derived their art from Egypt; but there is no satisfactory proof of this, however possible it may have been. It has been well remarked by Lanzi,* that

* La supposizione che gli Etruschi traessero dagli Egizii le loro arti e il loro disegno è priva di fondamento, poichè, come avverti il Lanzi, la rigidezza e il rettilineo dei segni non hanno bisogno di venirci dal

those peculiarities which have been taken for indications of relationship in art have no such character; the assumption of a connection being grounded, not on the presence of any common type or style so much as on the common absence of all real art-character. This is a very important distinction, not always made even by those accustomed to the examination of archaïc monuments.

Considerable variety will be found in works of the Etruscan school. In some examples the forms are very simple and almost undefined, and the accessories, as the hair and draperies, are arranged stiffly and in regular lines, bearing in these respects considerable resemblance to the works above described of the Persians. In others there is an exaggeration and affectation entirely distinct from anything found in the contemporary art of the time, excepting, occasionally, in the early Greek vases; a circumstance which might seem to indicate a connection at this period between the two nations. The peculiarity referred to is especially indicated in the hands, which are long and attenuated, and where the fingers are turned back in the most unnatural manner.

The prevalence of a marked style in the Etruscan

Nilo, e nei principii delle arti presso tutte le nazione si vede lo stesso carattere, *essendo quello stile non tanto arte quanto mancanza di arte.* —(Cicognara, *Stor. della Scultura*, vol. i.)

sculpture may be attributed to the same causes which, it has been shewn, influenced Egyptian, Assyrian, and, as will be seen, early Greek art. Their rulers, the "Lucomones," were priests as well as governors; and no doubt religious feeling consecrated certain forms and, for a time, prevented changes which doubtless would be considered in the light of profane and sacrilegious innovation. A distinction must, however, here be pointed out between original Etruscan works—that is, the production of native Etruscan artists—and works in the Etruscan style; by which is meant a peculiar mode of treatment that was retained by the admirers or followers of this school, long after the character of the true and original art of Etruria had been disturbed by modern introductions. It was a style particularly distinguished by the Romans, and called by them "*Tuscanicus,*" as applied to art; and it was not necessarily confined to works executed in Etruria or by native sculptors. All productions which exhibited the hard and dry manner of the earlier Etruscan school gained the title of *Opera Tuscanica.* A passage in Quinctilian affords an illustration of this nomenclature or mark of style, when he is speaking of the (technical) character of the works of some of the more celebrated Greek sculptors of the fifth and sixth centuries before Christ. Callon and Hegesias, he says, executed their statues or productions in a harder style than some other artists referred to, approaching very near to the Tuscan or Etruscan* forms.

It is extremely probable that this nation, considerably advanced in many respects, lent the aid of their superior intelligence to their younger neighbours the Romans; a subject to which further reference will be made when the early art of that people comes into review. It may be remarked, generally, that the works of the Etruscan artists are deficient in beauty. They have not even that simplicity and repose which, in spite of its deficiences in other respects, give a certain air of grandeur and dignity to Egyptian sculpture; still less is there any attempt at or approach to the fine forms which were the study and peculiarity of Grecian art.

Some Etruscan works have been found to differ considerably from the usual productions of this school, and from the style particularized in the foregoing remarks. This is especially observable in the compositions in painting and sculpture that have been discovered of late years in certain tombs of Volterra and other Etruscan cities. The sculpture in these consists of semi-recumbent figures reposing on sarcophagi. They vary in size, some being as large as life, others of small dimensions; and they usually form the top or lid of the coffin or receptacle in which the remains of the deceased were

* Duriora et "*Tuscanicis*" proxima Callon et Hegesias; jam minus rigida Calamis, etc. (lib. xii. 10. 7).

deposited. In these statues we no longer recognise the ordinary Etruscan style; and yet they have been found in localities and bearing inscriptions which would appear to carry them back to a very remote date. The forms usually are clumsy, and they are loaded with full and heavy drapery. The heads, again, are peculiar. They often have all the character of being portraits, and sometimes they are pleasing in expression, and even exhibit an approach to beauty. The first impression they convey is, that they belong to a low Roman school of art, to which indeed some antiquaries have unhesitatingly assigned them. There are, however, difficulties in the way of coming to a conclusion upon their date and origin. There is no doubt that the tombs of Etruria were opened, and, in many instances, plundered in very ancient times; and it is extremely probable that they were used also as depositaries for the dead by a people who were in possession of the country very long after the date of their original constructors. Objects, evidently of various ages, have been found in some of these tombs; a proof of their not being in their primitive integrity when opened by more recent antiquaries. From these circumstances it becomes exceedingly difficult to define the precise age of the works that occasionally are found in them; and where inscriptions of an ancient character occur upon sculpture that exhibits indication of the seeming decadence of art this difficulty is of course greatly increased.

SECTION IV.

THE foregoing rapid survey of sculpture has been rather a notice of an universally practised form of record than a history of a refined art, requiring the exercise of the intellect and of the educated hand, and having for its office to express elevated sentiment, and to illustrate noble subjects under appropriate forms of beauty. Important in other respects as was the employment of sculpture among the most ancient nations, and valuable as are the monuments that time has left us, it was not till the Greek mind perceived its capability of development that the entire value of the art was recognised as a most powerful æsthetic influence, and, at the same time, as a means of physically illustrating the perfection of nature's noblest work. It strikes us with wonder and astonishment, now that the existence of the art of design has been traced through such a long series of years, and among so great a variety of peoples, that so long a period could have elapsed between the first invention and rude practice of sculpture, and the perfection it was destined to reach among the Greeks. Sicyon was founded above 2000 years B.C., and Argos 1856 B.C., and yet it is not till between 700 and 600 B.C. that those first changes are perceived in the style of art practised in that region of the world, and with such especial success in the two localities referred to, which then led so rapidly to the consummation of sculpture, in the time of Pericles, in the great school of Myron, Phidias, and Polycletus.

It is among this people that its history as a *Fine Art* will be considered; and contemplated from this point of view it will be seen what a totally different aspect it assumes from that which it has where the art was simply mechanical and exclusively employed for monumental or religious objects.

The application of sculpture among the earlier settlers in Greece and Asia Minor in no wise differed from that of other nations by whom the art was exercised. Under whatever circumstances the first rude attempts at representing the human form were made, sculpture was used for religious purposes; and it everywhere experienced similar fortunes in its earlier history. The Greeks were subject to the same obstructive influence of the priesthood as other nations whose works have been referred to; and, though they eventually freed themselves from this domination, there can be no doubt that for a considerable period this power of preventing innovation in sculpture intended for religious purposes held its sway, and retarded the progress of the art. Still, with this people, it was but for a time; and it is here that the history of sculpture gains immense interest, for it henceforward became an art of progress.

Some writers, in endeavouring to account for the superiority of the Greeks, have thought it attributable to their climate; some to the government under which they lived; some to the fine physical development of the people, or to other external causes; but in considering the history of the several schools of Greece, it will be found that none of these influences existed universally in any of the localities where sculpture was most successfully practised, and that neither of them, singly, was sufficient to produce the effect attributed to them. Attica, which was especially the home of the fine arts, had a climate of great inequality. In some parts there was the greatest luxuriance of vegetation, while in others the soil was ungrateful, naked, and barren. Again, with respect to personal beauty, Athens held no decided superiority over other cities, and yet the Athenians were distinguished beyond all others for the excellence and extent of their productions of art. It certainly is remarkable that not one of the women whose celebrity for beauty has come down to us was a native of Athens. Phryne, for instance, was a native of Thebes, Glycera of Sicyon, Aspasia was born at Miletus, Laïs at Hyccara in Sicily; another of the same name, and accounted even more beautiful, was of Corinth. All these were renowned for their personal charms, and when Zeuxis the painter was occupied upon his famous picture of Venus, it is recorded that he studied not the forms of Athenian women, but those of seven beautiful virgins of Crotona. It is worthy of remark also that Cicero, speaking of the youths he saw at Athens, says he observed few who were handsome.* It is not intended to deny the existence of beautiful forms among the Athenians, but simply to point out that their exclusive possession of it was not the cause of their superior success in sculpture. The Lacedæmonians, whose admiration of beauty is especially remarked by Ælian,† proscribed the practice of sculpture and the fine arts in Sparta. Nor will the form of government, or the manners of the Greeks, account for the excellence of this people in the arts of design. The most widely contrasted political and social conditions existed in different localities where the arts flourished, as was the case at Corinth, at Athens, and Sicyon. The first of these was celebrated for its magnificence and refinement, and yet, while the comparatively feeble Sicyon held, with Athens, the first rank in the cities of art, Corinth was only of secondary consideration in this respect. Indeed if wealth and luxury could alone give the necessary impulse to the nobler arts of design, Asia

* Quotus enim quisque formosus est? Athenis cum essem, e gregibus epheborum vix singuli reperiebantur.—*De Nat. Deor.*, i. 28. 79.

† Var. Hist. xiv. 27.

should have been the seat of their most successful development. It is clear, therefore, that the aptitude of the Greeks for excelling in the fine arts is to be sought for in other causes than these.

There seems to have been one quality in the Greek mind which, independently of other circumstances, in a great measure necessitated, if it may be so said, the development of an imitative art to a condition of high excellence. This, in a word, was its sensibility to, and appreciation of the beautiful in all its various aspects. Other influences may have contributed to the result, but there can be little or no doubt that it was this feeling or temperament that established a principle upon which their imitative art—with which we now have to do—was founded, and which mainly, and indeed necessarily, led to its excellence. Why the Greek was the first to feel this, and how he was led to break through prescriptive forms in expressing it in art, need not be made a subject of speculation in this place, but the fact of its existence and influence is indisputable. He recognised sculpture as an imitative art, while with other nations it seems to have been considered little other than symbolical; and his acute and sensitive intelligence taught him that it was capable of improvement from the old types if that upon which it was founded, namely Nature, was carefully studied and copied. This was the secret of the superiority of the

Greeks over all other nations in art; and their selection or choice of what was most fit to be imitated led to the perfection of their sculpture, and to the establishment of what has been called in art-language, *ideal* Beauty.

A few remarks may be permitted corroborative of this view of the Greek idiosyncracy in this respect.

That the Greeks generally had this intuitive perception of the beautiful under all its aspects, and that they sensibly appreciated it, is proved by many curious facts. Allusion has already been made to the admiration felt for it among the Lacedæmonians. In other parts of Greece the same feeling appears to have existed. The priests of the temple of Jupiter at Ægium in Achaia, were chosen from youths who had received a prize for their personal beauty. The same distinction marked the priests of the Ismenian Apollo; and the boys who took part in the procession in honour of Mercury at Tanagra, were also chosen for the possession of this quality.* The Thebans had a law which subjected artists to a fine if they represented objects less beautiful than they were in reality.† It is remarkable how strictly the artists seem to have been bound by this principle not to represent repulsive subjects, nor indeed to express any passion or feeling under forms that were

* Paus. ix. 20. 22; vii. 24. 4.

† Ælian, *Var. Hist.* iv. 4; and see Junius *de Picturâ veterum*, and Lessing, *Laocoon*.

incompatible with the laws of beauty. This feeling influenced them in all they did. In their choice, as well as their treatment of subjects, the artists seem to have been careful never to lose sight of it, nor to express any passion or feeling so violently as to be at variance with the established canons of beauty united with simplicity; and as extreme expression would have interfered with its existence, it will be found that the ancients studiously avoided it in their best works. The distortion of agony would have shocked their sensibility. Laughing or crying figures can have the effect of being so excited but for a moment; afterwards the expression is but a grimace, as may be seen in many productions of later schools of sculpture.

A further proof of the attention which the ancients paid to beauty in works of Art, applying this equally to the choice of subjects and to the manner of treating them, is shewn in the contempt and derision to which those were exposed who confined themselves to representing common or inferior objects. Pauson, we are told, suffered indigence and neglect in his old age on this account; and an artist named Pyreicus, who painted barbers' shops, and such low and trifling subjects, with all the care of the Dutch or Flemish School, got the nickname of Rhyparographus.*

The habits of the Greeks fostered this appreciation

* Ῥυπαρὸς, *sordid, mean.*

of the beautiful. The mode of life of the people, and the constant occurrence of public exercises, taught all classes to be, in no small degree, judges of the human figure. The Gymnasia, or schools of training for the games, were universally frequented. The public found there their rulers, statesmen, philosophers, poets, and artists, taking interest in the exercises; and thus all were accustomed to see the human form in its highest condition, whether in action or repose. The education of young men who intended to take part in the great contests for prizes was also a subject of the greatest care. The fullest development was given to the muscles, and constant practice prepared them for those trials of agility and strength which were witnessed by the eager multitude of all classes; and from which the successful candidate issued not only a crowned victor, but the subject of the poet's noblest odes and of the sculptor's art. The highest honour that could be awarded, and this was only granted to those who had been conquerors a certain number of times, was to be allowed to dedicate an Iconic or portrait statue, representing the fortunate victor, in the Altis or sacred grove, near the temple of the Olympian Jupiter. These were to be seen by the crowds who assembled periodically to witness or take part in the games; and thus not only was the memory of the prowess or agility of the individual perpetuated, constantly inciting others to deserve a similar distinction, but a monument recorded also the fine physical development which had helped to gain the wrestling match or the race. The opening afforded by this custom for the exercise and improvement of sculpture is obvious. The established recurrence of these public games and combats, in which the competitors were for the most part naked, offered important advantages to the sculptors of Greece, and were of great assistance in enabling them to carry their art to perfection, from the intimate knowledge that was thus acquired of the anatomical construction, as well as the active powers of the figure.

Those who intended to compete for the honour of the games, their relations and friends, the public, and especially the artists, made these subjects their study; the causes of the superiority of the conqueror in the race or wrestling-match were diligently sought after, and the properties that were discovered most generally to exist in those who excelled in the various exercises were presumed to be best adapted for the purposes required, and were, therefore, adopted by the artists into all representations of the human figure in which the character of the subject demanded these qualities. Thus, for example, the sculptor found in the successful wrestler a peculiar development which was evidence of strong physical power; in the victor in the foot-race the clean limbs and light proportions which enabled him to outrun his competitors; while the combination of similar qualities of strength and lightness gave the artist the type of the general athlete. Here, then, are seen the elements of those fine creations which have stamped Greek sculpture with its enduring character of excellence. From such studies were produced what have been called the *ideal* statues of divinities and heroes; of Hercules and others of that class; of those of the light and active Mercury; or, again, of Apollo; and, in another class, of the more ordinary Discoboli and similar productions. Thus, from the skilful application of the principles discoverable in such forms, the whole range and variety of ideal subjects had their existence.

By these means, that pervading harmony, the natural and unfailing result of propriety, was attained which gives so peculiar a charm to all the best works of the Grecian School, and without which no production, however beautiful it may be in detail, can ever please. It must be remembered too, before we leave the subject of the public games, that, in witnessing them, nothing (during the best times of Greece) was ever presented to the spectators that was capable of doing violence to the finer feelings. No barbarity disgraced these amusements; for the introduction of the cruel and repulsive exhibitions of gladiators, and the fights with wild beasts, were reserved for a later period, when the public taste had become deteriorated and debased.

The noble objects to which sculpture was thus applied—to do honour to worth, and to decorate the temples of the gods—gave dignity to the art, and an honourable character to its practice: while the recognition of the principle that, as an imitative art, it was constantly to aim at reproducing and repeating the finest forms which were presented for its guidance, led to its perfection as an objective art. It was precisely this union, which had not before been established by any nation of artists, that gave to ancient Greek sculpture its extraordinary excellence; and which, it may be said, has maintained its superiority through a long succession of ages.

Another circumstance, highly conducive to the progress and development of art, must also be taken into consideration. This was the general appreciation of sculpture among a whole people sensitively alive to beauty in all its forms. Art was not here sustained by the opulent few, who bought the services of the sculptor to execute works merely to gratify the patron's fancy. In Greece the artist, himself a Greek, and having a common feeling for the beautiful with his countrymen, produced his works for the public. They were to represent divinities and heroes; to record noble actions; and they were to be erected in places of honour, or to be dedicated in the temples of the immortal gods. No mere personal motives influenced his labours. These were the conditions which carried the art to its highest perfection. When they were invaded, and the objects of art lowered to suit a less noble feeling, sculpture, as will be seen, immediately began to show symptoms of decline. It was not sufficient amongst the enlightened rulers of Greece to wait for the arts to flourish, and then to patronise them; their utility being fully acknowledged, their success was the natural consequence of the protection they received, and which led them up from their infancy to strength and maturity.

These, then, may be considered among the secondary causes that rendered the Greeks so well qualified for carrying sculpture to excellence; and it is to the presence or absence of these that the good or ill success of all art, wherever practised, is to be attributed. The *moral* influence of the fine arts was duly felt, and their operation in exciting to actions of virtue and honour, and perpetuating the glory of a people, acknowledged; they were fully appreciated as of public utility, and the artists in consequence were treated with distinction. They, in their turn, seeing the honourable purposes to which their productions were destined, were emulous to deserve this favour and to supply works worthy of their object and application. Thus exercised and encouraged, sculpture was not a mere mechanical pursuit; but mind was made to illumine matter, and the conceptions of rich and glowing fancies were embodied in the art-productions of the age.

It may be accepted as a fact, without at all underrating the collateral advantages of private patronage, that the highest conceptions and most strenuous endeavours of its followers will fail generally to carry art beyond mediocrity, unless their efforts to produce works of excellence be seconded by public encouragement. The history of the arts in Greece affords the strongest evidence that their extraordinary perfection among that people was mainly owing to this influence. It was this judicious encouragement that enabled them to produce those marvels of art in their public monuments, some of which, remaining to the present day, attest the elevated and refined taste, the genius and the magnificence of the Athenians.

The unsettled condition of Greece in the earliest periods of its history—divided into small states or provinces, each ruled by its own head or leader, jealous of their neighbours, and continually engaged in domestic or foreign disturbances—impeded the early advancement of the arts of design, and rendered them, comparatively with Egypt, of very late growth in the country. At their commencement they exhibited no peculiarities that gave indication of their future superiority, but were as simple among the Greeks as with other nations. Columns and blocks of stones were the primitive types under which they worshipped their divinities ; and even as late as Pausanias, A.D. 170, some of these were to be seen in different parts of Greece. This traveller speaks of having found some at Pheræ in Achaia. In like manner, Juno at Thespiæ, Diana Patroa, and the Milichian Jove at Sicyon, and even the Venus of Paphos, were thus represented. The addition, by degrees, of heads, and then of feet and hands—the latter close to the sides, and the legs united like columns—formed probably the earliest attempt at giving such objects a human form. It would be difficult to attribute dates to such early attempts at imitative design. In this respect, in the very infancy of art, the mode of representation was doubtless very nearly the same wherever it was attempted at all.

In the earliest attempts in sculpture among the Greeks there is a distinction discernible which separates it from that of other nations; and a skilful antiquary will rarely have any great difficulty in deciding whether or not the most archaïc specimen belongs to this people, or claims affinity with that of the more ancient races who practised the art. It is true the sculpture of the archaïc period offers but little that is attractive to the admirers of the beautiful. Rude and clumsy in form, stiff and limited in action, there is nothing in these respects to elevate them above the earlier productions of other nations; but, as already has been observed, in the Greek sculpture there is early indication of a feeling which, however limited by the obstructive conditions referred to, showed the existence here, not perceptible elsewhere, of a spirit of progress. The first improvement was in the attempt to give fuller action to the figures; and this led necessarily to a more careful consideration of the human form. The characteristics that are here most striking are on the side of exaggeration. The action is often violent and energetic, and the forms are over-developed, and the muscles full and charged. The proportions are wide or broad compared with the length of the figure. The treatment of the head in sculpture of the earliest period offers, also, some remarkable peculiarities. The eye is usually long and narrow, and slightly raised at the outer extremity, and the mouth is always represented open, with a somewhat silly smiling expression. The execution of the hair varies at different dates and in different schools. On some of the most ancient coins it is wiry, and in close parallel lines; in other examples it is represented in masses, and in heavy lumps or knobs. In male figures the beard and other hair is, on the contrary, frequently found marked by elaborate care. The drapery, in early Greek sculpture, is usually extremely scanty and thin, lying close to the figure, and scarcely showing any fulness or variety except at the edges, which are sharp and angular. The folds are for the most part arranged with mechanical precision; opposite folds corresponding, line for line and angle for angle, with each other, and exhibiting at their termination a regular zig-zag. In all these particulars the distinction between the earliest Greek art and that of Egypt and Assyria is strongly marked.

For examples of the peculiarities above noticed, the student may examine the early tetradrachms of Athens, the early coins of Oreste and Pellene, the coins of Poseidonia, the heads of the statues found in the island of

ARCHAÏC SCULPTURE.

Ægina, and the sculpture from Selinunte in Sicily. The British Museum possesses most interesting monuments of all these earlier schools, and, in the absence of the original works, the casts from the Selinuntine and Æginetan sculptures may be consulted with advantage.

Lately some very interesting monuments of the

archaïc type have reached this country from Branchidæ, in Miletus. They appear to have formed a portion of an avenue of sitting statues leading to the temple of Apollo Didymæus, and are extremely valuable as examples of the peculiarities of very early execution.

These sculptures offer curious subjects for speculation to antiquaries. From certain indications there may be a doubt whether they are all of the same date or hand; though in their general archaïc treatment and style all are alike. This may be accounted for by supposing the statues to have been votive, and erected at different times, as individuals were induced to dedicate them; it being understood that each work, as it was added, was to be of a prescribed form; that is, of the received religious type, and to suit the character of the series.* The style of art does not necessarily connect them with any one particular source or origin. In their extreme simplicity and uniformity of action, they are, at first sight, suggestive of Egyptian parentage; but in the heaviness of their forms they seem to shew more of the character found in the north-eastern or Assyrian sculpture; while, in some of the draperies, if such a term can be applied to their costume or dress, appear the distinctive zigzag edges so peculiar to early Etruscan art.

* This conjecture receives strong confirmation from certain inscriptions on individual statues.

In tracing the later history of sculpture among the Greeks, certain changes mark distinct epochs in the progress of the art. Four principal periods may thus be distinguished, each characterised by striking peculiarities of style or treatment.

The first may be said to comprehend all that uncertain age of which no reliable record remains, and of which our only knowledge is in the traditions preserved by ancient writers down to the period of the first art-movement exhibited in the archaïc monuments of the Æginetan school, at about 600 B. C. The second period extends to the perfection of sculpture, by Phidias and his contemporaries, at from 450 to 400 B. C. The third period includes the practice of the art from this time to about 250 or 200 B. C., when the more voluptuous execution and style of design of Praxiteles and his scholars, and of Lysippus and his followers, had effected most important changes in the condition of the art. The fourth, and, in this comprehensive summary, the last period of true Greek sculpture, is that of its decline under mere imitators or bad innovators; when manner took the place of style, and when the simplicity and grandeur that had hitherto characterised sculpture, while its object was noble and lofty, were superseded by minute details, tasteless execution, and by littleness and poverty of treatment.

Notwithstanding the uncertainty of the dates of

many of the earlier monuments of Greek sculpture, and of the artists to whom they have been attributed, it will be proper to notice briefly the usually accepted history and chronology connected with the subject. This will not be done in a dogmatic spirit, but simply with the view of assisting the student with such lights as we at present possess in a very difficult and controverted field of inquiry. Fresh discoveries of works of art and inscriptions, and scholarship especially applied to archæology, are constantly affording new and valuable information, and extending our knowledge on these points. Thus, the most approved theories of to-day may always be open to correction or change from later acquisitions; and it will be judicious not too obstinately to insist upon opinions which time may shew to be unsound.*

The earliest names that occur of sculptors of the Greek school are Dædalus, Smilis, and Endœus. The difficulty of giving anything like precise dates to the first artists who are recorded has already been adverted to; and with respect to Dædalus especially this diffi-

* The date of a work in sculpture cannot, as has already been intimated, always be safely inferred from the style of art, for this may be imitated in a time long posterior to the true archaïc period. Inscriptions are a much truer test of date, for at least the work inscribed must be anterior to or contemporary with the inscription. The inscription, if a true one, may be very much later than the work on which it appears, but it cannot be earlier.

culty is the greater, because there is so much reason to believe that it was a common appellation given to many persons remarkable for skill and ingenuity. The Dædalus usually considered as the first rightful owner of the name is said to have been of a royal race: the grandson of Erechtheus, king of Athens. He was said to be the inventor of various mechanical instruments—the lever, the saw, etc.; and as a sculptor to have been the first who ventured upon the innovation of giving action to statues by separating the legs and arms from their former stiff attachment to the body. Pausanias* says, "the ancients called (wooden) figures Δαίδαλα (Dædala);" and he suggests, that it is probable the artist was called after his works rather than by his own name; thus, again, making Dædalus a title or distinctive appellation denoting skill and ability. Pausanias was shewn some statues said to be by the early Dædalus; and he declares there was a certain air of grandeur in them, but no beauty. Their presumed great antiquity, added to the extreme simplicity of their style of art, may have given them this effect in the estimation of one who naturally connected the representation, however rude, with religious associations. Smilis, the second sculptor referred to, was a native of Ægina. He was the reputed author of a statue of Juno at Samos. Endœus was an Athenian, and scholar of Dædalus. Pausanias† records a colossal

* Lib. ix. 3, etc.

† Lib. vii. 5.

seated statue (of wood) of Minerva Polias, attributed to this artist, which was in the temple at Erythræ, in Ionia. He is said also to have executed various works in stone and ivory. The accounts of artists of this remote period are obviously very vague, and the chronology founded upon such traditions as Pausanias was able to collect cannot, it is needless to say, be implicitly relied on.

Phido of Argos is said to have struck the first money in Greece, in the island of Ægina, about 800 B. C. Some extremely rude coins of that island, having for a device a tortoise, are extant; and from the very primitive style of their execution, they have been thought to be not very remote from the period alluded to.

Gitiadas, a native of Sparta, some of whose works Pausanias saw, and Learchus, of Rhegium, are mentioned among the earliest artists who executed works in metal. He speaks* of a bronze statue of Jupiter at Lacedæmon, which was said to be by this Learchus, as the most ancient statue in that material known to exist. This can only mean that this statue was of very great antiquity, or the most ancient of those which Pausanias had seen executed in the manner he describes. The date of Learchus, owing to the very scanty notice of him, and the inconsistent statement in Pausanias respecting his supposed masters, has been a subject of considerable difficulty with antiquaries, but it is probable that he

* Lib. iii. 17.

lived in the eighth century B.C.* The fact of a sculptor of Rhegium being noticed at so early a date has led to the inference that the arts were more advanced at this time in Italy than in Greece; and some very early coins that exist afford ground for believing that the state of art in many of the colonies of Greece was more flourishing at this early period than in the mother country. The difficulties attending the right placing of Learchus are great; indeed if he was a scholar of Dipœnus and Scyllis, our mention of him should have been deferred till after our notice of those sculptors. Still, with respect to the supposed advanced condition of art in Italy in his time, no sure argument can be brought forward from the mere circumstance of the sculptor being a native of Rhegium; for even if the early date be correct, he might have practised his art elsewhere than at home.

The next names that occur are of considerable historical importance in the annals of Greek sculpture—these are Telecles, Rhœcus, and Theodorus. Their reputation was so great that they had the credit of being the inventors of many processes of art, but which it is obvious must have been known before their time; such, for instance, as modelling. Still, without claiming for them the discovery of this long-known art, they may have been the authors of many improvements by which sculpture was greatly advanced among the Greeks.

* See Sillig. *Cat. Artif.*

No names of artists of antiquity have given rise to more discussion among scholars and archæologists than these, and their date is still a subject of controversy. The most ancient sculptors called Rhœcus and Theodorus were said to be natives of Samos. The probability, however, is, there were several of the name, living at different periods; and that, from the varying traditions respecting them, and the few works preserved from which any fair judgment of the style, and therefore date, of their sculpture could be drawn, the productions of several artists were attributed to one only. It is clearly established that there were at least two very early and contemporary sculptors called Theodorus. One of these was son of Rhœcus and the other of Telecles. Of Rhœcus but little is known, and no works have been discovered that can with any degree of certainty be ascribed to him.

Herodotus* says Rhœcus, who was an architect as well as statuary, built the temple of Juno at Samos; and he is also referred to as the author of a statue called Night, preserved in the temple of the Ephesian Diana. Pausanias† records that Theodorus engraved the celebrated ring which Polýcrates, the tyrant of Samos, threw into the sea, and, according to the tradition, so marvellously recovered. The king, who had enjoyed a long course of uninterrupted prosperity, determined, it

* Lib. iii. 60. † Lib. viii. 14. 5.

is said, to make some sacrifice to prove his equanimity if any reverse of good fortune should befal him. Among his most highly-valued treasures was this ring, and he voluntarily parted with it, casting it himself into the sea. His usual happy fortune still, however, attended him. In a few days, a large fish that had been taken was presented at the palace for the king's acceptance, and upon opening it the much-prized ring was found in its belly. The son of Telecles was said to be the inventor of casting in iron.

A Theodorus is also said to have made a magnificent vase that was dedicated at Delphi by Crœsus, king of Lydia; a circumstance that has led to the belief that this Theodorus lived at a later date than that usually assigned to him. It is possible, however, that the vase presented by Crœsus may have been placed among the treasures of the king, a carefully-preserved work of an older age, and may, from its value and the fame of its author, have been considered a worthy object for the purpose to which Crœsus applied it.

Pausanias says he was unable to find any work of Theodorus, while Pliny mentions several that were attributed to him. In considering the testimony of these writers, it must be remembered that Pausanias took great pains to acquire information by his personal visits to and inquiries at the different places where remarkable works of art were said to exist. Pliny seems only diligently to have noted down every report that was made to him. In speaking of the older sculptors here referred to, it may be observed that Pliny records that they lived long prior to the expulsion of the Bacchiadæ from Corinth. As this occurred about 659 B.C., it has been conjectured that Rhœcus and the two earlier sculptors named Theodorus must have flourished between 800 and 700 before our era. It scarcely need be observed, after what has been said, that the dates of these artists have not yet been satisfactorily determined. It is, however, of comparatively small importance, as there are no known monuments remaining from which any information can be derived of the state of sculpture in their time, or rather as it was practised by them individually.

Among the very early artists recorded by scholars is Dibutades, a native of Sicyon, who practised his art at Corinth. He is said to have invented modelling in clay; and the following is related as the cause or origin of the art. The daughter of Dibutades, seeing her lover's profile cast by shadow on the wall by a lamp, traced the outline to secure the portrait. Her father, seeing this, filled in the outline with clay, and sent it to be baked in order to preserve it. This is a poetical and romantic story, but wholly inadmissible as the history of one of the most obvious art-processes; especially as the profession Dibutades is said to have exercised—namely, that of a potter—must have made him fully conversant with the uses to which his very simple material could be applied, and in which rude imitations of the human form were doubtless made at the earliest periods.

Dipœnus and Scyllis, who are supposed by some writers to have lived at this remote date, were considered the founders of the school of Sicyon. They had many scholars, among whom appears the Learchus of Rhegium before mentioned, and which will account for the early date given by some writers to these artists. It has been said of them they were the first who employed marble for sculpture; but the expression of Pliny,* upon which this opinion has been formed, more probably means that they were particularly distinguished in working in that beautiful material, and so increased its importance and popularity. It is recorded that Dipœnus and Scyllis were employed to make some statues of the gods for the Sicyonians, but owing to some offence that was offered them, they quitted Sicyon, leaving the statues unfinished. When a famine soon after afflicted the country the oracle declared it would not cease till the statues of the gods were completed. The sculptors were upon this prevailed upon to return and resume their

* "Marmore sculpendo primi omnium inclaruerunt Dipœnus et Scyllis, geniti in Creta, Olympiade circiter L."—Plin. *Hist. Nat.* xxxvi. 4. If we might imagine that L., in the above passage, was an error of the transcriber for I., the difficulty of assigning the older and more probable date to these artists would vanish.

work; and the statues of Apollo, Diana, Hercules, and Minerva, were finished by them. Among their more distinguished scholars appear Tectæus and Angelion, Doryclidas, Dontas, Medon, Theocles, and, especially, Learchus.* Some writers have imagined that these eminent sculptors lived as late as 540 B.C. Flaxman† considered the older date the more probable one.

The above artists of the earlier times of Greek sculpture necessarily claim notice in a history of the art, however limited may be the reliable information respecting their practice. The accounts of Pliny and Pausanias as to their probable date seem to defy adjustment. The most remote certainly appears the more probable one.

The names of Bupalus and Anthermus, who lived soon after Dipœnus and Scyllis, deserve to be noticed, as they distinguished themselves by a variety of works of a high character, which were preserved at Chios and other places. A group of the Graces by Bupalus, which was at Smyrna, is highly spoken of, and it is worthy of remark, that at this period the Graces were always represented draped. Pausanias says Bupalus was an able architect as well as sculptor.

Bathycles, of Magnesia, the author of the throne of Apollo, at Amyclæ, a work of sufficient importance to be especially noticed by Pausanias,‡ is supposed to have

* Paus. ii. 32; iii. 17, etc. † Lect., pp. 75-79. ‡ Lib. iii. 18.

lived about 600 years before the Christian era; though some writers have brought his date down rather lower, and have placed him at about 530 B.C.

Pliny,* recording all that he heard, says the plastic art (modelling) was introduced into Italy about 550 B.C., or it may be rather earlier, by Demaratus, who fled from Corinth accompanied by two artists of that country, named Eucheirus and Eugrammus, after the usurpation of Cypselus. This, however, is so improbable as to be inadmissible. Indeed, as has been observed, the composition or etymology of the names of the companions of Demaratus is suggestive of titles of skill rather than of family. They may all have exercised their art with ability and success, making for themselves a great reputation; but modelling was, of course, universally known and practised long before this date.

The period now reached is one of the most important in the history of Greece and its colonies, as regards the advancement of philosophy, the progress of literature, science, and art, and for the political changes that mark the time. With respect to art, the practice of sculpture, which hitherto had been carried on with great comparative success in Asia Minor, received a check which greatly affected its fortunes. The growing discontent and impatience of the people under the Persian rule exhibited itself at last in open revolt against Darius

* Lib. xxxv. 12.

Hystaspes, and the local consequences were most disastrous to the insurgents. One of the first measures of Darius, in his attempt to suppress the wide-spreading insurrection, was the demolition of the temples and many of the cities of the offending population. The inhabitants were driven to seek refuge in distant places; some became slaves, and others were punished with the utmost severity. Thus art had no resting-place where hitherto it had been flourishing; and Asia, so far, lost its prestige as the great school or home of sculpture. But as it fell here it rose in Europe. The artists of Sicyon, Corinth, and Ægina, especially, gave an impulse to the development of sculpture in those localities; and many names of eminent men are found practising their art with such success that the colonies were soon found to hold quite an equal place with what may be called the parent country.

To about this date may be attributed the execution of one of the most remarkable and interesting series of sculptured monuments that have reached our times. These are the statues, before alluded to, which were brought from the ruins of a temple in the Island of Ægina, and are now preserved at Munich. Before, however, describing them more particularly, it may be well to offer a few preliminary remarks, even at the risk of repetition, on the general character of the early monuments of this date.

From the most archaïc period to about 600 B.C., there probably was but slight change as regards style in sculpture, though no doubt improvements were effected in some of the executive processes. At the later date referred to, a great step was made in the art; and it will be seen that from this time (600 or 550 B.C.) the advancement of sculpture was continuous and rapid to a degree that is perfectly surprising.

Before proceeding, however, with the consideration of some of the more interesting of the earlier monuments discovered within the present century, attention may be directed to the ancient lions still standing over the gate of Mycenæ, and supposed to be the oldest example existing of Greek sculpture. This work is in stone, in high relief. The two lions are represented on their hind legs, with the front feet resting on the shaft of a column standing between them. Pausanias* says this was reputed to be the work of the Cyclops. In other words, that nothing was known of its date or authorship, and therefore it was attributed to supernatural agency. Many of the most ancient erections in Italy, especially in Etruria, as well as in Greece, have, from the absence of historical records, been awarded to the same mythical workmen. The heads of the animals are destroyed, and the other portions too much injured to allow of any judgment as to the style of the art,

* Paus. ii. 16.

beyond the general character of archaïc heaviness which is found in so many of the earlier works.

The statues from Branchidæ have already been referred to for the peculiarities they exhibit of archaïc design. They are of very great interest in an antiquarian point of view, but they offer nothing for the improvement of the student as works of art. They are only remarkable for the same character of heaviness and clumsiness of execution that has been noticed in the lions of Mycenæ, and which appears also in the sculptures of Selinus.

The Branchidæ sculptures have given us the name of an artist not hitherto known. On one of the seated statues is inscribed the name of Terpsicles.*

It remains to mention the very interesting archaïc sculptures discovered in Lycia in 1842-47, and now deposited in the British Museum. The statues and rilievi in this collection are of different periods, down to a comparatively late date; but the slabs on the tomb (called) of the Harpies, and some few fragments of draped statues, are of the most ancient type; curiously illustrating the infancy of Greek sculpture, and its distinctness of character from that of any other people. The consideration of these peculiarities forms an interesting and instructive introduction to the study of the highest type of Greek art; and we are fortunate in

* Newton, *Sculptures of Halicarnassus and Branchidæ*, vol. ii.

possessing in our national collection of antiquities undoubted monuments of the different schools and dates to which these important steps in the progress of Greek sculpture may be attributed. The earlier Lycian monuments are valuable links in the chain of archaïc art-evidence; but there are other still more striking examples to which attention must also be directed.

In alluding to certain characteristics of archaïc treatment in style, especial reference has been made to the sculptures of Selinus. These consist of some fragments of metopes from two temples discovered in Sicily in the year 1823. One represents a portion of a combat between a warrior and a female. Three others, from another temple, are of historical or mythological subjects. The art of all these remains is very rude, but extremely curious and interesting, especially with reference to the growing change in sculpture. The proportions of the figures are short. The waists are remarkably contracted, and the heads, thighs, calves, and feet, large and heavy. The legs and feet are represented in profile, though the figures are fronting the spectator. The execution of the hair is formal, being long, and falling over the shoulders. It is also in some of the figures plaited. As usual in archaïc design, all the figures, whatever their occupation, appear to be laughing. There is a total absence of beauty in all these sculptures. In the head of the fallen warrior some exceptional peculiarities will, however, be observed, which seem to refer it to a higher school of art than the others. So strong a resemblance appears in it to some of the

FIGURE IN ALTO-RILIEVO. SELINUS.

heads of the Æginetan sculpture, that it might be fancied that a portion of these works may have been superintended by artists from that rising school, while others may have been the productions of native artists. This is especially remarkable in the treatment of the statues from the western compared with those brought from the eastern temple. It may be that some of the artists employed were travellers from the Greek schools, and that some may have been drawn from the opposite coasts. This, if they were Carthaginians, would account perhaps for the peculiarly heavy character in the heads of two or three of the figures as compared with that of the dying warrior. The date of these interesting monuments may probably be reckoned at about 600 B.C., or perhaps a little earlier. The originals are in the Museum of Antiquities at Palermo, but casts from them are deposited in the British Museum. Selinus was founded about 620 B.C., and though it was taken and sacked by the Carthaginians, was not finally destroyed till about 270 B.C.

DYING WARRIOR.—SELINUS.

The above sculptures may be referred to a very early period of its history; and the student of the history of the art will be struck with the examples they afford of the progressive changes which begin now to mark the development of Greek sculpture.

The remarkable series of marble statues, already alluded to, that form the Æginetan collection of sculptures, of which also we only possess casts, was discovered in the year 1812 in the island of Ægina. They decorated the two pediments of a temple dedicated to Jupiter Panhellenius. They consist, in addition to numerous fragments, of sixteen statues, of which eleven belonged to the western pediment and five to that at the eastern end of the temple. The first eleven appear to complete the composition required to fill the space, and are therefore considered to be the entire number originally intended on that side. The eastern end is, of course, very deficient. The subjects of both are combats; and in the more extensive series Minerva appears in the centre as the presiding power. She is of somewhat larger proportions than the combatants, and is raised on a step or plinth. The colossal dimensions of the divinities, compared with mortals, are quite consistent with the descriptions of the poets. In the Iliad, in the combat between Minerva and Mars,* the goddess throws at her opponent an enormous mass of rock, which strikes him to the earth, and Homer says he covered seven acres. The goddess is here fully armed, with her helmet on, and on her left arm is a large circular shield. In her right hand, which was bent towards her front, was in all probability a spear. Her ægis covers her bust; the edge of it shews the winding bodies of the snakes, and these terminate in small points or tails, formed of metal. The figures extended on either side of the centre are engaged in battle; some are in violent action, some wounded and dying. It is remarkable that the figures of the eastern pediment are of a larger scale than those of the western side.

* Ἑπτὰ δ' ἐπέσχε πέλεθρα.
"And seven broad acres covers as he lies."
Hom. *Il.* xxi. 407, *et seq.*

These sculptures offer many points of great interest to the student. Their general style may be classed as archaïc, but there are peculiarities and varieties even here that shew the commencement of an important movement. The statue of Minerva is of a much more ancient or rude style than the rest of the figures; from which two important conclusions may be drawn:—*First*, that although all the statues are unquestionably of the same date, there was a style of art already known and practised superior to that which was sometimes employed; and, *secondly*, that in the statues or representations of divinities, the sculptors were still under some obligation to conform to prescribed rules. This seems to be proved in the present instance. While the combatants, who are mortals, exhibit every variety and generally entire correctness of action, the goddess is stiff and primitive; and she stands, as in the most ancient types, with both feet turned sideways, in the same direction; an attitude of extreme difficulty and insecurity, but which constantly occurs in very archaïc monuments. In the other figures there is a considerable display of knowledge of form, and an approach to broad treatment in the execution; and though the details are not yet equal to the excellence of the subsequent school, there is a feeling for true proportion, and an agreeable and harmonious balance of parts. Yet here again the archaïc element steps in in the character of the heads, which exhibit all the peculiarities of the more ancient schools before referred to However earnestly engaged, and even when wounded and dying, each warrior or hero has a smiling expression; the mouth being slightly open, as though the occupation of slaying and being slain was of the most pleasing and satisfactory nature. The hair is worked with the utmost care, in small curls and knobs, in the manner before described.

ÆGINA.—HEAD OF A WARRIOR.

These sculptures afford some instructive and interesting details of costume. Some of the figures are armed with defensive armour, composed of helmets, cuirasses, and greaves; and the manner of attaching the different parts of each piece is clearly shown. In many cases this was done with metal, for although the fastenings are lost there still are the holes to which the plates or buckles were attached. The dress of one figure is very remarkable. It appears to be composed of leather, which fits closely to the body from the throat downwards. This coat clings to the limbs, to the wrists, and upper part of the thighs. Here it overlies tight leggings or pantaloons, which terminate at the ankles. The feet are naked. The head-dress appears also to be made of folded leather, and a long flap falls down the back, as if to protect the neck. He is represented kneeling on one knee in the act of shooting from a bow, and a quiver, it may be of thin wood, or more probably of leather, hangs at his left side.

The subject of this remarkable series of sculptures is scarcely yet satisfactorily determined. Antiquarians differ as to their precise meaning and their date. Judging from the style, which approaches very nearly to that found in the works of the artists who immediately preceded the school of Phidias, considering also the high character of the Æginetan school and the eminent artists who composed it, it may be inferred that their date cannot be very remote from the period which our history may be said to have reached—namely, between five hundred and six hundred years before the Christian era. The learned Müller, indeed, inclines to the opinion that they were later, and draws his conclusion from the style of the architecture of the temple to which they belonged, and from the costume of the archer, whom he considers a Persian, and even thinks they may have been subsequent to the battle of Salamis.*

The originals of these interesting monuments are now in the Glyptotheke of Munich, but casts of them are preserved in the British Museum, where the groups are arranged as they were seen in the pediments of their respective temples.

* Illas enim post bellum Salaminium factas esse, tum ædis cujus in fastigiis positæ erant architecturæ ratio, tum vestis sagittarii Persici in Paride diligenter repræsentata, mihi quidem persuasere.—C. Odof. Müller, *De Vitâ Phidiæ.* The argument is by no means conclusive.

SECTION V.

BEFORE at once entering upon the history of sculpture of the greatest period of the art, a few remarks may advantageously be offered upon the schools and artists immediately preceding. The most celebrated of the former were those of Sicyon, Ægina, and Corinth; and from about 500 B. C. the succession of the sculptors and the changes each effected in the style of his art may be traced with tolerable accuracy. Callon was a sculptor of Ægina, and probably one of the earliest; but his precise date is uncertain, and the only work recorded as his is a statue in wood of Minerva. After him appears Onatas, who was both sculptor and painter, and Pausanias describes many of his works.* Amongst these were several of bronze; some were of colossal dimensions, and others of ordinary scale. At Pergamus was a colossal statue of Apollo; at Olympia a colossal Hercules; also one of bronze dedicated by the Thasians; also at Olympia a statue of Mercury, placed there by the people of Pheneos; and a statue of Ceres and

* Paus. vi. viii. ix. x.

others. Onatas executed some works in connection with other sculptors; Calliteles, for instance, assisted him with the above-named statue of Mercury. In another work—a chariot with accompaniments, which was dedicated at Olympia—we find him associated with Calamis; and in another with one Calynthus, of whose history nothing is known. Pausanias also states that certain of his performances in the sister art were preserved in the temple of Minerva Aræa. Canachus is also another sculptor referred to at this time. Glaucias of Ægina is to be noticed as one of the earliest artists celebrated for his metal works. The date of this sculptor is established by the fact of his having been employed by Gelon, king of Sicily, who lived at 491 B.C.

A mere list of the numerous works of the sculptors who gave celebrity to the school of Ægina would scarcely be of value unless the monuments themselves could be consulted to shew the peculiarities of practice which distinguished each artist. Few, if any, of these are extant, or can be identified; but there is sufficient in the statues from Ægina, already noticed, to exhibit clearly, in certain particulars, as in the larger massing of the muscles and the broad divisions of the parts, the preparatory steps which so soon led to the establishment of the grand style which is so striking in the sculpture of the age of Pericles.

Among the sculptors who illustrated the period now

arrived at, are Hegias or Egesias, Myron, Pythagoras, Phidias, Polycletus, and Alcamenes—the greatest names that occur in the annals of the art, inasmuch as these were the founders of the noblest school of sculpture that has been known to exist. The art was undergoing an entirely new phase, and an element was being admitted into its practice which hitherto had not been recognised—namely, the value of an improved standard of form. It was the development of this principle by this school that has given their great superiority and importance to the productions of the artists and time referred to.

It has been observed that the Æginetan statues indicate the steps by which this revolution in sculpture was brought about. This is exhibited in a very remarkable manner by the indirect testimony of unprofessional critics; and it is curious and not a little interesting to find ancient writers illustrating another art—that of oratory—by a reference to peculiarities in the practice of sculpture; by which we not only acquire some very valuable information upon the subject of the changes and progress already adverted to, also shewing how the art passed through its various phases, out of the early archaïc manner, into the more perfect school of which Polycletus and Phidias were the greatest ornaments; but are also furnished with an authentic list of names of the successive ancient sculptors, by whom principally these changes and improvements were effected.

Quintilian* refers to the style of Callon and Egesias, saying their works were hard and severe, approximating to the Etruscan manner, and that Calamis made his less rigid and stiff in their character. Then, again, Cicero refers to the characteristics of other sculptors, in like manner carrying on the sequence of names, and giving in his list two of the contemporaries of Phidias. The statues of Canachus, he says, are more rigid than is agreeable or consistent with the truth of nature; and that those of Calamis are also hard; but, it is added, they are softer than those of Canachus. The works of Myron, he says, are scarcely yet sufficiently truthful, yet they may be classed as beautiful, compared with the others referred to. Those by Polycletus, however, are admitted to be clearly of a higher and more approved quality, and indeed are pronounced perfect.† This series of sculptors, leading from the artists of an archaïc school to two of the most famous contemporaries of Phidias, is one of the highest importance in establishing the succession of the sculptors, and the steps by which the art was carried to perfection. Of Pythagoras, one of the artists above mentioned, Pliny says

* Duriora et Tuscanicis proxima Callon et Egesias, jam minus rigida Calamis, etc.—*Orat. Instit.* xii. 10. 7. The spelling of the second name differs in various writers. It is found as Hegias, Egesias, and Hegesias.

† Quis non intelligit Canachi signa rigidiora esse quàm ut imitentur veritatem? Calamidis dura illa quidem, sed tamen molliora quam Canachi; nondum Myronis satis ad veritatem adducta, jam tamen quæ non dubites pulchra dicere. Pulchriora etiam Polycleti et jam planè perfecta, etc.—Cic. *de Clar. Orat.* xviii. 70.

he was the first sculptor who expressed the veins and who treated the hair with peculiar skill or delicacy.* Some further remarks on the still remaining archaïsms in the style of Myron, will be made when that sculptor is more particularly referred to. These notices here cited lose none of their value from not being contemporaneous with the artists they refer to. They no doubt had the authority of tradition, and would not have been put forth by such eminent writers as Cicero and Quintilian unless they had felt they would be received as trustworthy. It is also probable that some of the very works alluded to were known at the time; indeed, the expressions used suggest that the reader might satisfy himself of the truthfulness of the critic's illustrations.

It will be proper now to consider more at length the history of the sculptors who appear in the earlier part of the fifth century B. C.

Myron was an Athenian, and a pupil, together with Phidias and Polycletus, of Ageladas. He is said to have introduced a greater variety in his art than those who preceded him; but Pliny says he was not considered successful in expressing sentiment or passion, and that in his art-treatment there was still much of the stiffness of the early schools. His style was, in all probability, hard and minute, but he must still be considered one of

* Plin. *Hist. Nat.* xxxiv. 8. Hic primus nervos ac venas expressit, capillumque diligentius.

those sculptors by whose assistance the art was brought to excellence. A very interesting specimen of this master's manner is seen in a marble statue in the British Museum, of a Discobolus or Quoit-thrower, generally believed to be a copy of the famous statue by Myron so minutely described by Lucian and Quintilian. Though there is considerable dryness of manner in this work, it nevertheless possesses qualities which claim for the sculptor a higher character than Pliny's account of him would alone have justified us in awarding him. The original was of bronze; and the copy referred to—one of three known to exist—bears out the somewhat severe judgment of the ancient critic. The statue is full of action, even to exaggeration, and the character of form and the style of execution associate it with the known date of its author. The figure leans forward, resting the weight of the body on the right leg, upon which the left arm, crossing the body, rests just above the wrist. The right arm is extended behind the figure, and the upraised hand, spread out, firmly grasps the disc, which is just about to be hurled forward with force. The head looks down. There is a peculiar expression, very true to nature, given in the dragging of the left leg, or rather foot, of which the toes are bent, shewing their under side.

The ancient comment on this work expresses the judgment of the writer, when he reflects on what he calls its distortion and over-elaboration.* Myron and Polycletus were rivals as artists in bronze works, and, as has been observed, they had their preferences for the kinds they used. Polycletus employed the bronze of Ægina, Myron that of Delos. Pythagoras has already been noticed as the first sculptor who was remarkable for his careful execution of certain details, as the hair and veins. He was a native of Rhegium, and supported the credit of the school of which Learchus was so distinguished a member. There is much difficulty in making the execution of some of the works attributed to this Pythagoras correspond with the date at which he is supposed to have lived; and it has led to the very probable belief that there were different sculptors of the same name. One of Samos is met with. The chief, or most celebrated, was said to be a scholar of Clearchus, also of Rhegium; and this would account for the archaïsm of his style. A statue by Pythagoras, representing a wounded or lame man, is recorded, in which the expression of bodily suffering was so admirably and forcibly given that the spectators were affected by it, and seemed to share the anguish of the sufferer. Many other works of this artist are mentioned by Pliny,† who in the same passage also

* "Quid tam distortum et elaboratum quàm est ille Discobolus Myronis," etc. Quint., *Trist. Or.*, ii. 13. 10. (Lucian, *Philops.* 18).

† Pliny says, "Vicit Myronem Pythagoras Rheginus." *Hist. Nat.* xxxiv. 8. See also Sillig. *Cat. Artif.*

refers to the productions of the Samian Pythagoras above alluded to.

One of the most famous sculptors in the annals of Greek art, and of whom many most interesting particulars are mentioned by ancient writers, is Polycletus. There are at least three of the name recorded, but the most eminent is called by Pliny *Sicyonius*. It is possible, however, as a sculptor equally celebrated was also called *Argivus*, that he may have been a native of Sicyon, but was considered an Argive from having produced so many of his most important works at Argos; and thus that the two epithets were bestowed on the same individual. The more celebrated artist of the name is noted for the great care and perfection of his finish; but it is said he wanted variety in his art. The precise force or meaning of this criticism is not easily understood, in the absence of works by which it might be tested; but it has been supposed to refer to the frequent repetition of the same attitude in his statues. This Polycletus was the author of one statue especially, a "Doryphorus," or lance-bearer, which was so perfect in its proportions that it was called by common consent "the Canon." Artists referred to it as a rule or standard of art.* An extraordinary number of works by this accomplished sculptor are described by the writers on art of ancient times.

* "Fecit et quem Canona artifices vocant, lineamenta artis ex eô petentes velut a lege quâdam." (Plin. *Hist. Nat.* xxxiv. 8. 55.)

From the extent of his practice, the high character of his productions, and the encomiums bestowed on them, he seems to have been distinguished in every branch of his profession, and was no unworthy rival of the greatest of the great artists who illustrated the age of Pericles. In one process he is pronounced to have surpassed even Phidias himself; for Pliny, in handing down a tradition of the practice of the *Toreutic* art, says that Polycletus perfected or consummated what Phidias had only commenced.* This remark, it has been conjectured, applies to works in *Chryselephantine* sculpture (gold and ivory); a mode of practising the art much patronised at that time, and in which both these artists were greatly celebrated.

Ageladas, or, as it sometimes occurs, Eladas, of Argos, is another sculptor mentioned with great honour by ancient writers. Many works by him are enumerated; but few particulars are given which can be of value to students respecting the peculiar style of his art. A mere list of his productions, with the conjectures of antiquaries respecting the time at which they were executed, must be considered as belonging to the history of the artist individually, rather than of sculpture generally. The subject is not, however, without interest; and much curious matter will be found in the article on this sculp-

* Hic consummâsse hanc scientiam judicatur, et *Toreuticen* sic erudisse ut Phidias aperuisse.—Plin. xxxiv. 8, 56.

tor in the catalogue before referred to of Sillig, as well as in Müller's treatise on the archæology of art. The frequent mention of Ageladas in ancient writers proves the eminent position he held in the history of the great masters of sculpture.* Perhaps the circumstance of the greatest interest connected with Ageladas is, that he was said to be the master of Phidias, Polycletus, and Myron —three of the brightest names that appear in the annals of art. This fact alone is sufficient to justify the belief that Ageladas was a sculptor of high reputation, and that his works must have been of no ordinary excellence to have attracted students of the class of these afterwards eminent masters to place themselves in his school.

Circumstances were peculiarly favourable to the development of art in the age at which this history has now arrived; and it was fortunate that there were such sculptors and architects as Phidias, Polycletus, Myron, Praxiteles, Ictinus, and Callicrates, to take advantage of and do justice to the opportunities offered for the highest exercise of their talents. The progress of sculpture received an immense impulse from the glorious fortunes that attended the patriotic resistance of the Greeks to the invasion of the Persians under Xerxes. A series of successes in this war gave them confidence in their own prowess; and the defeat of their powerful enemy not

* Plin. *Hist. Nat.* xxxiv. 8. Paus. vi. 8; vii. 24; x. 10. Junius *de Picturâ Veterum.* Sillig. *Catalogus artificum,* in verb. O. Müller, *Archæologie der Kunst, etc.*

only added to this feeling of national importance and reliance, but it also threw into their hands the means of effecting some of the most glorious achievements in art. An enormous amount of wealth flowed into the public treasury, much of which was applied to the production of the noblest public works in architecture and sculpture. It was a custom in Greece to dedicate a portion of all spoils gained in battle to the service or honour of the immortal gods; and at this time a tenth of that obtained from the Persians was appropriated to this high service.

Happily the opportunities this application of wealth afforded for the advancement of art were met and assisted by a greater amount of talent in the respective professions of architecture and sculpture than had ever before appeared.

The stimulus thus given had, as will be seen, the most important effect on all the arts of design. The extraordinary opportunity thus offered of distinction, among those who devoted themselves to the class of art especially required in works destined to do honour to the gods; to mark the gratitude of a nation; and, at the same time, to commemorate the glory of their country—excited a spirit of honourable emulation in the artists that called forth their talent, and led to that perfection in art which, still seen in existing monuments, strikes, even at this distant period, modern nations with wonder and admiration.

SECTION VI.

TILL the character of sculpture exhibited those slight changes in its mode of presentation, which is first observable, in any marked degree, in what has been called the Æginetan school, the art was only used as the means of recording events, or of doing honour to the gods by the dedication of religious statues in the temples. Iconic or portrait statues were indeed permitted, as has been already shewn; but these were in the category of semi-religious offerings. No interest had, as yet, been shewn in the representation of forms of beauty; and the whole of the sculpture, of whatever nation or time before this, seems to bear out the impression that it never was exercised with this object. No doubt can be entertained that, after the first difficulties of execution had been overcome and the mechanical parts of the art were understood, this natural step in an imitative art would have been taken by sculptors had there not been some repressing influence to check it. The whole history of the most early art suggests what this influence was. It appears in Egyptian art, in that of Assyria, of Etruria—

indeed, wherever the practice of sculpture can be traced. Being employed to incite religious impressions, and in the representation of religious subjects, the priests felt the importance of not allowing the popular sympathies or habits to be disturbed by offering to their submissive votaries objects of art that should obviously differ from those to which they had always been accustomed. An entirely new form would be suggestive either of a new divinity, or of a former object of interest and worship being superseded by a novelty which required explanation. Or it might be that if the senses were seduced or appealed to by sculpture representing attractive or beautiful forms, the mystical *ideal* of the god might be impaired in the popular mind; that the divinity might be too nearly associated with familiar forms; and, while the religious sentiment might be weakened, that it was possible the influence, the power, and the interests of the priests might also be compromised. Whatever may have been the cause, the fact is indisputable of the long continuance of a prescriptive and essentially conventional style of art; and it is not till the changes adverted to were made by the earlier Greek sculptors, and carried on, as has been shewn by the bold genius of some of those so recently noticed—as Myron, Pythagoras, and Polycletus—that there is any satisfactory indication that sculpture was considered capable of being developed into an art of the very highest class of imitation. It will now be seen how, and by whom especially, this great consummation was effected.

Phidias, a native of Athens, the son of Charmidas,* also an Athenian, was the greatest sculptor whose name and fame have reached modern times; and fortunately some undoubted works produced by him, or under his immediate direction, remain to attest the justice of the distinction that has been universally awarded him. He was born in the 73d Olympiad, or 484 years B.C. His masters were Hippias, of whom little is known (indeed he is mentioned but by one author), and Ageladas, above mentioned. At one time he is said to have studied painting, an art professed by some of his family; but it is as the greatest of all sculptors that the reputation of Phidias has reached modern times. It has been seen by preceding remarks that the sculptors of what has been termed the Æginetan school, immediately prior to this time, laid the foundation of a finer style of art which Phidias assisted in bringing to perfection. The preparation for this consummation takes nothing, however, from the honour due to this sculptor; for the superior quality of the art which he eventually produced stamps it with a character of grandeur and beauty entirely its own.

It was in Athens, under the enlightened administration of Pericles, that some of the most famous, because

* Φειδίας Χαρμίδου υἱὸς Ἀθηναῖος.

the most perfect, works in architecture and sculpture were produced that the world has ever seen. Immense funds were in the hands of the Athenians from various sources; and though Pericles subjected himself to severe animadversion, for this partial employment of the wealth accumulated ostensibly for other purposes, he boldly took upon himself to use a large portion of it to decorate the city, and to make Athens, what she really became, the admiration of all Greece. Artists in every branch of art were called in to give effect to this resolution; and while Ictinus and Callicrates, the architects, were employed upon the construction of the temples, the greatest of sculptors, Phidias, superintended all the sculptured decoration and enrichment, and controlled the general designs.

Plutarch and various other writers record the favour with which Phidias was especially honoured by this accomplished patron of art, and the great responsibility thrown upon him. Speaking of the more remarkable edifices erected during his government, he says, "It was Phidias who had the direction of these works, although great architects and skilful artists were employed under him;" and he adds, "as the various works were completed, they were not only admired for their scale and grandeur, but for the grace and perfection of art they exhibited; for every artist was ambitious that the excellence of the workmanship should equal the beauty of the design."* He remarks also upon the rapidity with which these great undertakings were completed, shewing the stimulus given by this noble employment, and the effect it had upon those engaged in it. The works here referred to are the statue of Minerva, and the sculpture for the decoration of the Parthenon at Athens; and the fame acquired by these alone is sufficient to establish the undoubted genius of their author. A still more important production of Phidias was the statue of Jupiter Olympius at Elis; and a short description of performances of such universal high repute will be interesting as shewing the quality of this sculptor's art.

Both these works were executed in what has been called *Chryselephantine* sculpture. This was a combination chiefly of two materials, gold and ivory;† of which, as applied to great works of this kind, Phidias, from the expression before referred to with reference to Polycletus having consummated or perfected that which Phidias began, has been thought the inventor.

These works, sparkling with gold, precious stones, and painted ornament, were produced when sculpture was in a transition state. It had by no means entirely emancipated itself from the stiff and severe style in which the older statues had been from time immemorial executed; nor, as will be seen from some facts connected with these productions, had the old prejudices regarding

* Plut. Pericl. 13. † From χρυσὸς *gold*, and ἐλέφας *ivory*.

what may be termed religious art been overcome. It cannot be supposed that statues, which hitherto had been of a prescribed type, were allowed at once to be treated altogether differently from the manner recognized as hieratic. Although the genius of Phidias, supported by the influence of Pericles, may have effected the fullest change in less important matters, in the architectural decoration of the sculpture of the Parthenon, for instance—that is, in the pediments, the metopes, and the frieze of the *cella*—it is not probable that the old feeling would be disregarded in the treatment of the statues of the presiding deities of the respective temples and localities. That there was much even here in advance of the former schools need not be doubted, but the very circumstance of the sculptor having to load his work with elaborate ornament, to use a great variety of materials, to make the parts of the figures themselves in small pieces of ivory, the drapery in gold, and this again to have flowers painted on it, suggests that these grand chryselephantine compositions are rather to be placed in the category of gorgeous idols, the offering and expression of popular devotion, than of works of the highest ideal art. They wanted, above all, that noble simplicity which is so remarkable in the marble sculptures referred to, and which, without prejudice, may be considered to constitute one of their greatest excellences. It is curious and not insignificant to find it recorded that Phidias himself seemed to prefer marble for the statue of Minerva for the Parthenon.*

Of these greater works for which Phidias is so celebrated, there are unfortunately no remains; but they were objects of such general interest and admiration in their time, that the most full and accurate descriptions of them have been handed down on most reliable authority; that is, either of eye-witnesses or by direct tradition.

Taking these works in the order of their scale and public importance, the statue of Jupiter, executed for the Eleans, claims prior attention. The exposed or naked parts of the figure were made of ivory; the drapery and other accessories being added in gold, and enriched in various ways; the former had on it flowers, painted in their natural colours. The ivory could, of course, only be used in small pieces; these were shaped according to a model previously prepared, and then closely fitted together at their edges, and fastened with pins over a rough, general shape or *nucleus* of wood. The god was represented seated on a throne composed chiefly of gold, and elaborately ornamented. At the back, over the head of the figure, were groups of the Hours or Seasons on one side, and on the other the Graces. At the four angles of the throne were small statues of Victories, and

* Val. Max., lib. i.; Quatremère de Quincy, *Le Jupitér Olymp.*, 3e partie.

on different panels and other parts, various well-known subjects were represented of ancient poetry and mythology. Among these was the destruction of the children of Niobe by Apollo and Diana; the Theban youths being carried away by the Sphinx; the contest between the companions of Hercules and the Amazons; and groups of young persons engaged in athletic sports. The number of figures stated by Pausanias to be exhibited in these various compositions is extraordinary.* Indeed, nothing can exceed the splendour and magnificence of the ornamental compositions described as part of this gorgeous work, of which the first intention evidently was to strike the spectator with wonder and astonishment, by its richness and sparkling effect.

The statue itself was of colossal proportions; being about forty feet high, exclusive of the pedestals; and some say it measured sixty feet altogether. This alone must greatly have contributed to produce the grand and awful effect which is ascribed to this noble work. The brows of the god were crowned with a wreath of olive, and the expression of the countenance was that of calm and majestic dignity. In his left hand he supported a statue of Victory, and in his right he held his sceptre. The Victory was composed of ivory and gold. The sceptre was of the latter material, and was surmounted by the eagle of Jove.

* Paus. v. ii. 1.

Phidias employed his half-brother Panœnus, a painter, to assist him in decorating this work. It does not, however, appear, that his services were required on the nobler parts of the figure itself, though, possibly, he may have painted the flowers on the drapery. The portion especially alluded to as his work was the painted parts of the throne or balustrade.

In this statue, Jupiter was represented rather as the local deity than in his usual character, armed with the thunderbolt, the supreme king of gods and men. The temple was erected in the sacred grove of Altis, in the immediate neighbourhood of the spot where the most important of the games of Greece, the Olympian, were celebrated, and it was surrounded by the statues and votive offerings of the successful competitors in these contests. Jove therefore appeared here as the presiding genius of the place and of the peaceful exercises which called together all the population of Greece who were disposed to witness those great trials of intellectual and physical excellence. The god, crowned with olive, was seen as the judge and the dispenser of victory and honour; supporting in his hand the type of success—the statue of a Victory decorated with a wreath, and extending in one hand the mark of honour, a crown, and holding in the other a palm branch. Pausanias says the work bore this simple inscription, "Pheidias, the Athenian, the son of Charmidas, made me."

The colossal proportions of this statue, compared with the temple in which it was placed, has occasioned a judicious criticism of Strabo. If it had stood up, he says, it would have been higher than the roof of the building, and, therefore, that the statue was disproportioned to the temple. This gigantic size, overpowering and dwarfing the building it inhabited, no doubt would give increased importance to the statue itself; but it was effected at the expense of the temple, and was at variance with one of the best of all rules; that of common sense and propriety in the due fitness or relation of things to each other.

The reader who desires further information respecting the mode of execution, the various subjects represented in its decoration, and the enthusiastic admiration bestowed by ancient writers upon this celebrated production, may advantageously consult the elaborate work of M. Quatremère de Quincy;* in which also many very interesting particulars upon the whole question of chryselephantine and toreutic art are collected.

An interesting anecdote is recorded by Pausanias, shewing the importance attached by the Greeks to this great national monument. Phidias, the story says, after the completion of the work, besought a sign from the god in whose honour it had been executed to intimate whether it was acceptable and pleasing to him. A flash

* Le Jupiter Olympien.

of lightning immediately descended into the temple, and struck the pavement in front of the astonished and gratified sculptor. This was at once hailed as a proof of the satisfaction of the deity, and a brazen vase was placed on the spot to commemorate the circumstance: Pausanias says it was existing in his time.

Although the accounts of the magnificent and varied decorations of this work convey rather an impression of barbaric splendour than of a fine style of sculpture, the encomiums passed upon it by the writers of antiquity, some of whom had an opportunity of seeing it, while others had the authority of tradition for their notices of it, prove beyond question the very high character both of the work itself and of the genius of its author.* It would be unprofitable here to enumerate the various notices, scattered over ancient writings, of the greatness and glory of the Olympian Jupiter, and the praises bestowed upon its sculptor. Phidias acquired the distinguished title of "the sculptor of the gods." An author records that "its beauty and majesty seemed to have added something even to the dignity of religion."†

After making due allowance for the religious sentiment with which the statue would be contemplated, and for the feeling of national pride in the Greeks in pos-

* "Jovem Olympium quem nemo æmulatur."—Plin. 34. 8, 54; and see Quatremère de Quincy.

† "Cujus pulchritudo adjecisse aliquid etiam acceptæ religioni videtur, adeo majestas operis Deum æquavit."—Quinct. xii. 10.

sessing a monument which, for the richness of the materials alone, was one of the marvels of the world, enough would still remain to warrant the belief in its value as a worthy performance of the great master. The undoubted remains of works known to have been produced under the immediate guidance of Phidias, testify to the noble character of his art, and to the perfection then attained in the representation of the highest type of human form. There need be no doubt that this was as far as possible maintained in the statue of Jupiter; although the old prejudice in favour of sacred prescriptive types had to be humoured to enable the sculptor to represent the god in the perfection of human beauty. But however worthy of admiration, with respect to this improvement and novelty in ideal beauty, it may be fairly supposed that much of the popular enthusiasm bestowed on this splendid production was owing, at this transition period, to the richness of its effect rather than to its merits in a fine-art point of view. The nobler parts being constructed of innumerable pieces of ivory, must have somewhat impaired the beauty of the face, hands, and feet, when examined closely, however perfect the general forms may have been. No skill or care could have rendered the joints altogether imperceptible, and there is no tradition that painting was resorted to by which these unsightly divisions could be covered. Indeed, had colouring been employed to conceal it, the use of ivory would have had no object.

The custody of this masterpiece of Phidias was entrusted to the descendants of the sculptor. They entered on their duties with sacrifices offered to Minerva (Ergane*). They were called *Phaidruntai;* and Pausanias records the interesting fact that the same office, held by the descendants of the original *Phaidruntai*, existed at the time he wrote, about six hundred years after the completion of the statue. The *studio* or workshop in which the statue and its accompaniments had been executed were preserved with great honour. In the centre an altar was erected consecrated to all the gods. The history of this far-famed work is traced through a period of about nine hundred years. It soon required repair. In the third century B.C. the statue was so injured, by the opening of the joints in the ivory, that Damophon, a sculptor of Messene, was employed to repair it. It was struck by lightning in the time of Julius Cæsar, but it is not stated that it received any material injury. Caligula desired to transport it to Rome, with other celebrated works of art; but so many difficulties, real or pretended, were thrown in the way of its removal, that this intention was abandoned. This remarkable work was in existence as late as the fifth century A.D. The temple of Jupiter Olympius was de-

* Paus. lib. v. 14, 5.

stroyed about the year 355 of the Christian era; but it is known that the statue itself had been transported, some time previously, to Constantinople. Its subsequent fate is very uncertainly recorded. It is generally supposed that what remained of it was destroyed by fire in the year 475 A.D.

The next great work of this sculptor was the statue, previously alluded to, of Minerva of the Parthenon, on the Acropolis at Athens. This, like the Jupiter, was composed of gold and ivory. The goddess was here represented standing; holding in her right hand a statue of Victory six feet high, and in her left a spear. She had a helmet on, and on her ægis was the head of Medusa. Her shield was elaborately decorated with a representation of the battle of the gods and giants, and the pedestal exhibited the birth of Pandora. The eyes of the statue were precious stones of a light colour. The whole height of this work was nearly forty feet. It has been calculated that forty-four talents of gold, in weight, were employed on this statue.

The above magnificent *chryselephantine* works are here selected for notice as being the most highly-reputed performances of Phidias; but a long list of colossal and other statues, in various materials—as bronze, marble, wood, as well as gold and ivory—by this artist, might easily be produced to shew the extent and the important character of his employment. As there are no remains of these works left by which posterity may form any judgment of their merit, it would unnecessarily occupy space only to enumerate their titles and subjects. It is, however, satisfactory to be able to contemplate some of the marble decorations of the Parthenon, which may without doubt be attributed to the master mind and hand of Phidias. These are remains of statues and rilievi which were on the exterior of the temple.* They consist of single figures and groups which were placed in the pediments, of several of the metopes, and a considerable portion of the frieze of the *cella*. These works are unquestionably the finest specimens of the art that exist; and they illustrate so fully and so admirably the progress, and it may be said the consummation, of sculpture, that it is important their character and peculiar excellence should be well understood by those who desire to make themselves acquainted with the true principles of this art. They exhibit in a remarkable degree all the qualities that constitute fine art—truth, beauty, and perfect execution. In the forms, the most perfect, the most appropriate, and the most graceful, have been selected. All that is coarse or vulgar in ordinary nature is omitted, and that only is represented which unites the two essen-

* The sculptures here described were brought from Athens by the Earl of Elgin, of whom they were purchased by Parliament, and placed in the National Collection of Antiquities in the British Museum. They are generally known as the Elgin Marbles, from the circumstance of their being first seen in this country as the property of that nobleman.

tial qualities of truth and beauty. The result of this happy combination is what has been termed ideal beauty. The statues of the Ilyssus or river god, of the so-called Theseus,* of Neptune, and the large draped groups, are all remarkable for the qualities referred to, united with grandeur of style and simplicity. Wherever the naked form is shewn there is the most profound knowledge of its anatomical structure and capabilities of action. The draperies, likewise, are everywhere treated with the greatest skill and with the most careful attention to effect, in their opposition to and contrast with the naked. These works deserve also special notice for the admirable management of composition in relief. The metopes afford the best examples of *alto* or high relief, and the frieze of that which is called *basso* or low relief. In the latter especially, the knowledge and skill exhibited in representing, without unseemly and unintelligible confusion, a crowded and busy procession of walking figures, mixed up with riders and horses in every variety of action, and with other animals intended for sacrifice, cannot be too highly praised. It may be observed here that the perfect acquaintance which the best sculptors of this time had with the anatomy and character of animals is worthy of remark. The list of works of this class, given by ancient writers, would in

* The learned antiquary, the Chevalier Brönsted, considered this to be a statue of Cephalus.

itself be sufficient to prove the extensive practice of sculptors, but the remains of art now existing shew also the very high quality of their productions of the kind. Myron was particularly celebrated for his accomplishment in this respect; and the horses in the sculpture of the Parthenon will be admitted by all competent judges of that animal to offer the most perfect representations of shape, action, and high-breeding.

On the Acropolis was another remarkable statue of Phidias. It represented the tutelary goddess of the Athenians in the character of Athene Promachos (Minerva the Defender). She was fully armed, and in the attitude of battle, with one arm raised and holding a spear in her hand. This work was of colossal dimensions, and stood in the open air, nearly opposite the Propylæa. It towered above the roof of the Parthenon, and it is said the crest of the helmet and the point of the spear could be seen as far off as the promontory of Sunium, by ships approaching Athens. Its height is supposed to have been, with its pedestal, about 70 feet. The material was bronze. This work is spoken of as standing in its place so late as the year 395 A.D.

Before entirely quitting the subject of Phidias and his works, an interesting circumstance may be mentioned in connection with the preservation of the two most important productions of the artist—the statues of Jupiter and Minerva. Pausanias says the former was surrounded at its base by a groove or channel of black marble containing oil. The object of this was, no doubt, to supply a small but sufficient quantity of moisture to preserve the ivory from shrinking or contracting, and at the same time also to secure the work from the danger of too much humidity, as the Altis was situated on marshy ground. The necessity for these precautions is evident, for it is recorded that the statue of the Olympian Jupiter was out of repair soon after its completion.

At Athens means were adopted to obviate the damage that might arise to the statue of Minerva from the opposite evil. The Acropolis, where the Parthenon stood, was in so remarkably dry a situation that the ivory composing the figure would be apt to contract from the want of sufficient moisture, and thus, unless this evil could be guarded against, the joints would be likely to re-open, to the great detriment of the appearance of the work, as well as risk to its security.

It is strange, after all the well-merited glory attained by Phidias for these and other great works, to read, that it is believed he was exiled from Athens; then that he died in prison; or, as other accounts say, that he was poisoned. It is recorded that the favour shewn him by Pericles raised up a host of enemies against him, who were envious both of his fame and good fortune; and further, that by attacking the favourite, the party opposed to Pericles felt that they were able to wound and insult

Pericles himself. The accounts of these half political and half personal feuds vary considerably; but ancient writers agree in stating that both the patron and the artist were subjected at this time to great indignities. The sculptor was accused of various serious offences against religion and the state. The first charge was that of sacrilege; inasmuch as he had presumed to introduce among the accessories of the statue of Minerva portraits of Pericles and himself. This being a votive work, and intended for the temple of the goddess, any representation of a mortal combined with the sacred or immortal was considered utterly inadmissible; and this attempt of Phidias to preserve the memory of his protector and himself by means so opposed to usage, and so offensive to public opinion, subjected him to this serious accusation. The next charge preferred against him was that of direct robbery; for having, as it was alleged, appropriated to his own use a portion of the gold which had been supplied to him for the same statue; and it was even hinted that Pericles himself had participated in the fruits of this crime. The prudent foresight of Pericles enabled the sculptor to meet the threatened danger and disgrace which this calumny might have brought upon him. Phidias had been advised by his patron, when the work was in course of execution, so to arrange the drapery of the figure—and it was on this the precious metal had chiefly been employed—that it might at any time be removed without destroying the rest of the work. By doing this the gold, should any question arise as to the quantity used, could easily be weighed, and its proper application proved. It does not appear, however, that this process was insisted on. This charge may have fallen to the ground, but there is every reason to believe that Phidias left Athens, at least for a time; and some accounts say he died, in exile, at Elis. It must be admitted that much difference of opinion exists among scholars and antiquaries respecting the fate of Phidias;* nor are they agreed as to the date and order in which his several great works were produced. His death is supposed to have occurred in the 57th Olympiad, or at (432 B.C.)

The style of sculpture which marks the school of Phidias is of the noblest order. The great characteristic of the works of the time is largeness and grandeur in the masses, and the very highest type of beauty in the forms. They are entirely free from the hardness and stiffness of the immediately preceding sculptors, but they are also equally removed from a soft and meretricious quality which is found in the productions of a subsequent school. In the few remarks made already

* See especially O. D. Müller, *De Vita Phidiæ;* Emeric David, *Examen sur les inculpations contre Phidias;* Sillig., *Catal. Artificum;* Quatremère de Quincy, *Le Jupiter Olympien;* Millin, *Dict. des B. Arts.* In these several works will be found valuable references to other authorities, ancient and modern.

upon the statues and *rilievi* from the Parthenon, some particulars of the artistic power of Phidias in the details are adverted to; and a careful examination of all this remarkable series will shew the student and the lover of art in what the great excellence of this school consists. Sculpture may be said to have reached its culminating point in this age. Never before were works produced, in this art, which so essentially exhibited the union of all the elements of excellence; and never, since that age, have any appeared, of an original school, that can bear comparison with the best productions of the Phidian era. In the first place, their purpose was of the highest. Works of art were not collected for mere pleasure or ostentation, but were required for sacred dedication; to do honour to the gods, and to express the national, religious, and patriotic sentiment. This noble impulse gave additional force to the artistic genius of the sculptor; and a new and most important principle being recognised in the mode of representation—namely, that as an imitative art, sculpture should aim at reproducing the most perfect forms to be met with in nature—the result was such perfection as to make the best art of that age unrivalled.

Among the most celebrated of the scholars and followers of Phidias were—Agoracritus of Paros, Alcamenes of Athens, Colotes or Colotas, Pæonius, and others. Of these, the two first appear to have held the highest rank, and these only need be particularly referred to. Agoracritus was, it is said, the favourite scholar; but Alcamenes, judging from the accounts left of him, was the most able artist. He is said, indeed, to have been second only to his master; and one author says, what was wanting in Polycletus was found in the works of Phidias and Alcamenes.* Agoracritus was so highly esteemed by Phidias that it is said he put the name of this artist on many of his own works. In a competition between Alcamenes and Agoracritus, the subject being a statue of Venus, Pliny says the former gained the majority of suffrages; but, he adds, this was not owing to the superior merit of the work, but to the personal favour of his fellow-citizens, who preferred their own countryman, an Athenian, to a stranger. Agoracritus immediately changed the title or name of his statue to Nemesis, and sold it, in order to prevent it remaining in Athens where this indignity had been put upon him. It was preserved at Rhamnus in Attica. It is curious to read that a statue intended to represent Venus should have been so easily converted into a fitting representative of Nemesis, a character so essentially different from that of the gentle goddess of beauty and love. If the story be true, it is possible that Agoracritus made some alterations in it before he changed its appellation; other-

* Plin. *Hist. Nat.* xxxvi. 5.

wise the preference of the fastidious Athenians for the statue of Alcamenes may be accounted for upon higher grounds than those attributed to them. The work of Agoracritus may have been of too severe a character to meet their approval.

There is a much mutilated marble colossal female head in the British Museum, which was brought from Rhamnus; and it is, without sufficient authority, called Nemesis. But it has a certain interest, however slight, in connection with the above tradition. There is so little of the surface left that it is not easy to pronounce a very decided opinion upon its merit. Its style, so far as it can be judged, is large; and the character of execution, in the portion left of one eye, a part of the cheek and forehead, and the hair, is consistent with the date of Agoracritus. It is also worthy of remark, that its proportions agree with the supposed size of the celebrated statue referred to.

Alcamenes held a distinguished place among the sculptors of this remarkable age, and Pliny and Pausanias mention several of his performances. It is to be lamented that no examples remain by which any judgment can be formed of his peculiar merit. Two works of this artist have been more particularly noticed for their excellence by the writers referred to. One was a bronze statue of a conqueror in the games, a "Pentathlus," which Pliny says was also called "Encrinomenos;" the other a "Venus of the gardens." It was recorded that Phidias himself had worked upon this statue.* Alcamenes, like other great sculptors of the age, executed works in ivory and gold. A statue of Bacchus so composed is mentioned by Pausanias.

It is not necessary to notice others of the scholars of Phidias, as no works are remaining known to be by them, and the style of their art would of course only illustrate the improvement which had been effected under the influence of the great master. It is, however, important here to refer especially to existing original works of this age and school, in which the qualities for which the Phidian period is famous are prominently exhibited.

The sculptures in high relief known as the Phigaleian marbles, and now preserved in the British Museum, are, on satisfactory grounds; attributed to this date, and they deserve the attention of students for the valuable art qualities they possess. They formed part of the decoration of the temple of Apollo Epicouros; and they were discovered, amongst its ruins, on the ancient site of Phigaleia, in Arcadia, in the year 1812. They are of great extent, and represent what was evidently a popular subject for art among the Greeks, namely, the contests between the Centaurs and Lapithæ, and the Greeks and Amazons.

There can be little doubt that these sculptures pro-

* Plin. *Hist. Nat.* xxxiv. 8, xxxvi. 5; Paus. i. 19, viii. 9, ii. 30, etc.

ceeded from the same source as the sculptured decoration of the Parthenon. Pausanias says the temple was built by Ictinus; and as he was assisted by Phidias in his great work at Athens, it is more than probable this sculptor also supplied the designs for the decoration of the Phigaleian temple.

The various groups in these compositions are striking for their vigour and expression; and though the forms are heavy, they exhibit all the character of a high style of art. Their comparative inferiority in some technical points—assuming that the designs were furnished by a master—may easily be accounted for by the probability of their execution being left to inferior artists, working at a distance from the personal superintendence of Phidias. The qualities most deserving the attention of students in this fine work, admitting the deficiencies in form, are richness in the masses, great beauty in the flow of lines in the different groups of figures, and energy without exaggeration in the action and business of the scene represented. Some of the episodes or incidents represented—such as the defence of the wounded, the carrying away the slain, and similar subjects—are exhibited with the most affecting truth and pathos.

SECTION VII.

Polychromy.

BEFORE entering upon a new phase of sculpture, inaugurated by Praxiteles, one of the greatest sculptors of antiquity, it may be desirable to consider, both historically and critically, the subject of *Polychromy*, or colouring, as applied to this art. The precise meaning of the word is *many colours*, from two Greek words signifying *many* and *colour*.* Strictly understood it means the application of pigments or liquid tints, but it may also signify variety of colour by whatever means produced. *Chryselephantine* and *polylithic* sculpture are therefore, in this sense, *polychromic*, quite as much as painted or tinted statues in which the colour may be given by staining, or by laying on red, yellow, or any other paint, with a brush. The reputation obtained by some of the works so treated by the great sculptors of the age of Pericles—as Phidias, Polycletus, Alcamenes, and others—challenges attention and will

* πολὺ, χρώμα.

justify a careful inquiry into the value of this extraneous application of a distinct art, as a means of decorating and assisting sculpture.

All ancient nations amongst whom image-making has been practised appear to have used colour, to enhance the force or effect of the representation. It was done, as has been shewn, by the sculptors of the most renowned school in the fifth century before Christ; and it is equally found in the productions of the most rude and barbarous people, wherever met with. Its antiquity and its universality are therefore incontestable; and, admitting this to be beyond dispute, the present inquiry will be directed to a consideration of the extent to which the great masters of sculpture applied it, and whether there is sufficient evidence to prove that they adopted and persevered in its practice as an admitted advantage and improvement to their art.

As the use of paint by barbarous nations preceded its employment by the more advanced and perfect schools, it is clear, in the first place, that the practice of colouring sculpture was not a development or a refinement induced by the progress of knowledge in art, or a discovery of a new element of beauty or effect, first struck out by the genius of those great masters who are admitted to have brought sculpture itself to perfection. It must, therefore, be received, in their use of it, as simply a continuation by them of an established custom.

This obviously places the employment of colour in sculpture upon an entirely different footing to that which it would have, had it been a peculiar feature in Greek practice, and originated by the great Athenian, Sicyonian, or Argive sculptors; when, of course, their taste would claim the credit, or would have to bear the responsibility, of a remarkable innovation. So far from this being the case, it was a foreign and very ancient element of design; and was either engrafted on the earliest attempts at sculpture by the Greeks, a mere imitation of the prevailing practice of older nations; or possibly it was original with them as with other rude beginners in sculpture. Once introduced, however, usage gave it a hold upon the prejudices of the people, who, as sculpture at that early period was, for the most part, if not entirely, employed for sacred purposes or illustration, soon closely associated all these modes of representation with the popular religious feelings; and thus, in the more barbarous ages of Greek art, painting the statues of the gods became a prescribed practice.

It may be observed here that there can be no doubt that painting, with all the earlier nations, as the Egyptians and Assyrians, was in a great measure hieratic and symbolical. In figures of mythological personages, or of kings and heroes, each colour so applied (and many of these are painted from head to foot) conveyed a distinct meaning, probably recognised by the people generally, but certainly understood by the priests, as having a peculiar and sacred significance.

Colouring sculpture, therefore, was not first introduced by the Greeks; nor was it confined to Greek sculpture; although the Greeks, like other nations, adopted the practice. It is important to observe this, because it establishes the fact that it was not a step in the progress or improvement of this art among the greatest sculptors whom the world has known.

But admitting that it was extensively employed in the best period of Greek sculpture, the question arises, first, Whether the practice was the general rule at the time? and, secondly, Whether it was employed by the most eminent sculptors in their ordinary works—works, that is, not executed for a particular purpose and under special conditions; a consideration of no slight importance.

If these inquiries should be answered affirmatively, it still will be a subject for discussion whether the practice was advantageous to the art to which it was applied; and next, whether the example, even of the greatest masters, should be implicitly followed in a case where they suffered the native and proper expression of their own art, sculpture, to be interfered with by the application of an extraneous accessory borrowed from an entirely distinct art. But if the arguments that can be adduced shall show, first, that where Polychromy was employed, it was either simply copied from other nations with whom the Greeks had come in contact; or that it was prescribed as a mode of hieratic or religious expression in statues and sculptured compositions that were to be placed in temples, or otherwise required for sacred purposes, and therefore that it had a traditional standing; but that it was not employed generally by the best sculptors in works on which they were free to exercise their own unbiassed judgment, it will be consistent to believe that, in the progress of sculpture from a mere rude manufacture of idols to its perfection as an art which aimed at imitating *form* only in its most beautiful and simple aspect, colour was not considered essential, or even desirable; and that when it was employed, it was exceptionally, and for some particular and especial reason, usually connected with architectural or merely decorative objects. The accumulation of rich accessories, and the profuse mixture of materials, ivory, gold, precious stones, and inlaying and painting, in the Olympian Jupiter, the Minerva of the Parthenon, and similar compositions, become then perfectly intelligible; and such works, though exhibiting also the most admirable art, will be considered rather in the light of splendid offerings to the honoured local deities, than as specimens of a rule which guided the sculptors of the greatest era of the art in their ordinary practice. It must be taken into account that these works were essentially religious sculpture, and as such were no doubt treated, in many respects, according to a prescribed formula.

It will be important to bear in mind that the application of colour to the sculpture of the ancients could not have been intended to add to the truth of the imitation. It may have been thought capable of adding to the *scenic* effect of a work, if the term may be allowed, or it may have been used subjectively, to inspire or awaken some peculiar class of thought where it was employed in temple or religious sculpture; but it never made the true and natural appearance of the object its aim. In the most perfect remains of sculpture of the highest school of art, which have reached modern times—namely, the statues and reliefs of the Parthenon at Athens—this truth of imitation and the reproduction of the most approved forms of nature constitute the whole claims of these works to the admiration of all competent judges of art. If they were covered with a coating of colour in the manner described, and as it has been found on some ancient monuments, it cannot be denied that all the most precious qualities for which these sculptures are now valued would be concealed. Some of these can scarcely be adequately appreciated by any but practical sculptors; for though critics long conversant with the excellence of the highest character of Greek sculpture may judge most correctly of results, it is not too much to say, there may still be subtle peculiarities of treatment and execution, into which those only who are conversant with such matters of practice, and have, at the same time, an intimate knowledge of anatomy and the human figure, can fully enter. But these works bear the closest examination, and are universally acknowledged to be the most perfect examples sculptors can be referred to for these very properties. No regret is felt by real judges of art, that the Ilyssus, the Theseus, the Neptune, the Horse's Head, or the figures in the Panathenaic procession in the frieze, or the vigorous and effective compositions of the metopes in this collection, are not painted; nor is it conceivable that they would be anything but injured by a process which would entirely prevent the study and examination of their actual surface. Nor, for the same reason, can it be desirable to have the Apollo Belvedere, the Laocoon, or any other well-known example of ancient sculpture, changed from the condition which has hitherto enabled the world to judge them on their merits, as the pure productions of their respective authors. It is obvious that if sculpture could by any possibility be subjected to the transformation that Polychromy of the ancient kind would effect, all the known principles by which it is now judged, as an art of form, must undergo also a total change.

In support of what has been said with respect to

non-natural imitation in the mode of colouring ancient sculpture, and that truth of representation was not the object of such accessorial treatment, a few facts may now be adduced.

In the first place, it is important to observe that in the very few instances in which colour has been found on ancient sculpture, there is no attempt at gradation, or to mix or unite the various colours. The pigment is always of one *uniform* tint, and appears to be laid on, or over, a thin coating of *stucco*, which covers, and of course must more or less clog and thicken, the surface of the material of which the statue is formed. Some fragments of statues were exhumed at Athens in the year 1835, on which colour was found laid on very substantially in this manner. Among them was a female figure, of which the face, the eyes; and the eyebrows, were coarsely loaded with thick colour.

In the official report of the discovery of the sculpture at Halicarnassus, a large proportion of which is now in this country, it is stated that colour was found on various objects. This being the impression of those who were present at the excavation of these interesting monuments, the presence of colour would only confirm the fact already admitted, that the ancients sometimes had recourse to this mode of giving effect to their works; but it is to be remarked that no trace of it is now to be found on any of these sculptures; unless, indeed, a very few spots of a reddish tint in one or two unimportant places may be considered to indicate where colour had been. It seems strange, if colour was distinctly preserved on these marbles from the time they were executed, above three centuries before the Christian era, to the date of their discovery—a period of more than two thousand years—that all traces of it should entirely have disappeared in the few months occupied in the transmission of the sculptures from Asia Minor to England. There being no ground or preparation left on the marble on which colour could, *more antiquo*, have been laid, is still further against the probability of any pigment having been generally applied over the figures. In the absence of such indications, it might be permitted to imagine that accidental stains, arising possibly from the marble having been so long buried in the earth, as well as from other causes, led to the belief that colour had been employed. But there is another fair ground of exception to the belief of the sculpture having been painted. In some of the architectural remains brought over from the same locality, the addition of colour in ornament, and in picking out certain details, is still distinctly visible; while in the sculptured figures found at the same time and place, all vestige of such an accessory is absent. Its preservation in the architectural portions, and its total disappearance from the entire series of statues and rilievi, is certainly remarkable if these latter were painted in the same manner as the other objects.

It may be observed here that in ancient works, the flesh or naked, where colour appears, is usually expressed by a dull dark red; though there are instances in works in *terra cotta*, where pure white is used. In the designs on Greek vases this is often the case, especially in the earlier specimens of this class of design, clearly shewing in both cases that the imitation of nature could not have been intended.

There are, however, some examples to be noticed of more carefully-coloured figures and reliefs in this material (*terra cotta*). They are covered, in the same manner as those referred to, with a thin coating of *gypsum* or *stucco*, upon which the various colours have been laid or washed, to imitate the flesh, hair, eyes, and drapery. So far, doubtless, they must be considered authority for *polychromic* sculpture. But too much stress must not be laid upon it. It must be remembered, in the first place, that these works can scarcely be classed in the category of sculpture proper. They usually are of small size, and were probably only made for decoration, and are not so much examples of sculpture as of ornamental plastic art. Being made of clay, gradually dried and baked in an oven, they are liable to a considerable change of form by the irregular contraction and expansion inseparable from these processes. This, of itself, offers one of the most powerful arguments against the general practice, as applied to fine works of art, as it proves that the refinement of surface and delicacy of form, so essential in works in marble, were not cared for in these productions, and that their being coated with an extra covering was not considered of any importance. It is evident also that they were produced in a very wholesale way, being simply what are called squeezes from moulds, easily multiplied as they were required, and not demanding any particular attention from the artist after the first composition or design was supplied. It cannot be supposed that the great sculptors in marble would have allowed the surface of their carefully-studied and highly-finished productions to be so thickened and obscured by a coating of *gypsum*, or any other material of the kind, in order to fit it for a *painter* to operate upon. The very idea seems preposterous, and to carry its own refutation. A process the marble did sometimes undergo, and to which particular reference will be made by-and-by, was quite distinct from this material interference with the integrity of the surface.

It certainly is remarkable, if the practice ever prevailed to the extent some advocates of Polychromy have supposed, that, among the very large number of marble statues of a fine period of art that remain to us, to attest the indisputable superiority of the ancients in sculpture (proper), there is not a single tolerable example of the application of colour. It scarcely will meet the objection to say this is owing to the great age of the works, and the accidents to which they have been exposed. Many of them have been found under circumstances that have insured their integrity a sufficient time to shew the original surface; and, as in the case of recovered painted architectural members, and of small works, such as those above referred to, it has been proved that age has not destroyed colour on some even of the most ancient specimens. Besides, there was a period when the works of the Greeks were studied and imitated in Rome with the most scrupulous exactness. The chambers of the Baths of Titus and of the Villa of Hadrian have given their long-concealed treasures of art to the light, after preservation from injury for centuries; and while the colours of paintings on walls have been found as bright and fresh as when they were executed, none of these even comparatively late works in sculpture have been found painted, or showing any indication of colour to warrant the conclusion, that even the Romans, in the days when a great effort was made to restore sculpture on the basis of Greek examples, considered it a characteristic of Greek practice to paint their statues.

The student is again reminded that it is not intended here to deny the mere fact that colour was sometimes employed; but only to dispute the universality of the practice, and its being usual in the best period of sculpture.

It remains now to make a few remarks on the ancient written authorities for colouring (Greek) sculpture. In the first place, the presumption is very strong that the assumed fact that the finest Greek sculpture, except when it formed a part of an architectural design, was ever systematically coloured, rests on very questionable foundation. It has been rather taken for granted, from certain vague expressions of comparatively late writers, than proved from contemporary authority, or from any experience we have of the fact as a matter of universal custom. Pliny and Pausanias, and a few other writers, living long after the date of the sculptors whose works they refer to, mention some so treated; but neither of these chroniclers were practical artists, on whose professional observation reliance can be placed, nor had they always the opportunity of verifying the accounts they read or the stories reported to them. Thus in later times the same uncertain testimony has influenced opinion, and the poetical and fanciful imaginings of certain writers have been credited and accepted by modern scholars, having themselves possibly little or no practical knowledge, and by artists, on their authority, as the statement of facts; and such statements having been repeated over and over again, unchallenged and without misgiving in those who have so trusted to such speculative accounts, have, there can be no doubt, led to considerable misapprehension.

A few examples of the description given of ancient statues, asserted to have been coloured in various ways, will show the character of some of the usually quoted authorities for the practice.

A sculptor named Aristonidas is recorded by Pliny as the author of a bronze statue which represented Athamas seated, and overcome with remorse, after the murder of his son. In order to express with greater truth the effect of confusion and shame, the artist, it is said, mixed iron with the bronze, and this, "by its redness shining through the bronze," caused an appearance on the surface like a *blush*. Pliny does not give his authority for this extraordinary statement. The explanation given of the mode by which this remarkable effect was produced, is sufficient to throw discredit on the whole passage. In the first place, the colour of iron is not red; though when it is oxydised or rusty, that tint, or rather an orange tint, appears upon it. Then the redness of the blush or iron is described as *shining through* the lighter colour of the bronze; as though bronze were a transparent substance or material. The passage is so curious that, in order to prevent mistake, or the supposition that the account of Pliny is misstated, the whole passage is given below.*

* "Aristonidas artifex, cum exprimere vellet Athamantis furorem,

Another ancient authority, Plutarch, is quoted* as recording that Silanio (an artist who lived about 320 B.C.) made a statue representing Jocasta dying, and that by a peculiar mixture of the metals used in the composition of this work, a cast of *paleness* was given to the countenance.

It is not desirable to multiply quotations from ancient authors; but the curious scholar may with advantage consult the original passage,† and he will there find how strong is the expression by which the effect of the pale colour is produced.

Any one who has the slightest acquaintance with founding or metallurgy must know that the effects thus described are at any rate utterly incompatible with the *fusion* of the different metals used for bronze statues: and even supposing, for the sake of argument, the possibility of keeping the metals distinct in a common melting, how then would it be possible to insure the blush or the pallor coming precisely in the right place? The ductility of certain metals is produced and modified by the action of heat properly applied, and their cooling is attended by effects not always uniform. Iron, if used alone, and bronze, are subject to different conditions,

filio præcipitato, residentem pœnitentia; æs ferrumque miscuit, ut rubigine ejus per nitorem æris relucente, exprimeretur verecundiæ rubor." —Plin. *Hist. Nat.* xxxiv. 14.

* Sillig. *Cat. Artif. v. Silanio;* and Quatremère de Quincy, *Le Jupiter Olympien*, 1re partie, par. 13.

† Plut. *Symp.* v. 2. 6.

which would prevent their perfect amalgamation in a common melting; unless indeed the whole became fused together in a mass, as in fact would be the case; but then, where would be the material for a blush?

It is scarcely necessary to say that these accounts must be received with great distrust; and so far as they assert that those expressive tints were produced by any possible mixture of metals—for the word used is "miscuit" in Pliny's account—it may safely be said they are not deserving of credit.

Another objection may also be urged against these statements. It is of a very commonplace character, but it is not without force, especially if truth to nature or exact imitation was the artist's object. It would not be easy to determine the precise colour such materials should assume when they are intended to represent such refinements as the complexion of persons under the influence of strong emotions. But the statue itself being of *chalcos* or *æs*, it is by no means clear that the addition of red cheeks or a pallid countenance would be an improvement to a bronze statue; and further, it might be asked, assuming for the sake of argument that the intention was to imitate the *natural* effect of these affections upon the countenance, would *red* be the appropriate colour of a blush in a green cheek? The colour of this composition (bronze) when it first leaves the furnace is usually varied, showing dark copper and golden tints;

after a time, by exposure to the air, it acquires a green colour, well known as the *patina* so highly esteemed and admired by antiquaries. In which of these conditions of the bronze—the copper or the green—would the preparation intended to express paleness or a blush have the desired effect? A subject of important calculation to the artist whose production was to exhibit this extra refinement.

It cannot, then, be denied that there is much which throws suspicion on these accounts, and suggests the probability that many of the details here described have their source in the imagination of the writers. The fact of one of these authors mentioning the peculiarity of the work alluded to as a "report," rather strengthens this opinion. There is everywhere the want of *direct* testimony; for Plutarch does not describe a work he had seen, or that even existed in his time. Its reputed author lived between three and four hundred years before the birth of Christ, and Plutarch not till nearly one hundred and fifty years after that event; thus comprising an interval of between five and six centuries. Considerable allowance must therefore be made for those who presume to entertain doubts as to the degree of reliance to be placed on such traditions. "They say," or "it is said," cannot, in a practical matter like this, where there is no adequate contemporary testimony, nor any remaining monuments to confirm it, be received as all-sufficient evidence or authority. In the other instance alluded to, of the statue of Athamas, Pliny says, "This statue is now existing at Thebes;" * but he does not say he had seen it.

Callistratus describes, among several similar examples, a Cupid, the work of the celebrated Praxiteles. In enlarging on its claims to admiration, he says there was on his cheeks a vivid blush.

This is a remarkable and very interesting tradition; and the date at which Callistratus lived gives a greater importance and value to his statement than can be accorded to those of most other writers. The description of this statue is quite in accordance with the style of sculpture which Praxiteles introduced, and which changed the whole character of art; but even here there is room for the supposition that the elegant and poetical fancy of the writer may have given some little extra touches in recording the impression made by a work of one of the most popular and successful sculptors of the age.

In marble statues the colour might easily have been put on; but this, as has been briefly shewn, was, wherever it has been found, done very coarsely and almost in patches. Nowhere is there any detailed or reliable account of ancient sculpture painted in delicate gradutions of tints, in imitation of the true colouring of nature.

Pausanias mentions various works of the kind

* "Hoc signum extat Thebis hodierno die."

painted with vermillion. Among others, a statue of Bacchus, that was made of gypsum, and painted; another of gold, or gilt, with the face painted red. It is difficult to imagine anything more grotesque and disagreeable, and certainly more utterly unlike nature, than a figure thus treated; and it would be surprising to find any competent judge of art considering a gilt figure with vermillion cheeks good sculpture, or worthy to be imitated by modern artists. It can only be classed as a conventional mode of treating sculpture, in its use as a votive offering, curious to the archæological inquirer and scholar, and quite irrespective of its merit or character as a work of art. Pausanias simply records the fact of its existence among the remarkable objects he met with. Another example occurs in a statue attributed to Scopas, of a Bacchante who held, instead of a *thyrsus*, an animal (a kid), probably sacrificial, with its entrails exposed. It is said the marble represented the livid flesh, and "one sole material offered the imitation of life and death." This evidently was not the effect of artificial tinting. The ingenuity of the sculptor may have been successfully exercised in adapting the accidental markings or variety of colour in the marble he used to give the general appearance of the dissected entrails of the animal. This probably would strike the vulgar as a very wonderful achievement of art; but it is not possible that a mere accident in the stone could give the representation correctly; and the employment of the means, a mere trick of art, seems quite unworthy of so great an artist as Scopas. It is, however, the only solution that is admissible, for the effect is said distinctly to have been produced by the self-same material, and not by the application of colour. This account is also given by Callistratus. The terms in which this writer speaks of the above work are not calculated to raise his character as an art critic; and, so far, the encomiums he elsewhere bestows on the coloured sculpture he describes must be received with some qualification.

The above are some of the leading ancient classical authorities upon which stress has been laid for the fact that the great sculptors of antiquity *habitually* coloured their sculpture. As a mere subject of interesting historical inquiry, the fact of Polychromy existing in the most prosperous era of the art may well occupy attention here; and sufficient evidence has been adduced to prove its practice, though not in the universal way in which some have supposed. The question has not, however, only been considered with reference to its historical interest. Arguments have been attempted to be drawn from it, that the same accessory should be introduced in modern sculpture; merely, it would seem, because the ancients coloured some of their works. Without entering, at least at present, upon a question of mere taste, which is to apply to the practice of an art exercised on entirely different grounds to that which guided the sculptor of antiquity, it may without presumption be said that the general practice of the ancient masters cannot be considered as established, upon such doubtful and vague expressions, and such insulated examples, as have here been quoted. As reasonable would it be to take the authority of antiquity literally, and to affirm that *living* busts could be produced out of blocks of marble, or that bronze may be made to breathe, because in ancient writers are found such expressions as "*vivos è marmore vultus;*" and "*spirantia æra,*" or believe that pictures and statues lived, because it is said—

> "Et cum Parrhasii tabulis, signisque Myronis,
> Pheidiacum vivebat ebur"—

with endless other instances of the kind.

One of the most frequently quoted authorities for the practice of systematically applying colour to sculpture, and even for employing a professional painter to complete the sculptor's work, is a passage also in Pliny. In order to prevent any question as to the value of the language used by that writer, the original Latin is given below.* In English, it runs thus, "Praxiteles, when he was asked which of his works in marble he most approved (or esteemed most highly), replied, 'Those to

* Dicebat Praxiteles interrogatus quæ maximè opera sua probâsset in marmoribus, Quibus Nicias manum admovisset; tantum *circumlitioni* ejus tribuebat.—Plin. *Hist. Nat.* xxxv. 11.

which Nicias had put his hand;' so much (value) did he attribute to his (mode of) rubbing or polishing (the surface)." There is no expression here that can with fairness or propriety be converted into meaning painting or the addition of colour; nor can the passage, by any stretch of ingenuity, be made to describe the process of painting or tinting with a variety of colours. Nothing can be more distinct than the expression used by Pliny; and it is not easy to understand how any scholar could translate *circumlitio* into colouring, or the simple assertion of *manum admovisse* (putting a hand to it) into meaning, that the hand was employed in the particular function or operation of putting paint on a masterpiece of Praxiteles. There may be doubt and difficulty in deciding, in the absence of all proof in remaining examples of sculpture, what this *circumlitio* was: but it seems tolerably clear what it was *not*. The assistance of Nicias may have been valuable in giving a certain richness of *tone* to the already finished surface of the statues, by rubbing in a varnish or some composition by which an extra appearance of softness was produced; and this, according to the passage above quoted, was effected by a circular or rotary action (*circum*); but this is totally distinct from anything like painting, or applying a coat of colour to the statues. It is a process very analogous to that resorted to by many sculptors in modern times.*

* Vitruvius, vii. 9, and Plin. *Hist. Nat.* xxi. 14, describe the means

The changes effected by Praxiteles will be seen to constitute a very remarkable era in the condition of sculpture. Any particulars, therefore, of the practice of so eminent an artist, if trustworthy, are of the highest importance in a history of the art; and the knowledge that he habitually employed a painter to *colour* his marble statues would form a most curious and interesting addition to the particulars already furnished on such subjects by the ancient writers. That this was his usual practice may safely be disputed, even if on some occasions, as in those referred to by Callistratus, the experiment was tried. The very specialty for which he is celebrated is the workmanship of marble. In this he was said to be *"felicior et clarior"* than any other artist. Could this have been said of him if his general practice was to call in a painter to paint his works? It may be permitted here to refer to one of his most celebrated productions in this material (marble), in which, had colour been an ordinary accompaniment to his sculpture, it might naturally be expected to be noticed. This was the far-famed statue of Venus of Cnidus. It was executed in Parian marble, and is particularly described by Pliny. Now, it is remarkable that he says nothing whatever to

used for preserving the surface of marble, "*uti signa marmorea curantur*," and of walls that were painted; but there is not the most remote allusion to *colour* being so applied. Vitruvius explains the process. It was a preparation of wax, heated and rubbed in with clean cloths—"*linteis puris;*" and he adds, "*hæc autem καῦσις Græcè dicitur.*"

lead to the supposition that it was painted; a circumstance or accessory not likely to have been ignored or overlooked in a production so universally criticised and admired. Lucian also speaks of it in detail, noticing the eyes and the hair; and yet he makes no allusion whatever to colour. But beyond this silence on the part of those writers who have so carefully described this work, there is curious evidence which would lead distinctly to the inference that the statue was not painted, but was simply an exquisitely-finished work in marble. Lucian, after expatiating, generally, on the excellence of this masterpiece of Praxiteles, refers to the extreme beauty of the marble in which the statue was executed. Had this been painted it certainly could not have been sufficiently seen to call forth this special admiration. But a further confirmation that the marble was not coloured seems to be afforded by a curious remark of this writer. He says that on one thigh there was a mark on the marble, but that it was not considered a defect, for, by contrast, it even improved the beauty of the rest of the figure. This must be taken as the opinion of the unprofessional commentator, for it cannot be supposed a sculptor would recognise any advantage in the discoloration, or in a dark stain on his block of marble; but the remark has this value, that there can be very little doubt—if, as Lucian says, this accidental defect could be seen—that it was on the surface of *unpainted* marble; and if it could have been removed or concealed there can be as little doubt that the sculptor would gladly have availed himself of the means of doing it. Here would have been the very opportunity for asking the assistance of Nicias, if painting over the marble was the accomplishment to which Praxiteles referred. There is no occasion to doubt that this very statue may have been benefited by the process for which Nicias obtained the high praise of the sculptor—the *circumlitio;* and yet that the marble was not painted. At a later period this statue is again referred to as the Cnidian Venus, in "*white* marble." There is a passage in Plato from which it is inferred there were persons in Athens whose profession it was to paint statues. This is quite consistent with what has been said above as to the employment of colour in many of the architectural decorations of the period; but it is no proof that when the great sculptors had executed a fine work in marble they sent for one of these painters to give it its crowning excellence.

In this place the practice of Polychromy has been considered only with reference to its general application to sculpture, in marble especially, in the best periods of the art. The question of its desirability as an accessory to sculpture is one of taste and feeling, and its discussion need not be entered on. It may be necessary again to recur to the subject in the employment of colour in some of the modern schools, when some further remarks may be made on the causes of its introduction, and the effect it may have on the character and prospects of the art.

SECTION VIII.

TO proceed with the history of the ancient schools, which, for sufficient reason, has been interrupted by the above short digression.—

The next great master who influenced the progress of sculpture introduced a new element into it, which could only have been accepted subsequently to the success which had followed the improvements introduced by Phidias. The latter had boldly freed his art from the more severe prescriptive types and the dry manner of the archaïc and Æginetan sculptors; but his style still maintained a character of grandeur and solemn dignity calculated to impress the imagination, and to awaken only the higher order of sentiment in the spectator. His works addressed the religious feelings; and from the sublime quality that marked his productions of the kind, he acquired the title, already referred to, of the "Sculptor of the Gods."

Praxiteles of Cnidus is considered the founder of the school that addressed itself more directly to the senses—an innovation that had a most important influence upon art. The object now was not so much to elevate and instruct as to please, by the representation of what was simply physically beautiful and seductive ; and the result was, of course, to induce a lower standard of taste and fancy in the public. Praxiteles is spoken of by all the ancient writers as one of the greatest masters who has professed this art. His works in bronze and marble are described as of the highest excellence ; and there can be no question that they fully merited the encomiums lavished upon them. It cannot, however, be doubted that his peculiar merit consisted, not in the imagination or the high purpose or aim of his works, so much as in the exquisite perfection of his execution. His selection of subjects appears to have corresponded with the softer character or style of art to which he was attached ; for, although in the long list of works attributed to him there are numerous statues of nobler subjects, by far the greater number are of Venus, Cupids, Nymphs, and others of the class which afforded opportunity for the exercise of his peculiar excellence, the representation of richly-developed form, and the delicate treatment of marble.*

Two of his works in this material are especially noticed for their expression. One represented an aged

* Praxiteles marmore felicior, ideo et clarior fuit. Praxiteles autem inter statuarios diximus qui marmoris gloriâ superavit etiam semet.—Plin. *Hist. Nat.* xxxiv. 8 ; xxxvi. 5, etc.

matron weeping; the other a courtezan, said to be a portrait of Phryne, whose features were lighted up with joy. These may appear, to artists of a later age, but ordinary claims to admiration; but in tracing the history of sculpture, it is very significant to find that the successful expression of human emotion or passion was considered to be so worthy of notice. It indicated, in fact, a new phase of art. It opened an entirely new field for the practice of sculpture, and brought it down to ordinary use in the representation of familiar subjects; instead of confining it, as in its former more dignified application, to the service of the gods and in heroic illustration. The fascinating element which Praxiteles now introduced—voluptuous form with the most exquisite surface-execution of the marble—had no essential place in the art which depended for its effect on the passionless majesty which pervaded the grand sculpture of Phidias. It was the charm of this rich treatment of the material which now constituted the recommendation of the art; and attractive and exciting, rather than elevating subjects, were sought for, in which these seductive qualities could be best exhibited.

It is impossible not to feel that this was an indication that sculpture was already leaving its higher and nobler purpose. While the art was exercised by sculptors possessing the genius and power of Praxiteles—artists whose feelings were still impressed with the traditions of the past, and whose practice was still influenced, in a great degree, by the noble examples extant—the danger of the change effected in the application of sculpture, and the great prominence given to exquisite manipulation, would be less likely to be perceived; but there can be no doubt that a less pure and a less elevated feeling for art was induced by it; and the subsequent history of sculpture showed that it led artists of inferior powers to rely on this sensuous element as a means of securing popular favour. The history of one of the most celebrated works of Praxiteles is strongly corroborative of the view here taken, both as regards the mode of treating art, and the change of feeling in the public.

Praxiteles executed for the people of Cnidus a naked statue of Venus.* This work was considered the masterpiece of the sculptor, and people flocked from all parts to see and admire it. No statue of antiquity, with the exception, perhaps, of the Olympian Jupiter, has received such universal and unqualified admiration as this example of a totally novel application of sculpture; for, before this bold attempt of Praxiteles, it is believed that no sculptor had represented the female figure undraped. It is recorded that, on this occasion, two statues of the goddess were made, and that the people of Cos were privileged to select the one they preferred. One was represented, in the usual way, with drapery; the other

* This is the work referred to in the last section.

entirely naked. The citizens of Cos decided to take the draped figure, as the more modest of the two; and the Cnidians then became the possessors of the rival statue. It is added, in proof of the high value placed on this work, that the Cnidians were at this time oppressed by a heavy debt they owed to Nicomedes, King of Bithynia; and that he, desiring to obtain possession of this masterpiece of Praxiteles, offered to liberate them from their obligation if they would consent to give up this far-famed statue. The Cnidians refused, however, to purchase their freedom from debt at this cost and sacrifice, and declined to part with a work of art the possession of which rendered their city illustrious. It was placed in a small temple or shrine (*ædicula*) open on all sides, so that the statue could be seen from every point of view. This celebrated work was, at a later period, carried to Constantinople. It fell a prey to the flames in the fifth century A.D., in the dreadful fire which destroyed so many of the valuable works of art that had been collected in that city.

Two statues of Cupid are also mentioned among the more attractive and admired productions of this master. From the description that has been handed down, they were treated in the same rich and voluptuous style that characterised the Venus, and which his great skill was rendering so fascinating to a highly sensitive people. It is worth remarking how these works were estimated, compared with the standard appealed to in the previous age. The Jupiter of Phidias was said to equal the divinity of which it was the type (*Deum æquavit*). These performances of Praxiteles appealed to the less refined sympathies, and it was their human, physical beauty that was admired. One of these statues of Cupid was considered worthy to be placed on an equality with the Cnidian Venus.

There is a story told by Pausanias,* connected with this work, which shows how great a value the sculptor himself set on this celebrated production. Phryne, a beautiful courtezan, whose influence over the sculptor appears to have been very great, and of whom he made at least two statues, was desirous to possess a work of Praxiteles; and not knowing, when she was permitted by the artist to make choice of one, which to select, she invented a little stratagem by which she might discover the opinion of the artist himself. One day she desired a servant to hasten to Praxiteles and tell him his workshop was in flames, and that his works were in danger of being destroyed. Praxiteles rushed out in the greatest alarm and anxiety, exclaiming that "all was lost if his Satyr and Cupid were not saved." The object of the ingenious beauty was answered. She acknowledged the trick she had played, and explained to the sculptor that all she wanted was to know which of his

* Paus. i. 20.

works he esteemed the most highly. She selected the Cupid. A statue of a Satyr, no doubt the work referred to above, was so excellent that it was called, by way of distinction, Periboetos (the *famous*). One of his statues, mentioned by Pliny, represented a youthful Apollo in the act of killing a lizard. It was from this circumstance called *Sauroctonos.* The well-known marble statue of this subject in the Museum of the Vatican is believed to be an ancient copy of this work. The figure is standing, with one leg bent, leaning with his arm against a tree; with the other hand, in which he holds a *style* or some pointed instrument, he is just about to strike a small lizard which is climbing up the tree. It is a composition of agreeable lines, great purity of form, and appropriate expression; but, if it is a faithful copy of the celebrated original, scarcely of so full and rich a character as might be expected in a work by Praxiteles.

It has been stated above that it is believed Praxiteles was the first sculptor among the Greeks who ventured to represent the female figure entirely nude. This appears now to be the generally received opinion among antiquaries. It was first decidedly expressed by Millingen.* He says it was an innovation somewhat startling, and at first was not generally adopted; but to reconcile, partially, the representation of such forms with feelings of propriety (for sculpture was not yet used

* Ancient Inedited Monuments of Grecian Art, No. x. p. 7.

merely to gratify indecorous fancy and prurient tastes), a compromise was effected by representing the lower half of the figure draped, as is seen in the fine statues of the "Venus" of Milo in the Louvre, the "Venus" of Capua at Naples, and the charming statue of Venus (or Dione) in the Townley collection in the British Museum.

It is, however, clear that, from this time, the exhibition of the undraped female figure was a common and popular exercise of the sculptor's art; and, as has been observed, perhaps the real decline of sculpture may be said to have commenced when its practice was directed to please the sense and supply objects of excitement, in what may be called "sensuous" sculpture, instead of addressing the nobler sentiments, as had been done by Phidias and his severer school. The object of this essay being the history of sculpture, and not the biography of sculptors, it is not possible to do more than touch generally upon individual artists; and that only in their character of leaders of schools. Otherwise the fame and extensive practice of Praxiteles would fully warrant a much more extended notice than is here afforded to so distinguished a master. Antiquaries and scholars have differed respecting the precise time at which Praxiteles lived. It is not very material in a general history, as enough is certainly known to fix his date within a few years, and to shew the direct succession of the great leaders of the schools of sculpture. This must have been between the 106th and the 124th Olympiad; that is, in parts of the fourth and third centuries before Christ. It has before been mentioned that his name is found among the sculptors who were employed to decorate the magnificent tomb which was erected by Artemisia in memory of her husband Mausolus. Praxiteles had many scholars, and he left two sons, Timarchus and Cephisodotus, who were also sculptors.

It is satisfactory to be able to direct the attention of the professed artist and the student to authentic works existing in England, illustrative of the great schools of sculpture. Already reference has been made to some of these, as the sculptures of the Æginetan school, of the Parthenon by Phidias, the Phigaleian marbles, and, lastly, the extensive remains from Halicarnassus. But there are also two other works of the later schools—of Praxiteles and Lysippus—which deserve especial mention here for the very high class of art they exhibit. One of these is a marble statue, but little injured, representing Apollo. It is of heroic size, and half draped from the torso downwards. The left hand supports a richly-decorated lyre. The head, though slightly injured, is of extreme beauty, and the style and execution of the naked portions of the figure are of the finest quality. This noble work was discovered at Cyrene, and is now in the British Museum.

The other work, also in the national collection, is a

female head, also somewhat injured. The style of beauty exhibited here is of the richest type. The proportions are rather larger than in ordinary nature, and it is supposed to be part of a statue of Demeter. The hair, parted on the forehead, is carried back in full waving masses, and then falls in long curls on the neck. On the head is a veil which partially encloses the neck and hair. The execution and the exquisite surface of this work are beyond all praise. It came from Cnidus, and might be worthily attributed to the hand of Praxiteles himself.

In the list of eminent sculptors living at this time the name of Scopas claims distinction. He is said to be the author of the celebrated group of "Niobe and her Children" in the gallery of sculpture at Florence; he also is named among the artists who executed the sculptures on one side of the quadrangular base of the celebrated Mausoleum. There is reason to think that the greater part of the statues composing the Niobe group are but ancient copies from the original work; but even as copies they afford satisfactory evidence of the ability of the artist who illustrated so dramatically this striking and affecting myth, while, at the same time, they are valuable examples of expression, form, action, and a fine style of art.

One of the reasons for supposing that the series of statues at Florence are only copies, is that portions of the same subject similarly treated have been found that exhibit features of greater excellence than appears in the corresponding figures in the above composition. There is a head of the principal figure, Niobe, preserved in England, which shews this superiority in a very marked manner.* Of the other work referred to—the sculpture of the Mausoleum—there are indisputable original remains from which, though unfortunately they are much mutilated, most important information as to the state of the art may be derived. They form part of the national collection of antiquities in the British Museum under the title of the Halicarnassus sculptures. They consist of a large collection of objects—as statues, rilievi, fragments of animals and of architectural details—and they certainly may be considered among the most valuable works of art that have been recovered from ancient times. They not only illustrate a very celebrated period and school, but are undoubted examples of the performances of individual sculptors whose names have been handed down to us by the writers of antiquity. They were found on the site of the ancient Halicarnassus, now called Budroum, in Asia Minor; and they formed portions of the famous commemorative monument, of which, till lately, nothing was known but

* It belonged to the Earl of Yarborough, and is engraved in the 1st vol. of "Specimens of Ancient Sculpture," published by the Society of Dilletanti.

by tradition, erected by Artemisia to her husband (and brother) Mausolus, King of Caria, who died in the year 353 B.C. It was called the Mausoleum from that circumstance, and it has given its name to all subsequent erections of a similar character. It was so remarkable for its scale and the magnificence of its decoration, that it was accounted one of the wonders of the world. Pliny describes this noble monument at great length. The whole composition, he says, formed of marble, stood upon an ample base. Upon this was a peristyle of thirty-six columns, of which, and of portions of the architraves, sufficient fragments have been found to settle an important point not mentioned by Pliny—namely, the order of the architecture, which is now shewn to be Ionic. From a centre or *cella* rose a pyramidal structure in steps, and this was surmounted by a marble quadriga. The whole height was 140 feet. The length on two sides, the north and south, was sixty-three feet, and on the others somewhat less. Many of the blocks which formed the base of the whole work, and shewing the manner of construction and of fastening the parts together, are preserved in the British Museum.

Among the sculptured fragments recovered are some of great interest, consisting of statues, portions of colossal horses, lions, and an extensive series of *rilievi*. Pliny acquaints us that Artemisia employed four of the most celebrated sculptors of antiquity to decorate this monument, and he records the names of the selected artists; Bryaxis, Timotheus, Leochares, and Scopas; Vitruvius gives Praxiteles instead of Scopas. They executed the reliefs that adorned the four sides of the Mausoleum; Bryaxis, according to Pliny, occupied the north face, Timotheus the south, Leochares the west, and Scopas the east. To Pythis, another sculptor, was entrusted the execution of the marble quadriga by which the whole was crowned. It is not necessary here to enter into the vexed question which has occupied, and still occupies, antiquaries and architects upon the precise architectural design of this celebrated work. The description given of it by the writer above quoted conveys a sufficiently clear notion of its general composition, as well as of its noble dimensions. It was erected on the high ground overlooking the entrance of the harbour, and the effect of the whole work must have been one of surpassing grandeur. The sculptures, notwithstanding the injuries they have received, afford the most satisfactory evidence of the quality of its artistic decoration; and it is this which gives these remains their great interest in a history of sculpture. The school they illustrate had already reached its highest point of excellence. These works carry out the idea of a more picturesque feeling in the flow of lines and variety of action than appears in the immediately preceding school; the proportions of the human figure are also more elongated than usual. Some of these even shew an excess in this particular; but, though it is a fault, it gives a character of elegance to the figures. It is possible, also, that some liberty may have been taken, in order to adapt the work to its situation and the point of view from which the composition would be seen. These *rilievi* vary considerably in merit, and clearly exhibit the difference of ability in the respective artists who executed them. Among the more prominent objects which claim attention are two draped statues of full heroic scale. One of these is of noble character, and it has been thought probably to be a portrait of Mausolus. There is much individuality in the head, and nothing in the way of accessory to give it an ideal or mythical character. It may, therefore, be supposed to represent the king in his apotheosised state. The other is a female statue. The forms here, especially on the right side and in the bent leg, are somewhat heavy and wanting in refinement; but there are passages in this work of great merit in the large or grandiose style of the art, and in the volume and adjustment of the drapery. The rich mass about the left arm of the figure, with the effect of the limb against it, is an example of consummate art. It would be gratifying to be able to think that this statue represents the noble Artemisia herself, who, by the erection of this magnificent tomb, has not only immortalized the memory of her husband, but has thereby secured a lasting fame also for herself. There is not, however, any authority for such belief, and the face is too much injured to admit of any opinion as to its subject. As a matter of speculation, the peculiar treatment of the hair in front, and the fact of the head being covered with a veil, might justify the assumption that it is a portrait statue; and if so, it would be a natural conclusion that a statue of such dimensions and quality could only represent the widow of the Carian monarch.

The *rilievi* represent various subjects, but chiefly contests between men and Amazons. They are full of action and expression, with the greatest variety of composition and most picturesque arrangement: a quality of very difficult and dangerous adjustment in the somewhat severe art of sculpture, but it is here achieved with the most skilful perfection. The slabs vary a little in width, and indeed in the scale of the figures, shewing that there either were different tiers or series of reliefs, or that the different sculptors exercised their own fancy in making their respective decorations of a larger or smaller size. The fragments of some statues of horses shew that these works are of a larger scale than any works of the kind that have hitherto been found in marble. There can be no doubt that two of these belonged to the quadriga, and it is evident that the horses were at rest, in a standing position, on all four legs. They were made of separate blocks of marble, for in both the fragments referred to there is a clean-faced joint in the centre. One exhibits a "forehand" with the head, but without the legs; the other a hind quarter. The former still has some of the original bronze bridle remaining, with part of a bit; shewing the not unusual employment of metal in the accessories of such works. There is another fragment of a horse in violent rearing action, with a portion of a mounted draped figure reining in the animal, or, it may be, in a fighting attitude. The whole is greatly mutilated, no extremities of the horse or rider, except the bridle-hand, being preserved; and the execution of this latter, though it is blocked in with great spirit, shews the work had never been completed. Generally speaking, it must be admitted that the horses, both in figure and execution, are of very inferior quality to the rest of the sculpture. Of the fragments of lions, and one or two other animals that had their place in the decoration of the monument, it is not important to speak. Many of them shew the sculptors' thorough acquaintance with the character of the subjects they were representing; but the execution is by no means thoroughly carried out, general effect and truthfulness having probably been preferred for works only to be seen at a distance.* The whole of the interesting works

* There is evidence throughout this remarkable series of sculptures that the work was never fully completed; and the traditions respecting it state that Artemisia died before the artists employed by her had finished their respective portions of the design.

above described are now in the British Museum; and although, from their injured state, and the disintegration of surface almost throughout, they can scarcely be offered to students as useful examples of form, they deserve careful examination for the vigour of their composition, their expression, and the variety they display.

The sculptor who may be said to have completed the progressive course of sculpture was Lysippus, a native of Sicyon. He worked chiefly, if not entirely, in bronze. Pliny, Pausanias, and other writers, furnish a long list of his works, and he is said by the former to have executed as many as six hundred and ten statues.

There are some particulars mentioned of the practice of Lysippus which throw considerable additional light upon the condition of the art at this its culminating point. He is noticed for the care he bestowed on completion and finish, and in working the hair. He also made the heads of his figures smaller than his predecessors (*antiqui*), and the bodies somewhat more slender, which gave to his statues the effect of being tall and graceful. His works were remarkable for a quality which Pliny describes by the word *symmetria*, and he appears entirely to have got rid of a certain squareness observable in the ancient school. A remarkable expression is attributed to Lysippus, which shews how thoroughly this sculptor understood the value of working for effect, without, however, any sacrifice of truth and correctness of detail. He said, "by other, that is the older artists, men were made as they are; by himself as they appeared to be." A most valuable rule, if carried out with judgment. When read in connection with another passage in Pliny relating to Lysippus, it evidently means that he preferred breadth and freedom in his art, such as Nature, viewed generally, exhibits, to the representation of such minute details and peculiarities as would be apt to destroy the large and grand effect that sculpture should have. To do this satisfactorily—to unite all the necessary attention to characteristic details with that generalization which constitutes a fine style—requires the ability of a great artist, and Lysippus seems to claim the honour of having produced this full development of his art. So unqualified an admission of his merit in this respect may seem to imply a superiority in the style of Lysippus over that both of Phidias and Praxiteles, and be thought overcharged when the great names of his precursors are considered; but however difficult it may be to explain in words the peculiarities which characterise *style* in art—and which, it must be remembered, often depends upon very slight distinctions—the difference does exist, and will be easily comprehended by those who can critically examine and compare good illustrative works of different schools.

It is quite consistent with the above remarks to find

the sculpture of this age influenced in its sentiment and character by the prevailing habit of thought of the time. The world was occupied with the conquests of Alexander the Great, who, arrogant, vain, and ambitious himself, gave the tone to the manners of his court and followers. It is found that the art of this time had a leaning to exaggeration. As the grand, solemn style of Phidias had been followed by the change to the sensuous treatment introduced by Praxiteles, so this latter was succeeded by the effort of a new school to produce additional effect by a more energetic display of action, and elaborate, though at the same time bold quality of execution. Portrait statues were eminently calculated to gratify the prevailing taste for personal distinction, and this class of art received immense impulse and encouragement during this monarch's career. Lysippus was in great favour with Alexander, who allowed him the exclusive privilege of making his statues. Pliny says "Alexander issued an edict that no artist but Apelles should paint him, Pyrgoteles engrave gems of him, or Lysippus make statues in brass of him." * Lysippus was employed to execute several portrait statues of the generals and favourites of his master. Among the latter he made one of Hephæstion, the great friend of the king. Many others of his works are men-

* Edixit ne quis ipsum alius quam Apelles pingeret, quam Pyrgoteles sculperet, quam Lysippus ex ære duceret.—Plin. *Hist. Nat.* vii. 37.

tioned, some of them of large dimensions. One of his statues of his patron Alexander was existing in Rome in the time of Nero, and a curious anecdote is recorded connected with it. The emperor had it gilt, but found its beauty, as a work of art, was so impaired by it that he had all the gold scraped off; and the statue, Pliny says, was preferred in its original state, notwithstanding the marks that were left of the scraping process. There is a small well-known bronze statue of Hercules, holding in his hand the apples from the gardens of the Hesperides, which is very characteristic of the style of art of this school. As Lysippus is known to have made many statues of this subject, it is not improbable that this may be an original work of this great master. It is in the British Museum. It may be noticed here that portraits on coins do not occur in Greek art before this age. Alexander the Great first caused his own likeness

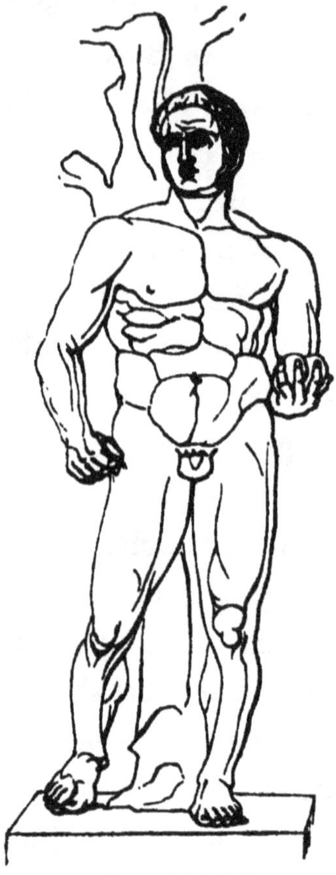

BRONZE HERCULES.
AGE OF LYSIPPUS.

to appear in these, in the character and with the attributes of Jupiter Ammon; an ingenious mode of introducing his own portrait on the coins of Macedon, and of indicating, at the same time, his own semi-divine origin; an assumption his pride had desired to establish in the minds of his own subjects and in the nations he conquered. Some of these are fine examples of medallic or numismatic art.

Lysippus left several scholars who were eminent sculptors; of these, three—Laippus or Daippus, Bedas, and Euthycrates—were his sons. Tisicrates, another, imitated his master so successfully, that it was sometimes doubted whether the work was by Lysippus or the scholar.

Art now began to migrate from Greece to the islands and coasts of Asia Minor; and Rhodes especially became a great seat of sculpture. Chares of Lindus, the author of the far-famed Colossus of Rhodes, had worked under this great master. This work was of bronze, and above a hundred feet high. It represented Apollo, or the sun, and stood at the entrance of the harbour, with its legs extended, so that it is said ships could pass between them. The execution of this gigantic work, which was accounted, like the Mausoleum at Halicarnassus, one of the seven wonders of the world, occupied the sculptor twelve years. It did not long continue to decorate the harbour of Rhodes. Fifty-six years after its erection it was overthrown by an earthquake, and was not again restored. It is worthy of remark how many celebrated sculptors were natives of Rhodes. Agesander, Polydorus, and Athenodorus, the authors of the group of "Laocoon," as well as Apollonius and Tauriscus, the sculptors of the well-known marble group representing Dirce being fastened to the horns of a wild bull, were all Rhodians. This very remarkable work, unique of its kind, is preserved at Naples. It is known as the "Toro Farnese," (the Farnese Bull). It will be more particularly referred to in a subsequent section. The claim of Rhodes to distinction as a great centre of art is established by the interesting fact that, from this small island, not more than forty miles long and fifteen broad, the Romans, when they conquered it, brought away as many as three thousand statues.

It is unnecessary to notice the long list of works by the scholars of Lysippus, recorded by ancient writers. Of one of these, Euthycrates, the son of the sculptor, it is said he did not entirely follow the example set by his master, inasmuch as he preferred the severer element of his father's style—if the expression of Pliny may be so rendered—to the more elegant or graceful treatment Lysippus had in some respects introduced.* The name,

* Ante omnes Euthycratem; quanquam is constantiam patris potius æmulatus quam elegantiam, etc. Plin. *Hist. Nat.* lib. xxxiv. c. 8.

or rather the school of Lysippus, seems to conclude the history of Greek sculpture up to its perfection; those who followed did little more than imitate what had gone before them, or, if they invented, their works were of an inferior description both in motive and execution. Many names of sculptors of great respectability still occur at intervals, but there was no longer that impress of genius—the seal of a true and original impulse—in their works, that demands for them a place equal to those eminent leaders who aided the development and perfection of the art.

Reference has already been made to the examples of sculpture of the archaïc era which have been found in Sicily. This was evidently a fruitful home of art, and the influence of great taste and feeling for the beautiful is finely exhibited in some of the later coins of this island. The best may be attributed to about the date at which this history has arrived. The large silver medals of Syracuse, having on one side a head of great beauty of Arethusa crowned, with neck and ear ornaments, and on the reverse a quadriga with accompaniments, are in a most perfect style of art. If the limits and intention of this work would admit of it, a much more extensive notice might with advantage be given of the history of Sicilian art, and of the different influences that prevailed to affect its practice. In referring to the archaïc monuments of Selinunte, and to the beautiful medallions of Syracuse of the later period, enough has been said to shew the existence of art in the country during a long period, and to prove to the student the claim of Sicily to his attention, as an important and most interesting school of sculpture.

SECTION IX.

IN the preceding passages it has been the object to mention only the principal artists of each period who were distinguished as heads of schools; and it has been considered unnecessary to give a list of all those less prominent sculptors whose names have been recorded by ancient writers. The degree of patronage that was extended to the arts would, of course, add considerably to the number of practitioners, and the excellence or celebrity of a master would increase the followers of the favourite style of the time. But the enumeration of these, however eminent they may have been, is not essential where their particular practice had not any material influence upon the character of sculpture. It would be natural to suppose that the conquests of Philip of Macedon, and of his son Alexander the Great, would have spread the light of Grecian intelligence and superiority in fine art over those countries which they visited, and which, compared with the invading power, were in a state of barbarism. But the advantages that might, with time, have been anticipated as the result of these successes of the more enlightened element, were not realised. The death of Alexander was the signal for disagreement and contention among those who had assisted him in his victorious career; and each of the leading generals, who had been content to serve in a subordinate capacity when the King of Macedon was their chief, aspired, on his decease, to an independent position and rule. By force of intrigue and violence, the vast possessions which Alexander had acquired were divided amongst the most influential of his lieutenants. The great empire the universal conqueror had attempted to establish fell to pieces; the successful competitors for the dismembered portions were soon engaged in domestic and foreign broils and wars; and the progress of art was everywhere arrested. Some attempts were made in particular localities to continue the practice of sculpture, and the honour of still upholding the art, as far as circumstances permitted, must be awarded to those who made this effort. Seleucus and his followers (the Seleucidæ) did this for a time in Syria; and Ptolemy supported the arts in Egypt, of which he had acquired the sovereignty. At Pergamus, also, they found favourable protection from Attalus and Eumenes. But the transfer of sculpture to localities where there was no national sympathy with the character of art which the Greeks had so successfully practised, ensured it no permanent or healthy condition in these countries. All the efforts which could be made by the sculptors, either in love for their art or for more material objects—namely, their own support and livelihood—availed little when the circumstances of the age were so unpropitious, and everywhere there was decline. In the frequent wars of the period, not only the sacred treasures were pillaged, but the edifices which contained them were despoiled of everything that was valuable; temples were destroyed, and the works dedicated in them dispersed; statues in marble were broken, and those of bronze melted down, and the material applied to other uses. The artists had the mortification to see the finest monuments of genius purposely defaced; and those among them who had a higher ambition than mere temporary profit, felt that all their efforts to gain distinction, by producing works of an elevated character, were hopelessly crushed. Though there were occasionally instances of private patronage, there was no general or public encouragement for works in the higher departments of art; and the sculptors soon found that the only remunerative employment was in portrait statues of those who happened to be in power, or who were the objects of popular favour—a precarious application of their talents in those times of change and violence, and from which the stimulus derived from the hope of future favour was taken, as the artist could have but little expectation that his work would last beyond the life of its archetype.

The feeling that this would be the probable fate of his best efforts would of itself be sufficient to depress the energies of the sculptor.

But although this political revolution, by which a vast empire was broken up, thus contributed to check some of the strongest impulses that had caused the greatness of sculpture in Greece, its exercise still occupied a large number of artists. It would require many years to stamp out all love of art among a people so sensitive as the Greeks, and among whom there must still have been a population of professional artists who could trace their descent from the schools of the greatest sculptors, and some of whom would fondly cherish the noble traditions of the past. Besides this, in many localities not yet reached or disturbed by violence, numerous masterpieces of art were still preserved, by which the interests of the artists were incited and kept alive, even when the less favourable circumstances of the times precluded them from the hope of seeing sculpture ever again holding the honourable place which it had occupied when Phidias, Polycletus, Praxiteles, and Lysippus, produced their far-famed works. Many of the artists now living might have worked under and derived their inspiration from Lysippus himself, and it is therefore not to be wondered at that as late as the 145th and 150th Olympiads (that is, from 200 to 170 B.C.), the names of several sculptors of ability are found in the annals of art. To this period antiquaries have attributed some deservedly celebrated works that have reached the present time. Among these may be mentioned particularly the "Hermaphrodite," now in the museum of the Louvre; the so-called "Fighting Gladiator," or Warrior, by Agasias, in the same collection; the well-known "Torso" of the Belvedere, bearing the name of Apollonius, the son of Nestor, as its author, in the museum of the Vatican at Rome; and the Farnese "Hercules," by Glycon, in the Farnese Palace at Rome. It must be admitted there is no direct authority for this appropriation or classification, the dates of the above sculptors being far from satisfactorily established. The opinion has, in all probability, been founded on the character and style of art exhibited in the respective works, which, excepting in the case of the statue called the Hermaphrodite, seem to shew the influence of the Lysippic school.

In the 157th Olympiad, or 146 years B.C., Corinth was taken and sacked by L. Mummius. This blow utterly destroyed the power and the hopes of Greece. Corinth was the principal city of the famous Achæan League, against which the expedition of Mummius had been directed, and its fall extinguished the last gleams of glory which had given renown and splendour to this hitherto favoured nation. The political consequences of their subjugation by the Romans were not the only mortification inflicted upon the conquered. The works of art were seized wherever they could be found; not, as might at first be supposed, for their value as the exquisite productions of the greatest sculptors, but simply as spoil. These trophies were transported to Rome, which soon became filled with the most noble monuments of Grecian taste and genius.

In the foregoing general survey of Greek sculpture, comprehending the period from Ageladas, about 480 B.C., and including the great schools of Phidias, Praxiteles, and Lysippus, down to the migration of the last of the sculptors of what may be termed true Greek descent, the history of real æsthetic art is brought to a close. Sculpture, as has been shewn, was still practised extensively, but it no longer bore an original character; and the best works that were produced, with very rare exceptions, wanted that impulse that had given their chief value to the masterpieces of the bygone ages. The gods still had their temples and worshippers, and their statues were set up in Rome as they had been in Greece; portrait statues also gave employment to the sculptors; but the exercise of a noble art seemed to degenerate into the mere making of images, and such works, even when applied to the representation of gods, were not the sublime types of divinity such as Phidias and Polycletus had conceived and expressed; and the portrait statues of a still lower type were as little calculated, generally, to redeem the character of the art.

One cause of the fatal change in the fortune of sculpture has been referred to. The grand manifestations of the age of Pericles had satisfied men's minds with the noblest forms, as the appropriate expression of the divine nature; and the most costly combinations were used as the fitting offering of religious devotion. But the natural tendency to change and the love of novelty, unhappily, led the Greeks to desire new objects of interest, and Praxiteles and his school found it for them in developing, even to excess, the discovery or rather principle of his great predecessor: that the essence of sculpture is truth of imitation applied to the best and most perfect class of form. Praxiteles especially devoted himself to this object; but he selected for its expression the voluptuous female and youthful male character, in its fullest beauty, to the sacrifice of the higher æsthetic quality which was dominant in the more severe works of Phidias. Lysippus appears to have returned to a purer and grander style, but he also was influenced by the spirit of the remarkable age in which he lived, and, not unnaturally, caught the exaggerated tone of the court and society from which he derived his employment and honours. The scholars of these eminent artists illustrated the prominent qualities of their respective schools; and while this impulse lasted some works of great merit were produced; but when this influence ceased sculpture still further declined.

It is impossible not to be struck, in considering its history at this time, with the remarkable fact of the comparatively short duration of the practice of sculpture in its highest perfection; that is, after the value of the best art had been fully recognised. The whole period of its existence, as a pursuit closely associated with the national glory, scarcely comprehends more than from 200 to 250 years. Its highest excellence was reached, as has been seen, by Phidias and Polycletus from 450 to about 430 B.C., and in less than 100 years the grand or sublime style, which had been hailed with the greatest admiration, and accepted as the perfection of art expression, was superseded by that class, or peculiar mode of representation, which made its address almost exclusively to the senses. This naturally had a strong attraction for and hold on the susceptibilities of so excitable a people as the Greeks; but it heralded in a false taste. The latest indication of the true Greek mind, in art expression, can only, with some little indulgence, be followed to about 200 B.C., when the disciples of the last of the great masters still helped to keep up the ancient prestige. If the Toro Farnese, the group of Laocoon and his sons, and some few works attributed to Greek artists, were executed at the date assigned to them, this late continuance of a school of good sculpture may be admitted. After this the art was carried on by mere copyists—weak interpreters of the ideas of others, and only differing in the greater or less success they exhibited in repeating or adapting ancient examples.

Athens, which had been the chief centre and the favourite home of the artists of Greece, had suffered many changes of fortune from the time of Pericles—under whom she may be considered to have reached the zenith of her glory; but she was able still to maintain, to some extent, her well-earned character for eminence in the fine arts. After the death of Alexander, she also began to feel the evil influence of the times, and, by degrees, to lose her ascendency even here. At length the all-conquering Romans invaded the chosen city of Minerva, and Athens had to bow her neck to the cruel and relentless Sylla. Subsequently still further humiliation awaited her. After the termination of the civil war between Pompey and Cæsar, in which Athens had sided with the former, her fate was for ever sealed. She had to submit to the common destiny, though it is recorded, to his honour, that her conqueror treated her with generous consideration, saying, in allusion to her former glory, "he would spare the living for the sake of the dead." But Greece never recovered her ancient state. She became a Roman province; and Athens only survived in her monuments and in the glory of the past.

SECTION X.

ROME was founded in 753 B.C., a date at which it would be vain to expect any indication of art, either original or borrowed. But even long after this there would be but little opportunity or disposition to cultivate a pursuit so foreign to the spirit and habit of a people constantly engaged in securing their own position and safety, and in endeavouring to extend their power and rule over neighbouring communities. There is vague allusion to works in sculpture of an early date in Rome, but if they existed at the time they were doubtless the production of foreigners; probably the Etruscans, who were already an established people, with their own form of government and laws, and from whose near neighbourhood the new settlers derived, as is well known, many advantages. One of the oldest monuments shewn in Rome—and it may be added one of the most interesting remains of antiquity, from its historical associations—is the bronze she-wolf with the two children Romulus and Remus, which is now preserved at the Capitol. It is of archaïc character, and no doubt of genuine and great antiquity. Mention is made of equestrian statues in Rome as far back as 300 years before the Christian era; but even if this were the case it would afford no evidence that they were the production of native artists. They are said to have been erected in honour of M. F. Camillus and Q. Mænius after their victories over the Latins. About the same date a bronze statue of Apollo was made out of the spoils taken from the Samnites, and placed in the Capitol. It is probable that works may have been procured for remarkable occasions from more cultivated sources, and the equestrian statues above referred to, if they had any merit at all as works of art, were most likely the production of more accomplished artists than Rome could at that time boast. At the period referred to sculpture had reached a very high degree of excellence in Greece, and it is difficult to believe that no indication of this could have reached Italy. It is quite consistent to suppose that the Romans themselves would be unaffected by its influence, so far as to ignore anything like the establishment of a school of artists among their busy population intent upon more material interests. It may even be assumed that the spirit of the government would be opposed rather than favourable to the encouragement of any of the more refined arts. The importance and the security of the nation being dependent on its military prowess and the respect it would command from its neighbours, it was of the highest consequence not to cherish any feelings or tastes which, in their estimation, might tend to soften the character of the citizens accustomed for so many years to a life of continual exertion and danger. The study of art would be associated in their minds with effeminacy, and might lead to a desire for that tranquillity to which all their instincts were opposed. This sentiment is often apparent in the writings of the Romans even at a much later period of their history. At the time above referred to it seems to have been distinctly exhibited in the feeling shewn to a native Roman who occupied himself with art. One Fabius, a member of one of the higher families, devoted himself to painting, and decorated the temple of the Goddess of Health with his works. He acquired the name or title of "Pictor." This accomplishment gained him, however, no honour with his fellow-citizens; for it is recorded that he was both laughed at and despised.* This low estimation of the more refined arts and their professors has been found among other nations, and even in modern times, where the influential classes—usually uninstructed in these pursuits, and therefore not very capable of appreciating their possible value to society—have only considered the arts of design in the false light of mere idle and useless accomplishments, of no

* In risu et contumeliâ erat.—*Val. Max.*

value in advancing the civilization and refinement of a nation. But if the Romans were too much occupied with their material interests, their wars, and the extension of their empire, to give much attention to the practice of sculpture among themselves, they appear to have accumulated immense collections of statues from the countries they subdued. After the capture of Syracuse, Marcellus sent home various works of art from Sicily, and numerous instances occur of the desire of the Romans to acquire such monuments. It is true that it cannot be said that the possession of the most beautiful productions which thus fell into their hands caused at this time any great improvement in the general taste of the people; the fact is, foreign cities and their temples were ransacked and plundered to enrich the treasury of Rome, or to swell the triumph of a general, and the most exquisite works of art were, it would seem, merely looked upon as so much spoil; the feelings, therefore, that the finest display excited amongst the people were far from those that were likely to generate a love of art for its own sake.

In this way, though large collections were formed, it was rather from ostentation than from any real feeling for, or appreciation of, the merit of the works they procured. It is, however, supposed, that about this time some artists from Greece were tempted to establish themselves in Rome, and they would no doubt exercise some influence in extending the knowledge of art. Sylla, it has been seen, had ruthlessly sacked Athens, and had, in mere mischief, demolished some of the principal monuments and temples of Delphi, Epidaurus, and Elis; but fortunately he had also sent a great proportion of the works of art which had fallen in his way as spoil to Rome. It would seem that either the establishment in the country of foreign artists, or, it may be, the possession of the fine productions of Greece, generated by degrees, if not a real feeling for art, at least a desire to possess objects to which others had formerly attached so much importance; and it may be assumed that in time this acted favourably on the fortunes of sculpture. Amongst the most celebrated of the Roman collectors the name of Verres has obtained unenviable notoriety. During his government as Prætor of Sicily he indulged this passion in a manner so rapacious and unjust that it excited the liveliest indignation, and he had to bear for it the disgrace of a public trial. Cicero undertook the cause of the oppressed Sicilians, and pronounced against him those celebrated orations which are still extant, and which drove Verres, who seems to have felt that no defence he could make could save him, into voluntary exile. At this time (when Rome was evidently becoming the asylum of those artists who could no longer live in Greece) flourished Pasiteles, a sculptor of no mean ability; also Arcesilas and Strongylion, celebrated particularly for his Amazon Eucnemis, or "with the beautiful legs," and his three Muses. Olympiosthenes and Evander are also among the sculptors, evidently Greeks, mentioned at this period.

A decided impulse was at length given to the success of sculpture and fine art generally, by the taste exhibited by Julius Cæsar; for he not only collected, as others had done, fine works, as statues and gems, but he caused Rome to be embellished with public buildings and other decoration. Nor did he confine his efforts to introduce a feeling for improvement in these respects to Italy only, but had many important public works carried on in various cities of Gaul, Spain, and other countries subject to Roman rule. After his death his successor Augustus equally encouraged art. He had all the most remarkable specimens brought together for his consideration, and he then distributed them in the most favourable public places, both as noble objects of decoration, and that they might be well seen by the people. He is said also to have had statues erected in honour of those who had distinguished themselves by any great actions, or had otherwise deserved well of their country. The impulse thus given by these emperors appears to have incited a praiseworthy emulation in others; for in this age the name of Agrippa stands pre-eminent for his public spirit and liberality in erecting, at his own expense, useful and ornamental public edifices in and about Rome. It is sufficient to mention the Pantheon, as the most striking monument of his munificence. This noble work, though despoiled of its original decoration, still exists to do honour to the taste and generosity of its founder. It is worthy of record here that Agrippa fully recognised the importance of sculpture in the enrichment of public buildings, for he is said to have employed Diogenes, an Athenian sculptor, especially to decorate this edifice. It is believed that all these works have perished. This artist is mentioned by Pliny as the author of some statues of Caryatides.

There were several artists of reputation living in the age of Augustus. Among these Vitruvius, an architect, holds a distinguished place both as an artist and author. In the latter character he may be advantageously consulted by the student in sculpture for some very curious and interesting commentaries on subjects connected with this art, as well as for some useful rules of proportion. Several sculptors of gems, chasers in metal, and similar works of a high character, are mentioned by Pliny. The most eminent of these are Dioscorides, Agathopus, Epitynchanus, Pythias, and Posidonius. Fortunately some of the productions of these artists are preserved and testify to the deserved reputation of their authors. It will at once be seen from the names of the above that the sculpture of the day was chiefly, if not entirely, in the hands of Greek artists, and it is equally evident that there were men of great ability still exercising the profession of art. The works of the time, of a larger scale, which claim attention, consist principally of portraits. In the smaller works above referred to the artists seem to have gratified their taste and feeling by recurring to the higher Greek types and subjects. In busts and portrait statues another influence is seen. They often possess great merit, but the true judge of art will easily perceive the difference that exists between the best of these and the productions of the pure Greek schools. Great attention was paid to individual character, as was natural where correct portraiture was required; and it must be granted that this was effected in the majority of works without loss of breadth, and without that poverty and minuteness of detail which often is found in later works of this description. The most striking deficiency in this Greco-Roman sculpture is the absence of ideal beauty. They are true to particular and individual nature, but they have not the refinement or selection so remarkable in the sculpture of the Greeks.

Reference has already been made to some fine examples of sculpture, supposed to have been produced at a comparatively late period of Greek practice by descendants of the great schools. It may be convenient, as some of these have been attributed to the Augustan age, to describe them more particularly. The first that deserves attention is the extensive group, which has already been cursorily noticed, known as the Toro Farnese, representing Zethus and Amphion tying Dirce to the horns of a wild bull. This work is in marble, and consists of the three principal figures, of heroic size, with the rearing and infuriated animal forming the apex of the composition. There is an accessorial female figure of smaller dimensions at the back of the design, and in front a small sitting male figure with other accompaniments. The forms are of a fine general type, the heads are treated in the manner of the best schools, and the drapery of Dirce, which covers the figure from the hips downwards, is in a good style of art. There is much in this production to justify the opinion of Winckelman, who considered the group might be the work of Greek sculptors before the time of Lysippus; but it is a point on which, with good reason, antiquaries differ. The style of a work of sculpture may truly indicate the character of a school, but, as it may be imitative, it is no sure or reliable criterion of the age itself of its execution. The negative evidence against this group being a production of the time of Praxiteles, is first, the silence of ancient writers respecting a work so important in size and subject. It is the most extensive composition in marble, of the kind, known. It differs altogether in its arrangement from designs in a series of statues such as the various well-known pedimental groups—as those of the Parthenon, of the temple at Ægina, the Niobe, and others of the class; and it is therefore difficult to believe that if it existed among the works of the great masters of the time referred to it would not have received honourable mention. That there were sculptors in Rome capable of producing such a work—successfully imitating, as is often done in modern times, the *style* of the most approved Greek examples—there can be no doubt; but certainly the loose and picturesque character of the design is a strong argument against its being a work of the purer ages of Greek art. The composition is unconcentrated, and without grandeur of design as to mass and breadth. The effect is, however, unquestionably very striking, and it may have been designed for some particular application where peculiarities that appear now to be faults may have assisted in answering a desired object. It is not easy for modern criticism to decide upon the full merits of ancient sculpture, when, instead of being seen *in situ*, and under the circumstances contemplated and prepared for by its author, it is only judged of in close galleries and embarrassed by surrounding and usually incongruous objects. It will be admitted that great power is shewn in this work, and that the story, though a very painful one, is well told.

From the great dimensions of this group, and the straggling character of the design, coupled with the very destructible quality of the material in which it is executed, this work has been greatly injured; and, unfortunately, the repairs and restorations have not always been carried out in harmony with the original style and execution. For many years it was exposed to the influence of the weather, being placed entirely unprotected in the public gardens of the Villa Reale at Naples. It has now, after many previous removals, been deposited in the Royal Museum (Borbonico). It may here be preserved from further injury; but, for the reasons above given, it can never be properly seen or fairly judged in so confined a space. It can only now be contemplated as a remarkable example of bold design, and, as far as the original work remains, of a fine school of form.

The well-known group of "Laocoon and his Sons," writhing in the folds of the serpent, has been attributed to this age, though it also has been thought to be of the time of Lysippus. The same difficulties that have before been alluded to here again meet the antiquary and critic. The style of the school may be evident, but not so the time of the production of the work; yet in certain particulars of treatment, as in the minute representation of suffering, by which so great a sacrifice is made of beauty and dignity, it would seem to belong to a different age from the nobler and simpler schools of sculpture. Pliny describes this group inaccurately, as consisting of only a single block of marble. It is, on the contrary, in various pieces, of which the joints may easily be seen on careful examination. There can be no doubt that this is the identical group referred to by that writer, as decorating the baths of Titus;* for it was among the excavated ruins of that building that it was found early in the sixteenth century. A very interesting account is given of this discovery in a letter written a few years afterwards by one of the persons present. When the architect, San Gallo, accompanied by Michael Angelo, then a young man, visited the excavation by command of the Pope (Julius II.), and saw this masterpiece lying amidst the dirt and rubbish turned up by the workmen, in a vineyard just beyond the walls of Rome, he immediately exclaimed, "*Ah! this is the Laocoon of which Pliny speaks;*" shewing how well acquainted the artist was with that writer's works, and the advantage such knowledge gave him in recognising at once a fine monument of antiquity. The figures in this composition vary much in their art-qualities. The centre of the group is occupied by Laocoon himself, and this may fairly be referred to as one of the finest productions of its kind in sculpture. It exhibits a most intimate knowledge of the human figure; the expression is intense, every muscle being in

* Ex uno lapide eum (Laocoon) et liberos draconumque mirabiles nexus de consilii sententia fecere summi artifices Agesander et Polydorus et Athenodorus Rhodii.—Plin. *Hist. Nat.* xxxvi. 5.

extreme action, and the hands and feet are convulsed with painful energy. One hand and arm of the principal figure are restorations. The youths are of smaller scale altogether than the father, and of an inferior class of art. It has been thought by some critics that the right arm of the figure of Laocoon was not extended as at present, but in the original work was bent back towards the head. This speculation gains much support from the fact that there is a fracture where it is possible the hand, or possibly a fold of the serpent thus held up, may have come in contact with the hair. It will be curious, if the missing limb should ever be found, if this conjecture should be verified. One of the most charming groups of antiquity, known as the "Cupid and Pysche," and preserved in the museum of the Capitol at Rome, is unnoticed by Pliny. It probably is a work of this age. Flaxman thought it possible that Pliny omitted to mention it because it was modern in his time, and not a standard production of any of those great masters whose works were sought after as the best examples of sculpture. This is scarcely a sufficient reason for his silence; but if it is admitted, it would account for many works being passed over by him which now occupy a distinguished place in public collections. It is, however, extremely difficult to decide upon the date of many of the works of art that have reached modern times; for where there was a taste for reproducing Greek sculpture, both in subject and treatment, and a class of artists capable of so doing, it would be almost impossible to discover whether they were really of a true, ancient school, or only successful imitations. A circumstance is related which occurred during the reign of Tiberius, which shews that the Romans were very jealous of their rights, even in the matter of public works of art, although they may not have been very earnest admirers of, or competent judges of their merit. Tiberius desired to remove to his own palace a statue, attributed to Lysippus, of an athlete anointing himself. It stood in the baths of Agrippa, to which the public had access, and it therefore was considered to belong to the people. Finding it had been taken away, the Romans shewed their dissatisfaction so unmistakeably that Tiberius, alarmed at the violent expression of feeling, and fearing a revolt in the city if he disregarded the public indignation, was compelled to relinquish his object. He commanded the statue to be replaced in its original situation, and the people were appeased.

Sculpture was now evidently held in some esteem, though it cannot yet be said to have been honoured in Rome, as an art either of noble purpose as regards sentiment, or attractive as the means of exhibiting beautiful form. But as the nation increased in importance, it became an object with successive rulers to add to the splendour and decoration of the city; and not only the public buildings but the palaces of the emperors exhibited all the marks of the increasing love of magnificence and display. The application of sculpture to the gratification of mere personal vanity shews how far the Romans were below the Greeks in the true feeling for this art. Caligula was most anxious to collect works of art from Greece, and it is said he shewed the strongest desire to transport to Rome the celebrated statue of the Olympian Jupiter by Phidias. This intention on the part of the emperor gave great alarm and offence to those who still clung to the possession of this remaining monument of their ancient glory. At any rate the design was not carried out. Fortunately, the architects and others who had been consulted as to the possibility of removing it, declared that it would inevitably be destroyed if any attempt of the kind were made, and Caligula was obliged to abandon his intention. This noble work was, therefore, saved from the desecration it is supposed was contemplated, namely to have the head of the emperor himself substituted for that of the god: a process Caligula had applied to many of the fine statues he had acquired. Many valuable works were thus maltreated, shewing that their accumulation in Rome was owing either to the desire of display, or, as in the case of Caligula, to gratify a wretched vanity, and not as memorials of an enlightened people, or as beautiful productions of art.

The reigns of Claudius and of Nero afford but little information as to the condition of sculpture among the Romans. The rage for collecting still continued, but it was not accompanied by any real appreciation of the excellence of the productions thus acquired. The only object seems to have been to accumulate monuments of Greek art from whatever quarter they could be procured. The latter emperor, notwithstanding what had already been taken from it, is said to have obtained no fewer than five hundred bronze statues from the temple of Apollo at Delphi. This, of course, must mean statues that had been dedicated, and placed in the precincts of the temple. The greater part of these works so removed were employed in the decoration of the celebrated golden palace on the Palatine hill.

How far the world is indebted to the Roman collectors for the preservation of many remarkable works of ancient sculpture it is difficult to say; or whether they might have been better preserved if left in their native soil than when transported to Rome; but it cannot be denied that several productions of the highest merit have been recovered from amongst the remains of Roman buildings. Besides the recovery of the Laocoon in the ruins of the baths of Titus, two of the most celebrated statues known—namely, the Apollo of the Belvedere, now in the museum of the Vatican at Rome, and the so-called Fighting Gladiator in the collection of the Louvre at Paris—were discovered in those of a villa or palace supposed to have belonged to Nero at Antium. The latter work bears the name of its author, "Agasias the Ephesian, son of Dositheus," in Greek letters. It is sometimes called the "Warrior of Agasias." The Apollo is considered, on very sufficient grounds, to be a copy in marble of a bronze statue, and the material is said closely to resemble, if not to be identical with, the marble of Carrara. If this should be so, the execution of this work would belong to a later age than the Greek schools, as these quarries were not worked before the time of Augustus. There were sculptors of great talent at this period. The names of Zenodorus and Menodorus occur. Zenodorus is mentioned as the author of a colossal statue of Nero, and is said to have been practising sculpture in Cisalpine Gaul, where he was sent for to Rome to execute this work. There were, probably, two sculptors called Menodorus. One of them was an Athenian, and is celebrated for his skill in a peculiar class of art—as armed men, athletes, and huntsmen. The circumstance referred to at an earlier part of this history—of Nero having had a bronze statue by Lysippus gilt, and then restored to its original state because he found its value as a work of art impaired by the addition of the more precious coating—speaks favourably for the taste of the emperor, who could forego a fancy for the sake of preserving the effect of the sculpture. Galba, Otho, and Vitellius, lived in times too disturbed to afford these emperors any opportunity, even if they had the inclination, to encourage sculpture. Their reigns were very short, and probably they took no interest in art. Busts of these emperors are extremely rare. One of Vitellius, in the Louvre, is very fine in its successful treatment of the full and coarse fleshy character; but antiquaries have suspected its authenticity. Otho is said to have given his assistance to continue a magnificent work of his predecessor Nero; having appropriated a large sum of money for the completion of the Golden Palace.

To this period, or soon after, may be attributed the introduction in Rome of *polylithic* sculpture, or the execution of works in different marbles. This became a favourite exercise among the now luxurious Romans, when the value or richness of the material was considered of much higher importance than the excellence of the design. It was quite in character with the unrefined and coarse feeling for display of the age and people, and indicated a false and bad taste which must prevent any successful prosecution of art for its own sake.

There was one short period in the history of the empire in which it seemed possible that the fine arts might have obtained an honourable position. In the reigns of Trajan, of Hadrian, and of the Antonines, an impulse was given to the practice of the arts, in all branches, which gave every promise of a fresh development. It may be called the golden age of sculpture in Rome. Though it is probable the ablest professors were not native artists, there must have been some residing there who were fully capable of executing the designs now made for the decoration of Rome and other cities. The Forum of Trajan at Rome, and the arch at Ancona, are monuments of considerable merit, and shew both the interest taken in such works by the emperor, and the ability of the artists to whom their execution was entrusted. It is said that a custom prevailed at this time of putting Roman names on ancient Greek statues. It is not easy to divine the object of this species of forgery, unless it were done with the hope of giving posterity a higher impression of the talents of the artists than they felt they were likely to obtain by their own performances. Their contemporaries could scarcely be expected to accept the works so marked as productions of the actual age; and it is difficult to reconcile the acknowledged passion of the better educated classes for ancient Greek sculpture as decoration for their palaces, baths, and villas, with this false appropriation of authorship.

The stimulus given to art lost none of its impulse under Hadrian. He was its munificent and zealous promoter, and his reign is distinguished for the variety and the extent of the works carried on. He did not confine his patronage to Rome. He restored in many cities of the empire the older temples which had been suffered to fall into decay or had been destroyed, and he also erected others. Among his more important undertakings was the completion of the temple of the Olympian Jupiter at Athens, which for centuries had remained unfinished. He had it decorated with a variety of works, and, not unmindful of his own glory and share in this great effort, had a statue of colossal dimensions of himself placed in it. In Italy he built his celebrated villa at Tivoli, and embellished it with all the finest remains he could procure of the great Greek schools, and with others that were executed especially for the purpose, under his own superintendence. This favourite palace of Hadrian is now only known by its extensive ruins. It was situated about eighteen miles from Rome, and the extent of ground still covered with the excavations, the remains of halls and chambers, and other indications of its scale, impress the visitor with the most vivid notion of its former magnificence. Its site has been most prolific in restoring to the world some of the most valuable monuments of ancient art. It was among the strange fancies of Hadrian to introduce into Rome many usages and ceremonies of Egyptian worship. The example of the emperor spread this new taste over many parts of the empire, and occasioned not only a great demand for statues and other representations of Egyptian deities, but, it is said, led to the introduction of many religious observances of the Egyptian form of worship. The villa of Hadrian has afforded a full harvest of these pseudo-Egyptian sculptures, in every variety of material, and not unfrequently in those offering great difficulty of execution.

Both Hadrian and Marcus Aurelius practised as well as patronized art; and it is said the architect Apollodorus owed his death to the imperial jealousy, in consequence of having had the courage and misfortune to find some fault in a temple which had been erected after a design furnished by the emperor himself. The statues and busts of these rulers of Rome, as well as the portraits of Lucius Verus, and, we may add, of the favourite Antinous especially, offer abundant proof of the power of the artists of this age. The statues of Antinous, of which two fine specimens may be mentioned in the museum of the Capitol—one in the Greek style, the other with the arms straight down to the sides, and having the well-known Egyptian head-dress—are of great beauty; broad in style, of grand, massive treatment, with careful choice and study of form. They carry the imagination back to the very best time of Greek sculpture. Here, however, and even during the period under consideration, the decline of art becomes too evident. The taste, if it deserves the name, and the liberality of the princes above named, gave an impulse which, for the time, seemed capable of restoring to art its former glory, but it was soon evident there was no true foundation for its re-establishment. The encouragement was personal, and had no support from the general or national feeling. No greater proof of this being a mere passing influence can be adduced than the difference observable, both in style and execution, of the two columns still existing in Rome of Trajan and Antonine.

The name of one individual stands out prominently about this time as an earnest and liberal promoter of art. Herodes, who acquired the title of Atticus—a man of immense wealth—expended large sums in embellishing Athens and other cities of Greece with public buildings and similar magnificent works. This noble example had not, however, any favourable or lasting result. Like other insulated efforts, it occupied attention at the time; and when the material stimulus offered by immediate and liberal patronage was withdrawn, there was again a collapse, and the practice of sculpture declined. Among the honourable uses to which he applied sculpture, Herodes caused statues to be made of the most deserving of his friends.

To return to Rome. At the time of Septimius Severus, about 200 A.D., the arts of design had rapidly fallen into a state of lamentable decay. They were no longer practised by any but the inferior classes; and not being considered fit occupation for persons of education or of good social position, they fell into contempt; and, from being recognised as *liberal*, and only to be exercised by freedmen, the arts came to be looked upon as a low kind of manufacture or handicraft. This in itself would be enough to degrade the character of sculpture; for, from want of education, there would be no power in those artists who exercised the calling to treat art in an elevated manner, nor any inducement to raise themselves above their base social condition. Some productions of this time shew plainly the deterioration of art. The sculpture on the arch of S. Severus in the Forum at Rome, as well as that on what is called the Arch of the Goldsmiths, is as poor in taste as it is feeble in execution. There is a great display of minute details, and abundance of littlenesses in carving and drilling, but a total absence of imagination and feeling in design, and of breadth in treatment. The sculptors appear still to have had some practice in portrait, and notwithstanding the general feebleness observable in inventive or illustrative sculpture, some of the busts of this time are not undeserving of notice. Alexander Severus appears to have taken much personal interest in one branch of art. Some extensive public buildings were erected in his reign, and he established schools for the study of architecture particularly.

The condition of Italy at this time, distracted by rival factions and disturbed by the usurpations of various pretenders to the purple, who were elevated or dethroned according to the caprice of an almost lawless army, gave little opportunity for encouraging or practising the arts of design. When Constantine was emperor it was decided to erect an arch in his honour. The poverty of Rome in sculpture is shewn by the fact that it was found necessary to appropriate certain portions of the decoration of a work erected two hundred years previously to another ruler in order to complete the design. The *bassi-rilievi* placed in the panels were taken from an arch erected in honour of Trajan to commemorate that emperor's conquests over the Dacians and Parthians. This affords sufficient proof that there were no sculptors in Rome capable of executing the appropriate decoration of a monument of that description. Constantine himself appears to have had a strong feeling for art, and if he had any acquaintance with its principles, it is possible he may himself have consented and even desired to employ older and better works on this occasion, rather than have the monument degraded by such sculpture as the practitioners of the day would have supplied. This emperor claims, however, a place with the distinguished few who earnestly endeavoured to re-establish the practice of the fine arts. But in Rome, as has been shewn, there was no hope of their recovery. Their existence here had never been secure at any time. They were treated rather as objects of amusement, or mere decoration, and were often degraded both in their subjects and application. In Rome, in its most palmy days, there never had been any real feeling for art as an elevated and ennobling pursuit. But the opportunity now occurred of forming a new home for its noblest exercise. The removal at this time of the imperial court to the new seat of government at Byzantium, and the subsequent division of the empire into eastern and western, gave a fatal blow to the grandeur and even security of Rome. This occurred at 323 A.D. Constantine determined to gratify his love of art by building and decorating the new imperial residence on a most magnificent scale. He attracted all the best artists to be found to his service; he instituted schools for their instruction, and engaged, by offering rewards and privileges, a number of youths to study architecture, especially, in order to insure the erection of creditable public buildings. It would appear, however, that the decoration of these edifices was to be provided in another way. Probably, although the more mechanical study of architecture might be taught with some success and rapidity, it was felt that a school of sculpture could not be so easily formed, and the buildings thus erected were enriched with all the best works that could be procured of the Greek sculptors. By the emperor's commands, the various cities of Greece and Asia Minor were again ransacked for their treasures of art for this object, and thus they were despoiled of any remaining monuments of their former glory. Trophies, statues of gods, heroes, poets, and philosophers, were collected from all parts, and were crowded together in this great centre of magnificence and splendour,* which then received the title of the city of the emperor—Constantinople. There were evidently some sculptors living who attempted works of a large scale, as mention is made of statues in bronze erected in this and the subsequent reigns of Constantine, Honorius, and Theodosius. No remains of these works are known, and it is not assuming too much to suppose there can be little cause to lament their disappearance. Even the names of the artists who executed them have been allowed to pass away unrecorded.

Italy was suffering various adverse fortune during this period of her history. She was constantly subjected to the incursions of northern adventurers. In the year 412 A.D., she felt the weight of the power of Alaric, king of the Goths, who, with his hordes, ravaged the country, and finally entered and took possession of Rome. In the year 456, Odoacer, a chief of the barbarians, who had called themselves allies of Rome, took upon himself the title of King of Italy. Rome was given up to pillage. Genseric, king of the Vandals, contributed

* Constantinopolis dedicatur pœnè omnium urbium nuditate.—Hieronym. *Chron.*

to its further destruction; and in 545 A.D., the Goths, led by Totila, again attacked it, became masters of the city, and set fire to it. It is said it continued burning for several days. Many of the wretched inhabitants having retired for protection into the Mausoleum of Hadrian (now called the Castle of St. Angelo), they threw down the statues which were in it on their enemies crowded together under the walls.

Constantinople had become possessed of an immense collection of works of art, many of them the productions of the most eminent sculptors of antiquity. A fire which broke out in the Palace of the Lausi, in the year 479, totally destroyed the greater part of these; and the world has thus lost some of the most celebrated monuments of the great Greek schools of sculpture. Among the most famous of those that perished was the Olympian Jupiter by Phidias; several others are also recorded, the productions of Lysippus and other artists of the noblest period of the art.

Justinian, who reigned from 527 to 565 A.D., had statues erected at the seat of government. Among these was one of colossal proportions of himself. It was placed on a column which was decorated with *bassi-rilievi*. It was during the reign of this emperor that the Church of St. Sophia at Constantinople was commenced.

In 661, Constans was emperor. He did not, however, long retain his power, but was driven from his capital amidst the imprecations of his subjects. He made his escape to Italy, and visited Rome. The city of the Cæsars, though so fallen from its greatness, had still, notwithstanding the reckless pillage and injuries it had suffered, several remains of its fine ancient monuments. Constans is said to have remained in Rome only thirteen days, but in that time he contrived to despoil it of everything that was of any value, and the statues he took were removed by his orders to Syracuse in Sicily, whither he himself proceeded, and where he terminated his wretched career.

It is remarkable how uniformly the spoliation and removal of works of sculpture accompanied changes in the whole of the Roman political history. It was, without doubt, a species of homage paid to art, even when there was no real love or knowledge of it in many of those who collected them. Statues appear to have been looked upon simply as movables of, perhaps, a superior quality; fitting accompaniments of imperial movements; and a species of furniture appropriate to palaces and the seat of government. This fancy, by no means confined to Rome, has doubtless been the cause of the preservation of many works of value, which otherwise would have perished from neglect.

The whole history of sculpture during the period of Roman dominion, affords sufficient proof that it received no valuable impulse from the national taste, or a feeling for imaginative or beautiful art. The first knowledge Rome acquired of the existence of fine statues was in its conquests, where such objects presented themselves simply as spoil, the reward of military prowess, and fitting accompaniments of a victor's triumph; or they were used as a ready-made decoration for the public edifices and squares of the mistress city of the world. When Mummius sacked Corinth, it was found filled with masterpieces of art. He, of course, secured these, but was so utterly insensible of their excellence, that he stipulated that if any of them were injured or lost in their transport to Italy, the persons who had the care of them should provide others to replace them. The truth is, the greatness and power of Rome were based on more severe exercises than the prosecution of the gentler arts; and painting and sculpture had no attraction for a nation whose function was war, and whose ambition was to extend the Roman name and glory wherever its legions could penetrate. As the riches and luxury of Rome increased, public buildings of magnificence were multiplied, and here the value of rich and costly decoration was recognised. But this was not provided by Roman genius. Greece supplied the taste and skill necessary for this refined work; and when temples, noble and spacious forums, public halls, and baths, were erected, under the impulse of that grand and colossal idea which characterised the Romans in all their works of the kind, it appears they were indebted for the more elegant details of statuary and rilievi, either to the trophies of foreign acquisition, or to the labours of emigrant artists who had sought an asylum and home in Italy. Those monuments of sculpture that may be considered Roman have no character in common with the imaginative art of the best Greek schools. They are essentially national. They either are portraits of individuals, or represent particular acts—as religious ceremonies, triumphs, sacrifices, and similar subjects—or they are mere friezes and panels of ornament and foliage. In this latter class, however, are found some works of very high merit. Of works of poetical fancy, or of a high type of beauty, there are scarcely any that can be ascribed to Roman origin. Wherever any striking or superior quality appears, it seems to be Greek. Even the allusions of some of the great writers of Rome to the wonders of Greek sculpture appear to have been incapable of exciting any real interest in the value of art in the nation at large; nor did the liberality of those emperors, or individuals, who shewed a disposition to protect and encourage it, meet with any response from the people. Rome was, however, filled with buildings of a scale and character that shew that architecture was extensively practised; and the monuments that still exist afford evidence of the greatness of a nation that could leave to posterity such almost imperishable records of its constructive power. Many of these works—amphitheatres, aqueducts, vast halls, baths, and temples—owe their ruined condition quite as much to the hand of man as to the ravages of time. It is in these manifestations of physical power in art, that the grandeur of Rome will be recognised. The sculpture, strictly Roman, to which reference has been made, has, it must be allowed, great value and interest independently of the higher qualities which are only originally found in the Greek schools. It has illustrated and explained many points of history which could not easily have been understood without such aid, and has afforded much information by its clear representations of the habits, the ceremonies, and the costume of the Romans, at different stages of their wonderful career. In this respect Roman sculpture has fulfilled a very useful mission of art, and though the student of sculpture and the refined judge of the beautiful may not find in its monuments either the highest standard for imitation or the nobler inventions of genius, the scholar, the historian, and the antiquary will gratefully admit its value in the particular objects in which they are interested.

With Constans the history of ancient sculpture is concluded. In Rome, as has been shewn, it had always held a mixed character; all the best that was produced among this people being either directly Greek, or made up of Greek subjects, expressed by Greek forms. Their own distinct contributions exhibited different qualities, which, though valuable in their way, prove, without question, that the art, from the time it left the genial atmosphere of Greece, deteriorated; and although, occasionally, efforts were made to restore it, that the true spirit of sculpture was extinct.

Constantly recurring wars, seditions, political and religious divisions, now fully occupied the government and people, both in the eastern and western world, and gave no leisure for the encouragement or protection of the arts, even if there had been any disposition to uphold them. The preservation of so many works remaining at this time is due rather to accident and good fortune than to design; for the anarchy that prevailed would be more likely to lead to the destruction of public monuments, as much from mere wantonness and mischief as from insensibility to their value. When the conquests of the Saracen Caliphs carried them into Sicily, the objects collected there fell into the hands of rude masters, who were quite incapable of appreciating their merit, and who, therefore, left them to the chances of war; either to be defaced and ill-used by an ignorant soldiery, or, as it might be, left untouched from utter carelessness as to what might befall them. The prejudices and violence of the Iconoclasts, and the inroads of barbarians in every direction, tended still further to forward the work of destruction. Occasionally individuals who held power exhibited a disposition to shew some respect and care for the noble remains of antiquity which everywhere challenged their attention; and, as was the case with Theodoric in the sixth century, and at a later period with Charlemagne, to put a stop to the ravages which had been so fatal, as various bands of savage and barbarous hordes took possession of the country. But their endeavours, however honourable to themselves, were quite inadequate to effect any great good, or to induce a respect for that which was totally unintelligible to their untaught followers. No mere personal influence was sufficient to arrest the rapid consummation that was consigning all the glorious memories of art to a long night of oblivion.

It is still interesting to watch the fortunes of sculpture, or rather of some of its products—for the practice had long fallen into neglect and disuse—before they entirely disappear. Even now, many masterpieces of the art were preserved, amidst all the confusion and disorders of the time, in Constantinople; to which remote corner of Europe the fallen Roman name was at length reduced. The hand of the destroyer was not, however, long withheld from this, the last asylum of art. Baldwin, Count of Flanders, and his allies, took armed possession of Constantinople in the thirteenth century.

The works of art were now systematically doomed to destruction, and the statues of metal were at once melted down and converted into money. It is melancholy to reflect that amongst them were a magnificent statue of Juno by Lysippus, a colossal Hercules, a statue of Helen, and a variety of works, the production of the most flourishing period of art, and of the most celebrated sculptors of ancient Greece.*

* A vivid account of the destruction of many of the noblest relics of Greek skill and genius is given by Gibbon, from the history of an eye-witness, Nicetas Choniates, *Decline and Fall*, vol. xi. p. 60.

PART II.

SECTION I.

THE history of sculpture is no longer a continuation of the noble and refined art of the ancients. This had for a long period been corrupted, in motive as well as expression, till it had gradually become extinct. The highest Greek practice began to decline, as has been shewn, in the fourth century B.C., when the more severe and chastened sentiment that had originally guided it had lost its force; and though many admirable works were produced subsequently, both in Greece and Italy—the latter chiefly, if not exclusively, by those artists who, on the subjection of their country, removed from Greece to Rome—there never was any real resuscitation of the fine schools of that gifted people amongst whom the art had had its fullest consummation.

In reviewing the later fortunes and condition of this art, it may be observed that modern sculpture must be judged by a totally different standard from that applied to the ancient practice, when art was the language of real feeling, and its technical perfection was progressive, and the result of successive stages of development. The character and changes of modern sculpture will be seen to depend upon external circumstances only; and as the impulse given to art has been almost always owing to *material* as opposed to *æsthetic* causes, it will easily be understood that the effect of modern sculpture, as well as the interest felt in it, will, with the one exception to be presently referred to, be of a different kind to that claimed by the more remarkable and original productions of the ancient schools. The comparative excellence achieved at various periods will justly command admiration for the ability displayed by the artists; but the impression the art produces will be found usually to be owing rather to the merit of the workmanship and the skill of the sculptor than the power of the work itself to awaken thought, or to excite affecting or noble associations. The single phase of sculpture which may be an exception to this, it will easily be understood, is the religious art of the early Christians after the Western Church admitted the use of sculpture and painting in their places of worship. The circumstances of its rise and progress give it a claim to particular consideration.

Italy may justly claim the honour of the new birth of art. This is usually dated at about the tenth century; but some writers have placed it much earlier, and Flaxman considered it might be dated as far back as the third or fourth century. It has been supposed that, after the miserable condition to which it had been reduced under the later Roman dynasties, art was only lying dormant till happier times should arise to give it fresh vitality, and that the monks and recluses of the early Greek and Latin communities were its real guardians, and kept alive its smouldering embers by illuminating manuscripts and church offices, or covering the walls of their convents and places of worship with rude paintings. There can be no doubt that the followers of the new faith employed art to express or illustrate the doctrines they professed, and in so doing used, at first, the forms that were supplied by the examples at hand; and, so far, this certainly would seem to carry back the practice of religious art, or rather art applied to a religious purpose, to a period quite as early as that referred to. But this must not be considered the rise of what may properly be called Christian sculpture. Such art was only a continuation, probably in a still more barbarous form, of the lowest pagan practice; while there is evidence that real Christian art was marked by distinct characteristics essentially its own. The first was, in fact, the remains of the old, debased, effete art, which had no present life or character; the second, rude as it was, had the stamp of true and real feeling. The term *revival*, then, which usually has been applied to the early practice of sculpture in the Christian time, does not truly express what was an entirely new birth of art, adapted to an entirely new class of feelings, and altogether independent of the older pagan monuments.

It may cause some surprise to find that when Christianity was more firmly established, and the aid of art was called in to enforce its teaching, that the artists did not avail themselves of the better class of examples that were to be met with on all sides, in the monuments that were still preserved of the best schools of sculpture. But however it may be accounted for—and reasonable causes may be found for it—it is not less true than remarkable that they were *not* so used and copied. The Christian artists took their own independent course. Their early sculpture was quite as rude, if not more so, than it had been in the third century; but with this remarkable difference, that the rudeness of this art of the ninth and tenth centuries had its own character, and was unlike anything that had preceded it, shewing that it had its source in original feeling. It seemed, in fact, to be a principle to ignore so far as possible the ancient practice. Many reasons may be found for this. In the early ages of the Christian Church its earnest and devoted teachers would see the desirableness of endeavouring to wean the minds of those who shewed any disposition to embrace the new doctrines from the dangerous associations and remembrance of the old pagan observances and rites. As a means towards it they would, of course, seek to throw discredit upon all the forms and superstitions which had served to do honour to the pagan pantheon; and a recurrence to, or preference for these, in their art expression, would be looked upon almost in the light of an insult to the purer spiritual worship which Christianity had inaugurated. That this principle was not always maintained is admitted, and the effect produced by departing from it, on the religious sentiment of the people, is deeply to be deplored; but there can be no doubt that in the early art referred to there was a desire in the artists, or their patrons, to strike out, for the service of the true faith, an entirely new and independent course; and that they succeeded in doing so is evident on a comparison of the productions of the time—that is, the tenth and eleventh centuries—with the Greco-Roman types of the third and fourth.

BASS-RELIEF.—PORCH OF A CHURCH AT CREMONA.

With reference to the prejudice that existed against recurring to the older forms of sculpture, there is curious evidence in the history of the early Eastern Church, where the prohibition against making statues with any appearance of beauty was in full force, so determined were they that no sensuous element should be allowed to invade the severity of religious art. But it may be allowed to suppose that common sense may also have had some effect in influencing art-practice. The ancient mode of representation with nude or semi-nude figures, draped in *togas*, could not awaken any sympathy in the people. There was no respect felt, in that age, for anomalies simply because they had ancient authority; and Christian subjects would not come home to the faithful if the actors in them were entirely removed, in appearance and costume, from themselves. The new faith, therefore, would receive no useful or edifying illustration which did not address the understanding and feeling of the mass of the people; and thus was laid the foundation of what may justly be termed an original school of art. The very fact of its rudeness is a proof of its not being copied; and its being earnest and simple in its object and character still further removes it from that art which preceded it, in which these qualities were obviously wanting. Christian art was as distinctly divided from the art of the Greek schools as the religion itself which gave it birth was, in its earlier and purer teaching, distinct from the numerous systems that had before filled the world; and it is important to assert this, as it will assist the student in understanding many of the causes of the changes that have characterised all the modern schools of sculpture.

Exercising art on this principle, the artists of this age may therefore consistently be considered men of original genius. Instead of merely copying, they drew from their own innate feeling, and produced works which, in spite of their technical deficiencies, gave the promise that had been realised in the best art of the Greek schools, where elevated sentiment had found expression in the highest class of form. In Christian sculpture this promise, unhappily, was not fulfilled, and the causes of its failure will be pointed out as the history proceeds; but this disappointment of its early tendency does not by any means affect its claim to originality.

Before, however, entering upon the real practice of the first acknowledged sculptors of the Italian school, it will be useful to mention some interesting and curious circumstances connected with the extinction of all art-feeling in the older systems. Amongst the most remarkable is the total disappearance of art in Greece, where it had been carried to its highest perfection; and its revival in a country where, in ancient times, its existence had been ignored, its practice looked upon with a feeling akin to contempt, and where collections of works of art, when made at all, were formed quite as much from ostentation as from any real interest that was felt in them. Again, when the early Christian communities began to employ religious art, the fathers of the Eastern Church strenuously opposed, on principle, the introduction of beautiful forms in sculpture in the representation of the Saviour and other sacred personages; while the Western Christians contended, on the other hand, that no form could be too perfect for this object. An eminent writer on Christian art* says upon this subject—"The regular development of art was arrested by the fatal (*funeste*) divisions which arose in the bosom of the Church. A question of the highest importance to the future of art was agitated amongst the bishops of the Roman Empire, some maintaining with St. Cyril, on the authority of Tertullian, that Jesus Christ was the most uncomely (*laid*) amongst the children of men† . . . while the contrary opinion was defended by the three great lights of the Latin Church."

This controversy was prolonged into the eighth century, when St. John of Damascus and the Pope, Adrian I., described Jesus under the most perfect forms. As the authority of Adrian was very great in the Latin Church, and was supported by that of Ambrose, Augustine, and Jerome, the choice or decision of this part of the Christian world was, Rio says, "irrevocably fixed."

* Rio, *De la Poesie Chrètienne*, chap. i.

† The expressions, as M. Rio observes, are extremely strong (*très fortes*)—"Ne aspectu quidem honestus."

In spite, however, of this powerful party, this decision was still disputed in the East, and the monks of the order of St. Basil insisted upon retaining their own opinions, and, out of respect to their founder, continued to represent the Saviour under the most hideous type of human ugliness. Thus the two fundamental types of Christian painting were differently conceived in the East and in the West. In the East, formerly the cradle and the home of all that was beautiful in art, but now where beauty as a means of illustrating divine and Scripture persons and subjects was unhappily proscribed, art was carried on in the most crude and even repulsive manner. The effect of this prejudice has been very remarkable. The religious paintings of the severe and "orthodox" Greek Church still shew its influence, and are even now of the most debased and barbarous quality; and in looking at the gaunt representations of the Saviour, the Virgin, the Apostles and Saints, it is difficult to believe they are not the rude productions of the most primitive and uncultivated ages. It would seem, however, that the feeling for the beautiful in art would occasionally break out, and that it had to be restrained by the action of the Church, or rather the clergy. Even in the Byzantine school an instance is recorded of this interference. It is related that an artist who had dared to imitate the head of Jupiter as a noble type to express the majesty of our Lord, had the hand which, to use the words of the writer of the account, had served as the instrument of such profanation suddenly dried up or withered. It is added, it required a miracle of the Archbishop Gennadius to restore its use to the painter. In Constantinople where an immense impulse was given to art in religious representation, it was found desirable by the rulers of the Church to repress its too liberal indulgence. A Council was held on the subject, whose object was especially to interfere, not in a matter of faith, but as to the manner in which an artist should represent the Saviour, as there was reason to apprehend that, in this respect, "the spirit or genius of the Greek mind might be tempted to refine too much." *

This is a subject of considerable interest, in some of its aspects; but it is not necessary to do more here than point out the questions that arose in the earlier stages of Christian art with respect to limiting the natural aspirations of artists to make painting and sculpture the worthy illustrators of the most sublime subjects. The state of art in the times adverted to was,

* It was "à craindre que l'esprit Grec ne voulut subtiliser sans fin." It is not easy to understand why this should be feared in a matter in which representative art could so legitimately have been exercised; namely, the attempt to reach the highest idealization in portraying the most perfect and divine character in the most beautiful form. A sentence in the canon gives indeed an admirable rule upon this very question. (See the passage in Rio, chap. i.) The Popes, it seems, at first refused to be bound by the decision arrived at, but subsequently the Roman Church adopted the terms of this Council.

of course, affected for good and for evil by such unseemly as well as senseless disputes, the practitioners on each of the contending fields being influenced by the local ecclesiastical authorities who commanded and directed their practice. Fortunately for the cause of art, such laws and edicts as would have entirely taken all freedom of thought and action from artists, on the pretence that Christian orthodoxy required the entire suppression of original feeling in this direction, had no lasting effect. The authority was not "irrevocably fixed," as it was said to be in the time of Adrian I.; and though the progress of sculpture and painting was impeded by many antagonistic circumstances, religious art was, in consequence of the more sensible and liberal view taken by the ruling authorities of the Western branch of the Church, in a fair way to reach a high degree of perfection.

It is to the travelling artists of this time that much of the practice of art in different Christian countries is to be attributed. Without questioning here the capability of each nation to originate such imitative art as it required for its own purposes, it is quite reasonable to suppose, considering the position of the whole Christian community in Europe with reference to the pontifical government at Rome, that all matters connected with religious services—as images, whether painted or sculptured, ornamental works and similar objects in churches

—would be more or less directed by the clergy. There was constant communication between Rome and its distant Episcopal sees; and amongst those who passed from Italy through Germany, France, and England, would be many, even among members of the religious order, who would be ready to decorate, with such rude art as was known to them, the various religious edifices that were erected. This would fully account for the resemblance generally found in the earliest sculpture employed for the above objects. In the first place, there was a common universal impulse in the motive of art, no country having any independent views to illustrate; and, next, it is not likely there would be, in the respective countries to which Rome sent her missionaries, any body of workmen or artists to compete with these foreigners, who, debased as was all art in their own country, had at least lived in the midst of monuments of sculpture. Thus, the general standard of early ecclesiastical art, in painting and sculpture, throughout Christian Europe, without doubt was found in the rude and coarse types introduced from Italy.*

No advantage or information would be gained by

* The early date at which Wells Cathedral was completed—namely, in 1242—suggests some very interesting speculations as to the artists by whom that remarkable edifice was erected and decorated. It will, however, be better to postpone any remarks upon that particular monument till the subject of early sculpture in England is more fully considered in its proper place.

describing the earlier sculpture to which dates have been ascribed, varying from the sixth to the tenth century. It has no character but that of extreme rudeness and coarseness. Its application alone gave it value among the simple and primitive Christian flock; but, as works of art, the examples that exist have and deserve no place. They received a sort of superstitious veneration from an uncultivated population, and, as had happened in the ancient nations, the old and well-known consecrated types were still adhered to, even after better forms were introduced. It has been seen how slowly innovations upon established usage in religious art were adopted in the most archaïc times; and but little surprise can be felt that similar prejudices, deserving, it may be, of all respect, should have prevailed with reference to art employed for the same end, amongst the devoted and not better informed disciples of the new faith.

The first artist whose works arrest attention for the real art-feeling they exhibit is Niccolo Pisano. He appeared early in the thirteenth century, and, as his name implies, he was a native of Pisa. It was usual in those days for the same artist to practise in all the three branches of the arts—painting, sculpture, and architecture; and many examples still exist of this combination. In the hands of Niccolo and his son Giovanni of Pisa, however, sculpture had its own distinct and important character, from the exclusive devotion given to it by these sculptors; and their employment in the decoration of the sacred edifices that were being erected in all parts of Italy enabled them to carry their art to a high degree of comparative excellence.

It has been supposed, in order to account for the superiority of these artists, that they derived considerable advantage from the opportunity they had of studying some remains of ancient sculpture which were collected in the Campo Santo of Pisa. It is highly probable, comparing them with the rude art of the earlier Christian artists, that they may have been impressed with the technical superiority of these ancient sculptures; but that their own original character of design or of sentiment, the latter so especially religious and Christian, was in any material degree affected by these works, is by no means apparent; and it is not till much later, when art was much more universally practised, that the influence of such examples can be traced. This is a subject which demands some careful attention, and it will be more fully treated of in its own place.

A reference to some few of the productions of the two leading sculptors of the school of Pisa will illustrate the view here taken. They abound in various parts of Italy, chiefly in detached rilievi, for altar-pieces, votive tablets, and similar objects; while in more extended compositions, the cathedrals of Pisa, Pistoja, and Orvieto especially, are rich in their works. The rilievi, in marble, which decorate the front of the cathedral of Orvieto, are particularly deserving of the attention of those who feel a real interest in art. The subjects are taken from the Bible, and represent the Creation of Adam and Eve, the Temptation, the expulsion from Paradise, and other events described in holy writ. These designs exhibit very rare qualities of beauty and expression, and are remarkable indications of the deep art-feeling which has made the Pisan school so celebrated. They exhibit the want of practice in the more mechanical requirements of art and in freedom of execution, but the higher qualities that abound in them go far to compensate for their technical shortcomings. Simplicity, grace, and feeling are all combined in these charming compositions; and in the figures of angels, especially, there is an exalted and pure character at once impressive and elevating. The draperies, which are light and flowing, are also treated with great taste and skill. Cicognara * thinks that these are the productions of some scholars of Niccolo, and not by that sculptor, but the question does not affect the merit of the works. A semicircular basso-rilievo by Niccolo, representing the "Taking down from the Cross," placed over a side door in the front of the cathedral of Lucca, is a composition of great merit; deserving attention, both for its design, in an artistical

* Il Conte Cicognara, *Storia della Scultura*, vol. i.

point of view, and for the deep religious feeling shewn in it. Another remarkable work by the same author may be seen at Siena, in a *rilievo* representing the

NICCOLO PISANO.—LUCCA CATHEDRAL.

Last Judgment and the final punishment of the wicked. Judging from the general character of the works attributed to Niccolo, the representation could scarcely have been congenial to the spirit of the artist. His special ability was in treating gentle, and touching and delicate subjects. This composition displays, however, considerable merit, in the bold treatment of the terrible scene; the crowding together and frightened expression of the guilty, the confusion so natural to the subject, and the intense interest that is excited by the life and character thrown into the whole design, afford unquestionable evidence of the genius and power of the sculptor. The skill occasionally shewn in the arrangement of particular groups deserves also especial notice. There are two figures of angels introduced, in which the artist has been able to exhibit all that grace and beauty of lines by which his style is characterised. Niccolo may justly be considered the founder of a school; for there can be no doubt that the principal artists who now began to find employment in the service of the Church went forth from the workshops of the Pisan master, and that such skill as they possessed was acquired under his guidance. He lived to an advanced age, and left many distinguished scholars and imitators, of whom his son Giovanni of Pisa, Arnolfo of Florence, Margaritone of Arezzo, and Guido of Como, gained well-deserved reputation.

These artists are only here mentioned as worthy pioneers in the march of modern sculpture. A list of their productions, even so far as they are known, would be of little service, and would not give any practical information upon the style of their art. The works of Agincourt, Cicognara, and the separate publications on some of the older churches of Italy, may be advantageously consulted on the details of their practice. Only a few, therefore, of the most prominent need be named who are particularly connected with well-known and celebrated monuments.

In 1330, Andrea, the son of Ugolino of Pisa, was settled in Florence, and executed one of the bronze gates of the Baptistery in that city. Though deficient, like the general productions of the time, in technical treatment, it is a very remarkable work, for its simple and expressive character. Some statues in marble by this artist still exist in Florence, but they are not equal in merit to some of his other works.

A sculptor of considerable power, Andrea Orcagna, was contemporary with Andrea Pisano, and executed, with him, various works in Florence. Some of these are still preserved in the small chapel or oratory, called Or San Michele, in that city, and justify the praise that has been accorded to this artist. His style partook of the dry and minute character of the early school, but he was superior to many of his contemporaries in his bolder treatment of drapery. Orcagna, like many artists of the time, did not confine his practice to sculpture only, but was known also as a painter and an architect. His biographers add to his other acquirements or accomplishments that of poetry.

Among the sculptors who greatly distinguished themselves towards the end of the fourteenth century Luca della Robbia claims honourable mention. His works represent, almost exclusively, subjects of a serious or religious character. He chiefly delighted in representing groups, in high relief, of the Virgin and infant Christ, or of the Saviour and St. John as children, Holy families, and similar subjects. There are many of his performances in England, from which a very competent judgment may be formed of the peculiarities of his designs, as well as of the artistic merit which characterises them. They will be found to exhibit a beautiful feeling for simplicity in treatment, and pure and touching expression. The forms are often somewhat stiff and primitive, and want *ideal* beauty; but in the modelling of the infant character, as in the Saviour child and the young St. John, there are unequivocal indications of a true appreciation of the beautiful in that particular class of representation which the artist probably had an opportunity of constantly studying from nature. Many of Della Robbia's compositions are enclosed in a framework of elaborate design, consisting of fruits and flowers, gracefully entwined and bound together by ribbons, which are inscribed with mottoes or texts. These accessories are often executed with great truth and boldness. Usually they are coloured black, blue, green, and yellow, but this is quite conventionally, and without any particular care as to the natural appearance of the objects. Occasionally, also, parts of the figures are more or less coloured; but if the eyes and the drapery are so treated, the uncovered portions are commonly left white; the whole being covered throughout with a lustrous glaze. The student of early Christian sculpture will find some excellent examples, illustrating the above remarks, in the national collection at the South Kensington museum.

There are two works of more ambitious character, attributed to Luca della Robbia, preserved in the sculpture gallery in Florence, which deserve particular notice. They consist of *bassi-rilievi* in marble, representing a choir, or a group of church singers; and they claim attention for their skilful composition, and for the truth of the expression in the different figures. Indeed, they only require elevation of form to place them on a level with the best productions in the art. Della Robbia is well known in the history of sculpture as the inventor of a peculiar mode of working in *terra-cotta*, the material of which almost all his groups are made. After he had painted his compositions, either with a coating of white, or with different colours as before described, he covered them with a beautiful and peculiar varnish, of which he made a great mystery. It is said by his biographers he never would impart the secret of this preparation to any one, but committed the process to writing, and then inclosed it in one of his clay models before sending it to be baked. Whether this was the case, can only some day be known by the accidental destruction of that one of his works which is the depository of a secret now, owing to modern discovery and skill in fictile manufacture, of little or no value.

Luca died in 1442, leaving behind him many imitators, but no equals in his peculiar style of art. There are many spurious reproductions of the mode of execution of Della Robbia, but the competent judge will usually find that the true feeling of the original artist is wanting in them.

In the gallery of Florence are preserved some very interesting compositions in *rilievo*, in marble, by other sculptors of this period, among whom Benedetto da Rovezzano may be particularly mentioned. In these works there is unequivocal evidence of a superior feeling in art. There is not only improvement in form, and in the care with which ordinary subjects were copied, but there is a sentiment in the treatment of drapery altogether new and very characteristic. In this branch of art the sculptors of the so-called revival soon shewed an exquisite taste, wherever the costume allowed of its exercise. It would not be easy to find, even in the works of the best modern period, examples of greater excellence in gracefully-composed masses, and flowing lines, than is to be met with in some of the draped figures of the sculptors of the latter part of the fourteenth and fifteenth centuries. It is true the dresses are usually those of the time, and the long robes of the religious orders and the costume of the better class of persons, male and femal afforded the examples which the artists followed whenever they were called upon to illustrate subjects that were of popular interest. Even when holier personages were to be represented—as the Virgin, angels, or saints—the costume of the day was commonly employed, with such slight modifications, chiefly in enrichment, as should elevate and adapt it to its purpose. The anachronisms constantly met with, of course, shock the taste of the scholar and antiquary; but the great object of such works being to address the people of the time, the mode of doing this was to accommodate art to their habits and understanding. It is, however, only to the graceful treatment of drapery by some of the mediæval sculptors that the above observations apply.

Of the works of this period no production in sculpture has obtained a greater reputation than that portion of the Gates of the Baptistery, at Florence, executed by Lorenzo Ghiberti. The subjects are in large panels enclosed in highly-enriched frames, and represent various scenes from the Old Testament. This is in all respects a very remarkable work, and so superior, as a whole, to anything that had appeared, that it well deserves the commendation that has universally been accorded to it. Several artists were employed on parts of this edifice, and the different gates boast the skill of different sculptors. These, generally, exhibit the usual peculiarities of a stiff, unformed style, though there are passages in them which claim careful attention, but the folding doors of Lorenzo Ghiberti so far surpass all the others that Michael Angelo is said to have declared, in his admiration of them, that they were "worthy to be the gates of Paradise." It is not at all surprising that this work should have produced a great impression at the time it was executed, nor that later critics should find in it much to interest them. It was, in point of fact, the sudden opening of an entirely new treatment of sculpture, possessing elements which were sure to attract popular admiration. The compositions abound with interest; the subjects are clearly expressed, and the arrangement is picturesque in the highest degree. These are qualities which all can understand, and they make an immediate impression on even the least cultivated. There is, however, much more than this to gratify the more learned and fastidious judge of art; and if he objects to certain technical errors, or, it may be, faults arising out of ignorance of principles in some parts of the work, he will still find much to admire in bold originality of design, the appropriate expression in the figures, the beauty of some of the forms, and especially the graceful arrangement and flow of the draperies. In all this he not only sees a very remarkable monument of the age, but also recognises in it the extraordinary ability of its gifted author; a power sufficient, it might be thought, to have carried the art to as high a perfection as it had ever reached even in ancient times.

This work is so exceptional, when compared with other productions of the fifteenth century, that it may be allowed to remark at some length on its peculiarities, and to show where, and why, when there is so much to be admired, it fails to fulfil all the requirements of pure sculpture. The first thing that invites criticism is the want of breadth and simplicity. The number of small parts and of unimportant details, and the crowding together of figures, trees and shrubs, and animals, tend to confuse the composition and disturb the attention, to the injury of the general effect of the subjects. This arises from the attempt in the artist to be over-picturesque in the design, and in the desire to show executive power; a not uncommon ambition in inexperienced sculptors, though it is one of very dangerous tendency. It is carried to a great excess in Ghiberti's admirable work, where he has also attempted what never has been and never can be achieved in sculpture—distant perspectives; in remote figures, retiring scenery, mountains, forests, and clouds. This cannot be satisfactorily done without the aid of atmosphere; and sculpture, which deals only in *form*, cannot give the colour by which alone the effect of atmosphere can be expressed in art. Had the artist consulted the remains of the best ancient schools he would have seen that there is scarcely an example to be found of an attempt at perspective or foreshortening.

In the arrangement and workmanship of these designs it is easy to recognise the influence of the practice of the time, where the artists were so much employed by the *Orefici* or goldsmiths. Careful and elaborate finish, and a rich accumulation of details, were here not only admissible but necessary. The works consisted, for the most part, of ornamental designs applied to caskets, salvers, cups, sword and dagger hilts, clasps, and similar objects, all subject to close examination, and therefore requiring minute treatment. This was also their habit in dealing with larger works; but it must be obvious that the same mode or process applied to sculpture on a large scale, and to be seen at a sufficient distance to embrace the whole subject, must be inappropriate, and calculated rather to injure the effect of the work. It does so in the performance now under review; and Ghiberti, though immortalised by what he has achieved, has fallen short of excellence by attempting, in the first place, too much elaboration, and in the next, by confusing the distinct properties of two arts, in the endeavour to produce picturesque effects which sculpture alone cannot give. This sculptor was less successful in some bronze statues he executed than in this celebrated work for the Baptistery. The judicious criticism of Flaxman has been directed to one of these, a statue of St. Matthew. He says,

"It wants the severe chastity of the apostolic character, and the head is inferior to those in the spandrils of his gates; the attitude also is affected, and the drapery unnatural." The judgment is sound as regards the particular work; but the St. Matthew is not without merit as a production of the time. Any performance of Ghiberti would naturally be compared with his greater achievement in the Baptistery gates, and, thus viewed, the inferiority in his other works is unquestionable. Lorenzo Ghiberti was born in 1378. The precise date of his death is not known, but it must have been at a very advanced age, as his will is dated 1455.

The next sculptor who claims especial notice is Donato da Betto Bardi, better known by the abbreviated form of his name, Donatello. He was a Florentine, born in 1383. The large number of his works still existing proves how extensively he was employed, and the character of his productions justifies the reputation he seems to have enjoyed. He struck out for himself an original style of treatment, which gives individuality to his performances. It is chiefly seen in his works in *rilievo*, in which the design is sometimes so slightly raised from the ground that it appears to be little more than drawn or engraved on the marble; or as if the ground had been slightly lowered to leave the drawing distinct. The true effect of relief is, however, given, and great breadth insured by the flat unbroken masses of the parts which it is desired to render apparently prominent. Two of his statues claim especial notice. These represent St. George and St. Mark, and they still form part of the decoration of the small church or oratory, before spoken of, of Or San Michele, in Florence, for which they were designed.

The former, though dry and hard in style, is remarkable for its simple action and calm but determined expression, both strongly suggestive of the bold and vigorous manner which characterised the productions of the immediately succeeding school. The figure of the soldier-saint stands firmly planted on both legs, which are separated; but the effect of angularity this action might produce is met by the arrangement, in front, of his long narrow shield. This, having the cross marked in slight relief on its whole length, rests with its pointed base on the ground; one hand grasps the horizontal top of the shield, the other slightly holds the side of it. The figure is dressed in conventional costume, composed of armour, combined with drapery, so that none of the form is shewn except the head and throat and the hands, in which, however, there is great character. Of the statue of St. Mark it is sufficient to record that, notwithstanding the shortcoming of its technical details, it received the high compliment of Michael Angelo's admiration. He is said to have been so struck with its truth to nature that, as he stood before it, he addressed it, "*Marco, perchè non mi parli?*"—*Mark, why dost thou not speak to me?* The works in *rilievo*, by this sculptor, are very numerous. They are chiefly found in the north of Italy, though some examples have been brought, of late years, into this country. Florence possesses some peculiar and, allowing for the imperfect state of art of the time, extremely interesting productions by Donatello. One set of these, in the *Galleria*, deserves especial notice. The subject is children dancing. The groups are most effectively arranged; the action full of movement, with great variety; and the expression of the figures is lively, without grimace or exaggeration. Where the forms are shewn naked, there is both knowledge and a feeling for beauty, and the draperies are composed with great skill. This work is in marble, and the background is curiously treated, being closely covered with small circular pieces of goldleaf, like coins. Donatello executed numerous compositions, in the peculiar flat mode referred to, of the Virgin and infant Saviour, and of the Virgin and child with St. John. Usually they are in the stiff and conventional style of the sculpture of the time, and they are designed too much like pictures; but there is a character of simplicity and purity in the expression which invests them with a peculiar charm, and gives them a value which works of far superior technical treatment often want. The manner of Donatello, in executing *rilievi*, has been imitated by modern practitioners, for trading purposes. These counterfeits are often so well executed that it is not easy to distinguish between the true and the false. Occasionally, compared with the performances of his immediate predecessors, there appears a degree of exaggeration and *mannerism* in the works of Donatello which approaches affectation. This occurs chiefly in the bendings of the wrists, and in the articulations of the bones. It may have been caused by his desire to avoid the timid and undecided execution of the earlier artists, and so far it is an indication of original power. There can be no doubt that a much higher feeling for character and expression began to prevail at this time than had previously been entertained; and among the sculptors who are distinguished for this advanced sentiment, Donatello and Lorenzo Ghiberti take honourable places.

An anecdote is related by Vasari strongly corroborative of this view, and it will not be read without interest, as it marks an important era in the progress of art. The artists of whom the story is told are Brunelleschi and Donatello, both at that time practising as sculptors. "Donatello had recently made for the church of Sta. Croce, at Florence, a crucifix carved in wood, with extraordinary care; and, proud of his performance, shewed it to his intimate friend Filippo Brunelleschi, in order to have his opinion of it. When Filippo, who, from the previous description of Donatello, had been prepared to expect a work of much greater excellence, saw it, he could not wholly suppress a smile. This did not escape the notice of Donatello, and he conjured his visitor, by all the ties of friendship, to declare to him his real sentiments. Brunelleschi, who possessed great frankness of character, replied 'that the figure he had placed upon the cross appeared that of a day-labourer, rather than a proper representation of Jesus Christ, whose person was of the greatest possible beauty, and who was in all respects the most perfect man that was ever born.' Donatello, already disappointed of the praise he had anticipated, could not brook the unexpected severity of this remark. 'It is easier to criticise than to execute,' he retorted; 'do you take a piece of wood, and make a better Crucifix.' Brunelleschi said no more; but upon his return home, secretly went to work, and after the labour of several months, he finished a Crucifix in the most perfect manner. This done, he invited Donatello one day, as if accidentally, to dine with him, and he having accepted the invitation, the two friends walked together towards the house of Brunelleschi, till they came to the old market-place, where the latter purchased various eatables, and giving them to Donatello, requested him to go on with them to the house, where he would join him presently. Donatello, therefore, having reached the apartment of his friend upon the ground-floor, had his attention immediately arrested by the Crucifix of Brunelleschi, which that artist had taken care to place in an advantageous light; and, standing before it, became so absorbed in the contemplation of its superlative merits as entirely to forget the provisions committed to his charge; for opening by degrees the hands which supported his apron, down came the eggs, cheese, and other things, upon the floor. Notwithstanding which he still continued in the attitude of one overcome with admiration, until the arrival of Brunelleschi, who, laughing, asked him how they were to dine, now that he had spoiled everything? 'I,' answered Donatello, 'have had quite dinner enough for this day. You perhaps may dine with better appetite. To you, I confess, belongs the power of carving the figure of Christ; to me, that of representing day-labourers.'"*

Brunelleschi, at a later period, relinquished the practice of sculpture, and, as is well known, became one of the most celebrated architects of his day.

Donatello lived to a great age, and left many scholars, of whom, with one exception, it will not be necessary to give any particular account. The steps in the progress of sculpture will be sufficiently marked by a reference to some of the works of the time. Giovanni di Pisa†

* Vasari, *Vite de' Pittori*, etc.; and Ottley, *Italian School of Design.*

† There are several artists so called, without any distinct surname being given.

was the author of a *rilievo* over an altar in a small chapel of the Church of the Eremitani in Padua. It represents the favourite and popular subject of the Blessed Virgin and infant Saviour, with three saints standing on each side. It is remarkable, besides its other merits, for the style of relief, which is higher than the generality of those of similar designs by Donatello; the figures being much flattened on the surface, with the edges returned on the background at a right angle. It is a very effective mode of treatment, and is similar, in many respects, to that seen in the frieze of the Parthenon. In some particulars there is stiffness and poverty in detail, which place it below the productions of the master; but the bolder character of the scholar in the masses and the relief of his work deserves attention.

Andrea Verrochio, painter and sculptor, is the author of several works preserved at Florence. Among these are many of classical subjects—an application of art to the *unreal*, as respects any sentiment in which the people could feel an interest, which does not often occur in the practice of the earlier Christian sculptors. It will be seen that this employment of sculpture was productive of a great revolution. It led, there can be no doubt, to considerable improvement materially: in the greater attention that was paid to form, in the introduction of a larger style, and in execution; and the works of Verrochio, many of which have great merit, afford proof of the effect of recurring to illustrations which allowed of a more bold use of the human form than had hitherto been required. There is, no doubt, more freedom of art; but what they have gained in this respect is at the sacrifice of feeling. Technically, they are superior to the sculpture that had been produced by the revivers of the art; but they are as deficient in sentiment and meaning, compared with some of the early Christian productions, as they are inferior in every respect to the fine ancient works which they affect to imitate. Verrochio is distinguished as having had among his scholars the celebrated Leonardo da Vinci, and Pietro Perugino, the master of Raffaelle. It was at this time that he professed the art of painting, which he is said to have relinquished from a feeling of jealousy of the ability shewn by Da Vinci, in a work in which the master had required the assistance of his scholar. Whether or not this is the true reason of his having abandoned his first profession, Verrochio appears to have devoted himself, in his later years, to sculpture. He died in the year 1550. Among those who studied under him as a sculptor, Rustici holds an honourable place. He was distinguished by Francis I., who invited him to go to France.

The general character of modern art had, up to this time, been essentially religious; and in the expression of deep sentiment, in simplicity, in a chaste character of form in sacred and holy subjects, in the arrangement of drapery, and the harmonious flow of lines in the treatment of this important accessory, no school of art of any time or nation can shew works of greater promise than occur in the productions of the mediæval artists. The deficiency in their sculpture was in the technical requirements of the art. It has been seen that, for some cause or other, little or no advantage was taken of the remains of ancient sculpture, as guides for modern practice. The Christian sculptors seem to have worked out their own ideas, beginning as it were *de novo*, as if sculpture had never before been known. At first the representations were little better than mere types, scarcely deserving the name of sculpture. Practice gave some degree of facility; and the simple and earnest sentiment which originated the art of the time then found expression in comparatively improved forms. The nude was, of course, unthought of, and the human figure was little, if at all, studied by the artists; but in a certain grace of action, and in the characteristic drapery which was introduced, there was evidently the indication of a rapidly increasing knowledge of all that was necessary eventually to establish a deeply interesting as well as excellent school of art.

This hopeful condition of sculpture, so full of promise for the future, was destined to be interrupted; and that by the very means which might have been expected to carry it to perfection.

At the period which this history has reached, the discovery of the long-lost treasures of classical literature had given an extraordinary impulse to the study of the ancient Greek and Roman writers. The family of the Medici, in Florence, took the greatest interest in this movement, generously assisting in the expense of recovering ancient manuscripts wherever they could be found, and, at the same time, offering liberal encouragement to men of learning to take up their residence in the capital of Tuscany, which thus became the centre of the revival of Greek and Roman letters. The Medicis had acquired a commanding influence by their success in commerce. They had accumulated enormous wealth, and by the power this had given them, aided by the great abilities of many of the members of the family, they had raised themselves by degrees to the highest honours of the state. They had on various occasions done great political service to Florence; and Cosmo, who died in 1464, had had conferred upon him the honourable title of "Pater Patriæ," the father of his country. The most distinguished of this great Florentine house was Lorenzo, the grandson of the above Cosmo, and who, from the splendid way in which he lived, and from his princely liberality in the encouragement of learning and in advancing the fine arts, acquired the high-sounding but well-deserved title of "Il Magnifico"—The Magnificent.

The fifteenth, and the early part of the sixteenth

centuries, comprehend a period of the greatest interest in the intellectual history not only of Italy but of the world; and the condition of art will be found to have been much influenced by the impulse given at this time by the prevailing passion for the restoration and study of ancient classical literature. No history of sculpture of this period would be complete, or indeed intelligible, if the cause of the change it now underwent were not distinctly described; and the personal interest shewn by Lorenzo de' Medici, in the studies referred to, and the munificent patronage he extended to those who were attracted to his court, entitle him to this especial notice as the great supporter, if not originator, of the movement which revolutionised the literary, and, with this, the artistic *status* of the age. So powerful, indeed, was this influence, that it led to much affectation, and, notably, in the employment of the dead languages in the writings and correspondence of learned men, to the exclusion of their native tongue, which was considered quite unworthy the study or use of real scholars. Latin and Greek were the only recognised medium of communication between these learned pedants, while the native Italian was left to the vulgar. Among churchmen and diplomatists Latin had long been generally used; but it was not elevated by classical correctness and refinement, as was expected to be the case at the period now arrived at, when the highest ambition was to imitate the elegance, the point, and the terseness of Cicero, Horace, and Tacitus.

Florence was essentially the birthplace and the centre of this pseudo-classical revival; but the passion soon spread abroad, and was not confined to only one part of Italy. Rome soon rivalled the city of the Arno in its anxiety to re-establish the style and feeling of the illustrious Greek and Roman schools, in literature, in philosophy, and in art. The Church at this time was governed by pontiffs who thoroughly sympathised with the elegant tastes of the Medicis. Julius II., who was elected to the tiara in 1503, gave the greatest encouragement to the artists and *literati* who visited Rome. Leo X., who succeeded him in 1513, was the son of Lorenzo the Magnificent, and inherited the classical predilections of his family. He made Rome a centre of attraction for all that was learned and epicurean. He was succeeded by another scion of the house of Medici, Clement VII.; for the intermediate Pope, Adrian VI., who had been elected to the papal throne after the death of Leo, scarcely held his sovereign honours one year. Clement continued to encourage classical studies and art with the same liberality that had distinguished his predecessors. That those competent to appreciate the excellence of the ancient writings should exert themselves to extend their influence, cannot be a matter of surprise; nor can any wonder be felt, that when the works of the great sages and poets of antiquity were receiving all this attention and honour, the remains of ancient sculpture should also begin to claim the notice of these enthusiastic admirers of the genius and taste of the Greeks. In Florence and Rome, collections were diligently formed of antique sculpture; less, probably, at first, for the perfection of art they exhibited—for as yet there must have been but insufficient knowledge in this direction—than as monuments of that wonderful people whose intellectual superiority was so clearly established. There was thus a new art-movement, and a hitherto unrecognised standard of excellence was offered to sculptors. The consequences were soon apparent, and claim attention here.

Whatever advantages may have been derived from the recurrence to fine ancient examples, there can be no doubt that the immediate effect upon sculpture was to arrest its development in one very important particular—namely, its power to address modern sympathies. The study of the best works of antiquity was capable of producing, and no doubt did occasion, great changes, and even improvement in the technical parts of sculpture; but it is equally indisputable that it also brought with it certain disadvantages. The religious sentiment that hitherto had marked nearly all productions of art, no longer characterised the works of the sculptors. The object, now, was to imitate as closely as possible the subjects and forms that had occupied the ancient artists; and, if history is to be believed, Paganism was more the creed of the upper classes than Christianity, which, probably, like the vulgar tongue, was left to the lower and the less cultivated orders. The Court of Lorenzo was composed of so-called philosophers, who appeared to make little or no distinction between the *Dii Majores* of the ancient mythology and the founders of the Christian faith; except, perhaps, to hold the former in higher estimation as the gods of their favourite ancients; while the general infidelity and immorality of the Court of Rome seemed to give authority to license, and certainly helped to extend the baneful influence of a misdirected taste. That the practice of artists, dependent upon the patronage of the great, should be influenced by the fashion of the time cannot be a matter of surprise. In order to meet this, classical subjects were sought for illustration, because in these a closer imitation could be made of the Greek mode of representation; and the conventional treatment of the ancient schools, exhibiting nude male and female forms, was introduced—however incongruous its application—to gratify a *dilletante* taste, as absurd, in that age, as it was artificial. The simple and expressive character which had previously been so remarkable, and had given so great a fascination to some of the works of the rising school of religious designers, was thus forced to succumb to the overwhelming influence of the classicists; and as the motive that now impelled the artists was factitious, the sculpture produced was utterly unreal in its sentiment, and therefore inexpressive and meaningless in its style of presentation. However indisputable the charm of beautiful forms in the abstract, their true value can only be appreciated after much study and reflection. Unless also they are employed in art in expressing intelligible ideas, or subjects which can be easily comprehended, the general public—to whom art should address itself as a language—can derive neither pleasure nor profit from their display. It is the *sentiment* and intention of a work of art that first attracts the attention, long before the *form* in which it is presented becomes a subject of examination or criticism; a fact constantly proved by the fascinating power exercised by some of the productions referred to of the earlier Christian designers, which are pregnant with meaning, but in which almost all the technical requirements of art are wanting. These observations are by no means irrelevant or without their use in the history of sculpture, as this art has always been greatly influenced by external causes. They will, moreover, assist in accounting for the entire change which marks the "motive" of the sculpture of the age; leading it away from the real to the false and merely academic.

The period under review, in which the enlightened

Lorenzo de' Medici, in Florence, and the equally accomplished pontiffs, Julius II. and those of the Medicean family, in Rome, were so nobly encouraging the arts—for it would be unjust to deny them this character, though the impulse was wrongly directed—boasts an extraordinary crowd of distinguished artists in every branch of practice. Among the sculptors who lived at this time are found the names of Michael Angelo Buonarotti, Torregiano, Baccio Bandinelli, the Ammanati family, Sansovino, Benvenuto Cellini, and Giovanni de Bologna; and others might easily be added who have left behind them works which have honourably illustrated their age and country.* The opening afforded by the study of the antique to the more intimate acquaintance with the human figure, and the habit of drawing from the living model, which the academies now founded greatly facilitated, incited some artists of original genius to extraordinary efforts to imitate the ancient modes of art without always repeating the subjects of ancient sculpture. No one of the crowd of eminent men who illustrated this age holds so distinguished a place as the remarkable individual whose career is now to be considered.

* It might be permitted, perhaps, to supplement these with the illustrious name of Raffaelle, for he is reputed to be the author of a statue of Jonas still preserved in a chapel in Rome, though some say he only supplied the small model or sketch, and that the work now shewn as his was executed by another hand.

The powerful genius of Michael Angelo Buonarotti has secured for him a fame and station in the history of art which no artist of his own age, or of a subsequent time, has been able to reach; and probably, when the extent of his attainments are considered—as a sculptor, painter, architect, and civil and military engineer—it would not be too much to say he had no equal even among the illustrious masters of the best ancient schools. Some of the most distinguished names known in art were either living in his time or were formed by him, but none have approached that lofty eminence which he so triumphantly occupies, and which even those who find good cause for criticising some defects in his style allow to be justly accorded to his surpassing and comprehensive ability. In the present history Michael Angelo will be reviewed as a sculptor, and it is in this capacity only that his merits and failings will be discussed.

Michael Angelo was a member of the noble family of the Buonarotti of Florence, and was born in the year 1474. He very early shewed a determined feeling for art, and when very young was placed under the care of Ghirlandajo, one of the most eminent painters of the time. When Lorenzo de' Medici, in his noble desire to foster and encourage art, established an academy in the gardens of his palace, to which students might resort for instruction and practice, he soon distinguished the young Buonarotti, and being struck with his genius, honoured him with particular marks of favour, and gave him apartments in the palace. With such encouragement the natural talent of Michael Angelo, improved under the guidance of Ghirlandajo, soon was displayed in the production of works which at once stamped the high character of their author. His performances afford excellent examples of the condition of sculpture at this period. They indicate unmistakeably the influence of the new opinions that were gaining ground, marking most distinctly the transition from the simple and original feeling that had supplied the motive to the first Christian sculptors, to the artificial stimulus given by the admiration that now was exhibited for the remains of ancient sculpture. But Michael Angelo has left works as striking for the inventive power displayed in them as for an original character of execution. In the school established by Lorenzo de' Medici he no doubt acquired both a feeling for fine form, by the contemplation of the remains of antiquity which Lorenzo had got together, and something of the classical taste which was the fashion of the day and of the learned society in which he lived. Many of his works decidedly shew the effect of this association, but, as will be seen, not to the extent of destroying or suppressing his own powerful genius, as original as it was characteristic both in invention and design. Extraordinary merit, like that which distinguished Lorenzo Ghiberti and Donatello, broke through the dryness of the earlier practice, and one or two succeeding sculptors carried on the improvement; but it was reserved for the gifted Florentine to effect that total revolution in style which, with all its peculiarities, has stamped the art of his school with a character exclusively its own, and which, as applied to his own works, has been happily and expressively termed "*di Michel Agnol' la terribil' via.*"

The artistic power and the peculiarities of this great master will be best exhibited by referring to some of the best-known productions which bear the impress of his remarkable genius. Among these is an affect-composition of two figures, known as the *Pietà*. It is in a small chapel in St. Peter's, at Rome. The Virgin is here represented sitting, and supporting across her knees the dead body of Christ. The head is full of expression, and the whole action of the figure, even to the hands, indicates the *abandon* of intense grief. In the statue of Christ the tranquillity and perfect repose of death are portrayed with great truth and feeling. A sentiment of desolation pervades the whole group; it abounds with the deepest pathos, and appeals powerfully to the sympathies of the spectator. As a work of art it exhibits the great knowledge and facility of hand for which Michael Angelo was so conspicuous. The head of our Saviour is inferior in its form to its expression, and a little of the exaggerated manner of the artist appears in the extremities, and in the articulations of the joints; but notwithstanding these drawbacks, it is impossible not to feel that this is a work of great power. A group in marble, of the dead body of Christ supported by Nicodemus, with the Virgin, and Mary Magdalen, also deserves to be pointed out to the student for its high merit. One of the most striking of the productions of Michael Angelo is the statue of Moses, a sitting figure, originally intended to form a part of the magnificent monument (still unfinished) of Julius II., in the church of *S. Petrus in Vinculis* (*S. Pietro in Vincoli*) in Rome. This work, though by no means free from the fault of exaggeration, so justly objected to in the style of Michael Angelo, is one of the grandest efforts of genius. Studied with attention, its merits, which are not so evident at first sight, will be found amply to compensate for minor faults which the *manner*, as artists call it, of Michael Angelo threw more or less into all the productions of his chisel or pencil. The broad and simple lines of the composition, chiefly disposed at right angles, give to the design a character of force and stability, while the expression and turn of the head, notwithstanding the strangeness of the forms, convey the impression of intense energy and dignity. It is easy to criticise the peculiarities that give its exceptional character to this noble work, but, while admitting these as grave defects, it is quite consistent to feel the utmost admiration for the higher qualities it possesses as a work of striking originality of conception, and at the same time of consummate artistic ability. Another well-known production of Michael Angelo is his marble statue of Christ in the church of La Minerva, at Rome. The Saviour is here represented standing, and holding the cross. The figure is life-size, and is in the revived classical or academical style, almost entirely nude. There is a pleasing, though somewhat melancholy expression in the head. Of their kind the forms are good; but as a representation of the Christ this statue is unsatisfactory. It is deficient in appropriate elevation of character—a defect scarcely to be expected in a religious work by Michael Angelo—and with all its excellence as a work of art it is little more than a careful and successful study of the naked model. The two statues of Giuliano and Lorenzo (not "Il Magnifico") de' Medici, in their monuments in the mortuary chapel of that great family at Florence, merit attention. The second of these works is the most remarkable for its character and expression. Lorenzo is represented seated and absorbed in thought; he leans his face on one hand which partially covers the chin and mouth. The rest of the figure is in repose, and throughout there is the sentiment of deep thought. It is impossible to look at this statue without being impressed by the *mind* that pervades it. For deep and intense feeling it may be pronounced one of the finest works extant. The semi-Roman costume is conventional, but treated in a manner quite free from all commonplace. There is no resemblance to the antique, but it rivals the best excellences of the ancients in expression, with repose and dignity; the happy result of the study of nature, or real life, contemplated by genius and imagination. The lower part of this monument consists of two statues intended to represent "Early Dawn" (or "Morning,") and "Evening," of which the application is not quite clear. They form a strong contrast to the dignity and simplicity of the figure above them; but though they are grandly conceived and boldly executed, there is a violence of action in them which is at variance with the repose of the pensive statue of Lorenzo, and which seems indeed to have been adopted rather for the

LORENZO DE MEDICI.—M. ANGELO.

purpose of exhibiting anatomical knowledge and manual skill than of adding to the real interest of the design. The monument of Giuliano is composed on the same principle as the above, and it also has two accessorial statues called "Day" and "Night." They all bear the impress of the master-mind and hand of their author, but equally with the statues of Morning and Evening they challenge criticism for a certain amount of effort and exaggeration. In the same chapel there is also an unfinished group in marble, called "Charity," or, it may be, the Virgin and Child, by Michael Angelo. It surmounts a monument, and is a striking work for its bold though somewhat forced composition and vigorous execution. A masterly composition in *rilievo* of the Virgin, with the Saviour and St. John as children, preserved in the gallery at Florence, and another, very similar to it, though extremely unfinished, in the Royal Academy of Arts in London, deserve attention as examples of Michael Angelo's treatment of this class of sculpture. The latter is a circular relief, the figures are small life-size, and it is a highly valuable example of the master. It has the peculiarities of Michael Angelo's manner, but it is, at the same time, full of grace and feeling. It is believed to be the only work in marble, in England, of this great artist. Another very remarkable composition by this sculptor is in the Vatican. It is an allegorical design connected with Florentine history in the time of Cosmo de' Medici. The relief is very low, and the crowding of the figures occasions a confusion which renders it difficult to comprehend the object of the design. It displays, however, wonderful knowledge and great facility of execution. A well-known work of this sculptor, the statue of David, in the Piazza del Gran' Duca at Florence, may not be entirely passed over, although it cannot fairly be adduced as altogether a performance of Michael Angelo. It was executed under very unfavourable circumstances. The figure had been commenced by another sculptor, and was found to be so unsatisfactory that Michael Angelo was employed to finish it. The vigorous hand of the master is visible, and, though the statue cannot be quoted as by any means a perfect or pleasing work, few can look upon it without being struck with the noble air it has, as a whole, and especially with the turn and expression of the head. One of his statues, of a classical subject—a Bacchus—in the gallery of Florence, is admirable for its expression of inebriety, and for its execution. It reminds the spectator of the "antique," but to its own detriment. It is wanting in purity of taste, and the forms, though most carefully studied, and admirably modelled, are deficient in that beauty and character which the ancients, of the best time of sculpture, considered appropriate in representations of the young and joyous god.

In contemplating the works of Michael Angelo, the

intelligent spectator is so struck with the invention, energy of character, and vast knowledge of form and anatomy displayed in them, that he scarcely can define, at first, the cause of their not fulfilling the conditions which should command entire approval. But it is undeniable that the sculpture of this great master does not yield that full satisfaction afforded by many ancient productions, by no means of superior merit in technical excellence. The great and deserved reputation of Michael Angelo will justify the attempt to account for this. Sculpture, to be perfect, requires to be practised on certain principles; and if these are disregarded, it is found, whatever other qualities may be present, that it has not the power to satisfy or to make a lasting agreeable impression. The chief of these qualities, in this art, is simplicity. It is the absence of effort and obtrusive display of means which gives their charm to all the best productions of the ancients, and even to many works of a later age; and there can be no doubt that it is to the disregard of this essential property or element that the unfavourable effect produced by many otherwise excellent works of Michael Angelo must be attributed. All who have seen it remember with admiration and satisfaction his "thinking" statue of Lorenzo. In the first place it addresses itself to the feelings of all. It is nature, simple and unaffected, but nature dignified by the highest power of imagination. Few recollect more of the statues of Morning and Evening, and of Day and Night, than their attitudes. They make no appeal to the sympathy of the spectator, and, however readily the competent critic may acknowledge their artistic merit, the want of simplicity in their design and expression disturbs and distracts the attention.

There can be no doubt that the intimate knowledge of anatomy and acquaintance with the human form, possessed by Michael Angelo beyond all the artists of his time, led to his excesses in giving expression to the suggestions of his energetic and daring imagination; and that this mastery over the technical difficulties of his art not unfrequently tempted him to indulge in its display at the expense of that sobriety and simplicity so valuable in sculpture, and which are so uniformly found in the finest examples that have come down to us of the Grecian schools.

The influence exercised by this artist, not only on his own age but on later schools, would justify a much more extended notice of himself and of his productions, than can be supplied here. It must suffice to refer, thus shortly, in this place, to the works selected as subjects well deserving the attention of the student in sculpture, and more especially beginners, for the useful lesson that may be derived from a careful consideration both of the merits and the defects of so distinguished a master.

Although Michael Angelo has here been considered as a sculptor only, he has also left behind him noble works in the sister arts of painting and architecture. It is not consistent with the plan of this short history to enter into the merits of Michael Angelo in the other branches of art, in which, perhaps, he has gained a higher reputation than in sculpture; but it may be permitted to make a passing reference to the more remarkable of his productions as a painter. Among these, the well-known compositions in the Sistine Chapel at Rome, illustrating the grand scheme of Scripture revelation, from the Creation to the Final Judgment, are unrivalled in invention, profound thought, knowledge, and a grand style of design. These truly sublime performances, whether taken alone or in connection with the other proofs of the power and vast range of his genius, place their author far above comparison with any known artist, ancient or modern. As an architect, he was scarcely less great, both in boldness of conception and constructive power, as many of the edifices erected under his direction amply prove. Nor was it in the fine arts of design alone that the great ability of Michael Angelo was conspicuous. The political circumstances of his country called forth his talents in other severer exercises; and it was in strengthening the defences of Florence that he added to his well-deserved reputation as an artist also that of one of the most accomplished masters in military engineering and fortification. The few remains that have reached us of his literary works, in his letters and sonnets, exhibit him likewise as an elegant writer and poet.

Pietro Torregiano was a distinguished sculptor of this time, the contemporary and rival, in some respects, of Michael Angelo; of whom his jealousy was so great that on one occasion, in a fit of passion, he struck him in the face with a sculptor's hammer and broke his nose. Torregiano was invited to England, and was employed upon the tomb of Henry VII. in Westminster Abbey, a work of great interest, and a sufficient proof of this artist's ability. In the Rolls chapel is a statue by Torregiano which deserves notice. It is in *terra-cotta*, life-size, and painted. It represents a judge, dressed in his robes, and recumbent, his hands on his breast. It deserves the student's attention for its truth to nature. Torregiano afterwards went to Spain, where he died.

Tatti, better known as Sansovino, appeared at this time. Several of his productions—statues and *bassi-rilievi*, in marble and bronze—are preserved at Venice and Padua, and, although they want simplicity, they display considerable talent. A group by this sculptor, of a naked Faun, with his arm upraised, holding a tazza, and a young satyr at his feet looking up at him, though a little weak in style, and affected in expression, shews a refined feeling for form and great delicacy of execution. He was a popular sculptor of his time, and his scholars were numerous. Some of them, particularly Danese Cattaneo, the Ammanati, Lombardi, and Vittoria, distinguished themselves by the success with which they practised their art. Many works by these sculptors are seen in various parts of Italy, and justify the honourable mention of their respective authors.

Baccio Bandinelli was a native of Florence, and takes a high rank amongst the artists of this age; he was the scholar of Rustici, the intimate friend of Leonardo da Vinci, a connection from which Bandinelli must have derived great advantage. His style was very bold, his general designing vigorous, and his works display considerable knowledge of form; but they abound also in the *mannerism* which characterises the art of this time. Several works in sculpture by Bandinelli exist in Florence, which, though they do not place him on a level with Michael Angelo, to whom he was always opposed, attest the skill of the artist. Amongst his most highly esteemed productions may be reckoned a number of figures in compartments, in very low rilievo, which decorate the base of the screen round the high altar in the Duomo of Florence. A *basso-rilievo* in marble on a pedestal which stands in the Piazza (or Square of) S. Lorenzo, also at Florence, though in many respects open to criticism, has many claims to distinction, and may be considered a fair illustration of the art of the age. He introduced a portrait of himself in a statue of Nicodemus supporting Christ. This was a group in marble, the size of nature, intended for his own monument, and it still exists in the church of the Annunziata, at Florence. In the Palazzo Vecchio are two statues by him of Adam and Eve, with the tree and the serpent between them: the former of these works is superior to the last mentioned, but both are stiff, poor in form, and much inferior to those above noticed. Baccio Bandinelli, either from his excessive conceit and pretension, or from the jealousy of his disposition, of which many instances are mentioned by Vasari, appears to have been exceedingly unpopular among his brother artists, and his performances were severely satirized by his contemporaries. The sting of these remarks has, however, passed away, and his works remain to claim for him the distinction to which his unquestionable ability as an artist entitles him.

The productions of this period claim respect for many great qualities of art; but it must be admitted that the *motive* of sculpture was fast losing all claim to originality. The names of the artists already referred to attest the artistic power of the time; but it is impossible not to feel that their productions are more or less imitations, and not the expression of individual thought or impulse. It would answer no good purpose to give a catalogue of the performances of all the eminent sculptors of this century, so prolific in art and artists; the notice of those most generally known being sufficient for the present purpose. It is seldom that any really original ideas occur in their works, the sentiment as well as the style of treatment being more or less borrowed from the antique, with a manifest imitation of some of the least commendable peculiarities of the school of Michael Angelo.

Among the prominent artists of the time Benvenuto Cellini claims a distinguished place. He was a sculptor of great power, though his works, partaking of the character of the age, are marked by some exaggeration of action and an unnecessary and injudicious display of academical study. Amongst his larger and more important works, his statue of Perseus especially, in the Loggia del Gran' Duca at Florence, notwithstanding its faults, is a production of great merit. The figure is of heroic size, entirely naked, but having on its head a picturesque mediæval winged helmet, and the *talaria* or wings are attached by sandals to his ankles. In his left hand, stretched out before him, he holds the bleeding head of Medusa, whose body is lying at his feet; in the other he grasps the peculiarly formed faulchion or sword, called by the Greeks *harpe*, lent him by Mercury. Though the action is somewhat theatrical, and the forms overcharged, this work will always claim attention for its bold conception and expression. It exhibits invention in design and considerable power of execution—great qualities in art. Benvenuto Cellini is, perhaps, chiefly celebrated for his smaller works in metal (gold, silver, and bronze,) and precious stones. Some of these, consisting of richly-ornamented cups, salvers, shields, and similar objects, are of great excellence, and shew the undeniable skill and taste of the artist in this branch of his profession. Some fine medals of the time have also been attributed to him. Cellini was an author as well as artist, and composed a treatise on his art, describing in the most graphic and picturesque manner his own practice and experiments in the then imperfectly known processes of metal-founding. He also published his autobiography; one of the most curious and amusing works, illustrating the manners of the sixteenth century, that have come down to us.

A peculiar mode of working in metal, omitted in the earlier description of the different processes of sculpture, may properly be introduced here, as it was a branch of art most successfully practised by Cellini and the artists of the sixteenth century. It is known as *répoussè* or "pushed out" work. The design is drawn on a thin plate of metal, properly prepared, and relief is given to the figures or other objects by pressing or pushing the parts from the back of the plate, till the required projection is obtained. The details are then carefully finished on the upper face by the means usually employed by chasers.*

Guglielmo della Porta, the friend of Michael Angelo, and of Sebastian del Piombo, held a high position as a sculptor. Among the best known of his works is the monument of Pope Paul III. in St. Peter's at Rome. Two statues in this composition, representing Prudence and Justice, establish this artist's claim to consideration. The latter statue especially has great beauty, and is admirably executed. It must be remarked, at the same time, that these figures are not in harmony with the character and requirements of a Christian monument, nor are they at all fitted, from their mode of treatment, to be placed in a church. But it appears that little respect was shewn to the proprieties at this period, and the religious feeling which had distinguished the earlier art had long given way before the fashion of adopting classical and pagan forms of expression, even in the most serious application of sculpture. The scandal attached to this representation—the naked figure of Justice on the monument of a Pope—led to the statue being partially draped since Della Porta's time. This accessory has been applied in bronze. The influence exercised on art by the genius of Michael Angelo is seen in the works of this sculptor. Guglielmo

* This practice is being again introduced with great success in the present time; and already there are some very distinguished artists in *répoussè* design.

della Porta is celebrated for his restorations. The ancient statue, known as the Farnese Hercules, when found, was without legs. Della Porta was employed to restore them.

Among the prominent sculptors of the age appears a native of France, Jean Goujon. The precise time of his birth does not seem to be ascertained, but he was much employed in the reign of Francis I., when he commenced a remarkable work for the decoration of a public fountain, and which was not finished till the year 1550. Other of his performances are still preserved in many parts of France which testify to the ability of this artist. The most important of these were prepared for architectural decoration, and were in relief. Two large *bas-reliefs* of sacred subjects, one a Deposition now in the museum of monuments in Paris, afford a fair example of Goujon's manner, which evidently was founded on the mixed principles of the Italian school of the time. The figure of the dead Saviour is represented naked, lying on a sheet, and supported by two male figures, kneeling. At his feet are five female figures draped, crouched down in various attitudes of grief. There is a good feeling for form in the naked figure. The draperies are carefully studied, and artistically arranged, but over elaborated. Some statues of Caryatides, also in Paris, claim for him honourable notice. Goujon met his death while literally occupied in the execution of one of his works. He was mounted on a scaffold at the Louvre, carving a *rilievo*, when a shot from a carbine terminated his life. This was on the fatal day of St. Bartholomew, in August 1572, when the atrocious massacre of the Huguenots by the Catholics took place in Paris. It has been said the sculptor was shot by accident, but Goujon, it appears, was a member of the reformed and proscribed church, and there can be little doubt it was intended that he should share the fate of so many of his co-religionists on that memorable occasion. Goujon was not only an able sculptor, but an architect also, and a distinguished medal engraver. A work of this class which he produced for Catherine de' Medici, the wife of Henri II., king of France, is rare and curious. Pilon is another French sculptor of the time whose works illustrate the art of the sixteenth century, shewing the artistic ability of the sculptor, and the peculiar style of what has been called the Franco-Italian school.

A female artist of this time, Propertia de' Rossi, may, with great justice, be noticed, as the author of some statues on the façade of the church of S. Petronio at Bologna. There is also a *rilievo* by her, in marble, of considerable merit, still preserved at Bologna, representing the history of Joseph and the wife of Potiphar. It is recorded that this was the last work on which she was engaged, when she died; and that the subject was suggested by personal circumstances. She became enamoured of a young artist who did not make a suitable return to her advances, and the disappointment and mortification she felt threw her into a languishing disorder which brought her to her grave. She occupied herself by executing this work, in which the object of her love was represented as Joseph, and in the other figure, it is said, she portrayed herself. She is reported to have been one of the most beautiful as well as accomplished women of her time. In addition to her talent in sculpture, she painted well, and was a good engraver. She died in the flower of her age, in the year 1530.

The quality for which the sculptors of the end of the sixteenth and the seventeenth centuries are chiefly remarkable is a love of display in the executive parts of their art. This led to the decline of sculpture. The object with them was not to improve the public taste, or to elevate the minds of the people, but simply, it would seem, to astonish the spectator by their bold and skilful ingenuity. The three sculptors who were most distinguished for their merit and for their faults in this respect are Giovanni de Bologna, Bernini, and Roubiliac; and it may be useful to students and others who desire to understand the influences that affected sculpture at this time—and of which the effect was not confined to their own age—to give some special attention to their works. These artists were essentially men of genius, and though their disregard of the true principles upon which alone sculpture can be successfully practised must be deplored, it would be unjust to withhold from them the notice to which they are entitled for such merit as they undeniably possessed.

It must also be remarked, to the credit of these too popular and, therefore, spoilt artists, that, although in the presentment of art there was much to be desired in a purer taste for design and in the character of form, they do not appear to have lowered their productions to incite or to excite or gratify the lower feelings of the public. The academical tendency led to a great display of knowledge of anatomy and action in their statues; and the fashion of the court of Rome (influential throughout Italy) biassed the artists, who had to live by the patronage they could obtain, to prefer classical illustrations to the more serious and simple character of sentiment, by which the earlier Christian sculptors had made their appeal to the religious feelings of the people at large. Still sculpture maintained its character as an art to be applied rather to elevated than to frivolous and commonplace representations. The sixteenth century artists addressed the educated classes; and as these were, now, only favourable to the imitation of ancient sculpture, the art conformed to this standard. But it was not yet prostituted to unworthy purposes; nor was it so far degraded as to descend to the representation of mere ordinary, domestic incidents, in which neither beauty of subject nor of form are considered to be essential objects of the sculptor's art.

The artists whose works are now to be considered may be viewed as great innovators on the style of art which hitherto had been practised. Not, as has above been observed, that they essentially lowered their art by objectionable representation, as to *subject*, but the whole purpose of their practice was to prefer the merely mechanical or material part of sculpture to the nobler objects to which it had, in the best times, been applied.

Giovanni di Bologna, a native of Douai, affords in his works a good illustration of the style of sculpture of the day. He is by far the best of the school, and deservedly holds a high place in art. The famous bronze statue of Mercury in the gallery of Florence is an honourable monument of his skill. It is conceived in the true spirit of poetry. The action is buoyant and full of energy, and the form, generally, is light and graceful, though it may be objected that the muscles are rather too round and full for the character appropriate to the messenger of the gods; and in this respect it does not bear comparison with the true Greek creation in the charming Mercury in the Museo Borbonico at Naples. It may be added that the mode of indicating that the god is borne by the winds—one foot being supported by expanding rays (but very material, and like a bundle of sticks) issuing from the puffed-out cheeks, or rather mouth, of a zephyr, whose head only is exhibited—is a conceit quite in keeping with the fancy of the age, but altogether offensive to good

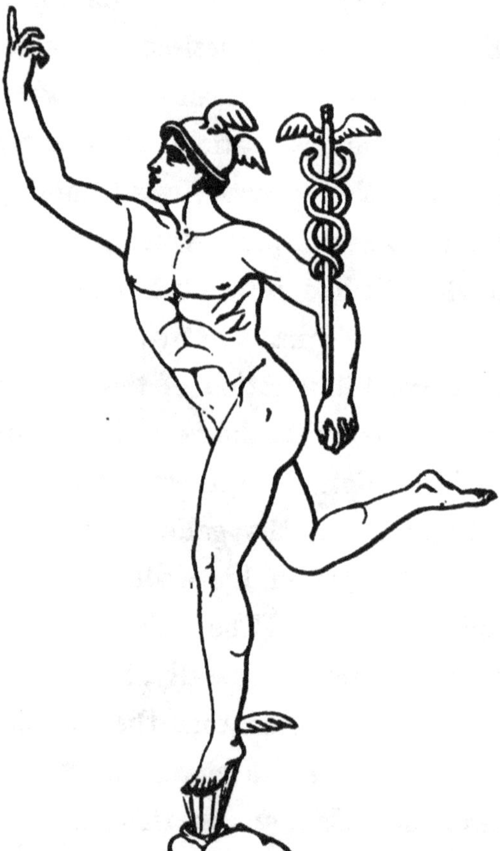

MERCURY.—GIOV. DI BOLOGNA.

taste. The well-known group in marble in the *Loggia* at Florence, called the Rape of the Sabines, consisting of a nude athletic figure carrying off a naked female, another crouching male figure below them, affords further illustration of what has been observed of the character and style of sculpture of this time. As a specimen of invention it is full of energy and expression, and the forms display great knowledge and mastery of art; but the composition partakes too much of the *corkscrew* form, and is extravagant. It is impossible, however, not to admire the courage as well as ability of the artist who ventured to execute so daring a work. Other statues and *bassi-rilievi* almost without number—so extensively was he employed—exhibit in like manner the power of mind and hand, but at the same time the defects of style, of Giovanni di Bologna. One of his most remarkable productions, for size as well as its bold treatment, is the colossal statue called L'Appenino (the Appenine), executed by command of Francesco de' Medici, for the Grand Ducal Gardens at Pratolino, near Florence. The figure, quite naked, is seated and leans over a small lake; a stream of water flows from a rock upon which rests one of his hands. A long beard partially covers the form. The material out of which the gigantic statue is carved is a grey-coloured rock. The effect of this work is at first very striking, but it is so disproportioned to everything around it that it injures rather than decorates the gardens. It must, however, be admitted that it is a production of no ordinary power, and shews the ability and energy of its author. Giovanni di Bologna had numerous imitators, and, as usually happens, his faults of overcharged action and display of means were the points copied, but without the genius that excused in a great degree the peculiarities of his style. One of the most distinguished of his followers was Francavilla, a Fleming, whose works are distributed in many cities of Europe. The chief object in mentioning him here is to point out that some of his productions are preserved and may be judged of in this country. A group in marble representing either a Venus or a water-nymph, above life-size, with two accessorial figures of less dimensions, one on each side, and two marble statues probably of Seasons, decorate the gardens of the Royal Horticultural Society. They have been injured by time and neglect, and in some parts they exhibit indifferent modern restorations, but they are characterised by boldness of design, a knowledge of the figure, in which the sculptors of this time were eminently accomplished, and vigour of execution. They fail in simplicity and in the sober taste which is so remarkable and admirable in all the finer specimens of Greek sculpture. In the art of this time subjects of ancient poetry were adopted, it would seem, as a mere convenient medium for the sculptor to display his academical training, and his skill as a workman.

Bernini was a Neapolitan, and was born in 1598.

His imagination was fertile, and his power of execution of the first class. Unfortunately, this power was uncontrolled by submission to the necessary principles of his art. Bernini delighted in the most curious and daring experiments upon his materials, and treated marble as if it had been clay or wax. Under him all the distinctive bounds of sculpture were transgressed, and the chief object seemed to be to rival the painter's art. Clouds, landscape, perspective, and other unattainable representations were attempted, till the whole subject became confused in the flutter of unintelligible details. That he was an artist of unquestionable genius cannot be denied, yet no one probably did more to precipitate the fall of sculpture than Bernini. The immense patronage he received during a long career (for he lived during nine pontificates) filled Italy with his productions; and it will be proper to notice some of them more particularly in order to give a just impression of his style of art. Among the most remarkable, a group in marble of "Apollo and Daphne" deserves attention, for its bold invention, the forcible manner in which the story is told, and the "bravura" of its execution. The god is pursuing the unwilling fair one, who, at the moment of his reaching her, is, in answer to her prayer for protection, changed into a tree. The passion of the lover is displayed in his eager action and by his flying hair and drapery, while the timely metamorphosis of Daphne is shewn by her floating tresses, her fingers' ends, and her toes, all sprouting forth in elaborately-executed laurel branches

APOLLO AND DAPHNE (MARBLE).—BERNINI.

and leaves. The bad taste of this picturesque treatment is only equalled by the extraordinary executive talent displayed in the representation. The "Extacy of Sta. Teresa" is another work of the kind, in which, amidst the flutter of drapery and clouds, it is difficult to discover the principal figure. There are, however, some passages of great beauty in this production, especially the expression in the fainting figure of the saint, who falls back "in extacy," as an angel, hovering before her, is about to touch her with his dart.

In St. Peter's the magnificent monuments of Urban VIII. and Alexander VII. are examples of the merits and defects of this sculptor. They are wonderful for their execution, but debased by the most meretricious taste. The colossal statues of the Four Doctors of the Church, in bronze gilt, supporting the chair of St. Peter, are also by this artist. The idea is grand, but the attitudes are affected and the forms exaggerated. In his statue of "David preparing to hurl the stone at Goliath"—a work of great energy and expression, and executed when he was quite young—Bernini is said to have introduced his own likeness. Among the numerous strange and daring performances of this artist, a large fountain with figures and accessories in the Piazza Navona at Rome is conspicuous. No sculptor ever had greater opportunities, and but few greater talents, than Bernini; but the variety of his pursuits, and his inordinate craving after picturesque effect, ruined the art he professed. His influence and popularity were so great that his example was followed by all who desired distinction or profit, and thus the very worst school of sculpture was perpetuated, owing to the extraordinary powers, and it may truly be said, genius, though misapplied genius, of its originator. It would have been better for this art had Bernini never lived. In proof of the versatility of his talents, it is recorded that, in a theatrical entertainment given by him at Rome, he designed and built the theatre, painted the scenes, made the statues, constructed the engines, wrote the drama, and composed the music.

It will easily be understood that sculpture was now rapidly declining when artists of the ability of Bernini so misused their facility of execution and their inventive power as to employ it only on works that would exhibit their merely mechanical or technical attainments. It will be useful to follow out the consequences of this condition of the art by referring to a few of the most prominent sculptors who attained celebrity in the period immediately subsequent to that which had received Bernini as the great authority in sculpture.

Alessandro Algardi was a native of Bologna, and contemporary with Bernini. The work by which he is best known is a *rilievo* in marble over one of the altars in St. Peter's at Rome. It is of large proportions, measuring about thirty feet in height by fifteen in width. The subject is the miraculous appearance of St. Peter and St. Paul to Attila and his hosts. The apostles are represented floating in the air over the crowd of soldiers, who, with their leaders, are struck with fear and astonishment at this unexpected divine interference. It cannot be denied that there are passages of considerable merit in this composition. The fault in it is its confusion and want of breadth. It is treated throughout upon the principle of a picture, but all true pictorial effect is wanting owing to the absence of colour. The parts being relieved throw shadows where they ought not to be seen, and necessarily the most distant groups and the sky and clouds have no remoteness, from the want of atmosphere, which can only be given by air tints.

In the church of St. Severo at Naples are some curious examples of patience, executive power, and, it must be added, of the bad taste engendered by the feeling and patronage of the time. Two of these are statues by sculptors named San Martino and Corradino. One represents Modesty, a female figure entirely enveloped in a thin veil, through which all the forms may be discerned, as if the covering were made of some transparent material. Another represents what is called Falsehood. It is enclosed within a net, of which all the meshes, with their knots and the construction of the ropes forming it, are most carefully carved and, in many instances, quite relieved, so that the figure appears almost insulated within them. There is another statue in this collection treated similarly. It is of the dead Saviour, who is represented extended on a couch with a sheet or cloth thrown over the body. To the ignorant, and those whose taste in sculpture is undisciplined and uncultivated, these triumphs of execution appear marvellous and deserving of all praise. To those conversant with the mechanism of sculpture they are known to be nothing more than specimens of the patience and technical skill of the carver. Such works, with few exceptions, can rank little higher than mere exercises of ingenuity; and for this only they never can receive, nor do they deserve it, the admiration of real judges of art.

It is not intended here to illustrate the condition of the schools of sculpture in different countries, but only to trace the progress of the art itself, with the changes that characterised its practice wherever new or peculiar features appeared. For this reason, no attempt will be made to classify the schools, as they have somewhat pretentiously been termed, of particular nations; as the German, the French, the Spanish, Flemish, and others. They exhibit at this time no individuality or originality that entitle them to distinction as founding any great principles. All the sculptors who deserve notice at all exercised the art more or less in accordance with the semi-pagan and wholly artificial practice of the day, and the more prominent of these artists can only claim it for their ability and success as imitators. France can boast some very eminent sculptors, especially in the seventeenth century—as Anguier, Puget, Girardon, Le Gros, Pigalle, Coustou, and others—who have left works honourable to themselves and their country; the peculiarity remarkable in them being the tendency to florid treatment and the common devotion to executive properties detrimental to the simplicity so essential to sculpture.

A sculptor was living in this century who deserves notice for the fancy and knowledge he exhibited in his statues and reliefs of "*putti*," or children. This was Francis di Quesnoy, better known in the history of art as "*Il Fiamingo*," the Fleming. He had great employment in this class of sculpture, in which it may be said he almost stood alone. His treatment of the round plump beauties of infancy, and the character he could throw into the heads and attitudes of his subjects, which, for the most part, were introduced as cherubs, in decoration, exhibit him in a most favourable light. A larger work by him, a draped marble statue of S. Susanna, in the church of La Madonna di Loreto at Rome, may also be noticed as a production shewing very pure feeling and a fine sense of beauty. The head especially merits attention. The colossal marble statue of St. Andrew, in St. Peter's at Rome, is also by this sculptor, and is a bold and striking work.

It would appear almost impossible to illustrate more fully the degradation of sculpture, than has been done already by the review taken of the art, from the *man-*

nerist imitators of Michael Angelo, down to the fanciful, elaborate, and mechanical sculpture of the leaders of the seventeenth century. It is painful to be obliged to trace this fact in the works of so many artists of undoubted genius and power, who, if they had exercised their indisputably great abilities in obedience to those principles which the judgment of ages has stamped as sound, and of which the excellence of the sculpture of the Greeks has established the unquestionable value, were capable of restoring the art to all its former perfection. A history of the full consummation of its decline would, however, be incomplete if the influence of one other leading sculptor were left unrecorded. This is Roubiliac. The fact of his having had great employment in England affords the most ample opportunity of judging his style of art. It would be injustice to deny him the merit of fancy, knowledge, and technical skill; but the possession of these valuable qualities was injured by the utter absence of good taste and his studied disregard of the rules that should guide the true sculptor. Two of his most celebrated works are in Westminster Abbey. One of these is a monument to the memory of a Duke of Argyle; the other, of Lady Nightingale. In the former is a statue representing "Eloquence." It is full of character; earnest in expression, and energetic in action; but its effect is spoiled by the flutter and confusion of the drapery, and the absence of simplicity. The monument of Lady Nightingale possesses the same valuable qualities, as regards expression; but the artist has injured the work by his bold attempt to give form to a sentiment, beautiful in itself, but which is here materially weakened by the very means taken to illustrate and intensify it. The husband, in this composition, endeavours to arrest the approach of Death, and while he supports his fainting wife on one arm, he extends the other to prevent the fatal dart from striking the victim. Death is represented by a human skeleton, the size of nature, in full action, preparing to hurl a very substantial weapon of destruction against the dying woman. Here the mere bones are made to assume the functions of a living, active body; and the gentler sympathies of the spectator are painfully disturbed, first by the disagreeable and repulsive object intruded upon the attention, and next by the confusion and mixture of fact with allegory. By this mode of treatment, in which the mere accomplishment of a technical success, in the carving of the skeleton, is made so prominent, the most important object of the design is injured. The *intention* is lost sight of in the wonder and, it may be, the admiration felt at the workmanship in which it is exhibited.

A statue of Sir Isaac Newton, in the ante-chapel of Trinity College, Cambridge, is one of the most celebrated works of this artist. The great philosopher is represented standing in meditation, with his head slightly raised and his attention intently occupied with some subject of study. The action of the hands is admirably contrived to assist the expression; a finger of one being laid on the extended finger of the other hand, as if aiding in making a calculation, or in demonstrating a proposition. The figure is habited in the academical gown, worn over the ordinary costume of the day. This is so well managed that, though the forms are unfavourable, so far from vulgarizing the statue, they lose their most objectionable element by the assistance the dress gives to the individuality of the likeness. The treatment of the accessories is in the usual fluttering, over-charged manner of the sculptor, but the execution throughout is most careful. Another work of Roubiliac, of somewhat the same character, inasmuch as the object of the artist has been to portray powerful and earnest expression, is preserved in the Advocates' Library at Edinburgh. It is a sitting figure, a portrait of Duncan Forbes. This statue is in marble, life-size. The costume here—that of the day—consisting of wig and gown, ruffles and knee-breeches, takes from this work all claim to what the admirers of Greek sculpture, only, consider true art; but its fine treatment as a work of expression—in the head, in the earnest leaning forward of the figure, and the extended hand, all acting in concert to give force to the address or oration he is supposed to be making—place this statue among the finest works of its kind.

Another admired work of this sculptor is the monument of Bishop Hough in Worcester Cathedral. It has all the characteristics and peculiarities of the artist and the age. As a composition it is arranged with good picturesque effect, and the execution is, as usual, most careful and elaborate. A female figure, very fully draped, is deserving of great praise for certain remarkable qualities of art which, in spite of its want of simplicity, the competent critic will easily recognise. A marble statue of Shakspeare, at present in the hall of the British Museum, may chiefly be referred to as a specimen of the executive power of Roubiliac. It is by no means without merit for its expression and intention, but it is simply a portrait statue, and the most striking part of the work is the immense facility exhibited in dealing with a difficult material, and giving movement and picturesque effect to the details of dress the most unfavourable for pure sculpture. The student may also derive both instruction and warning from another very remarkable work of this artist in Walton Church. The care bestowed upon every part of this production, which represents a modern military figure, with a tent for a background, and innumerable accessories of war thrown about—as trumpets, drums, guns, and cannon-balls—shews how much diligent attention was given to the conscientious representation of details; while, in the confusion and total absence of simplicity and concentration, a lesson will be learnt of the danger of sacrificing these essential qualities to the desire to produce all the effect by a too free use of merely subordinate elements. There can be no doubt that the taste or prejudice of the time required this of the popular sculptor of the day. It is impossible not to feel, in contemplating the works of Roubiliac, that he possessed the genius and power of a very great artist; and that, had the field of his labours been more favourable to the development of his natural instincts, instead of cramping them within the caprices of fashion, or had he himself had the moral courage to use his great ability to elevate the character of his art, he was capable of taking rank with the most eminent sculptors who have lived. With all his remarkable power, he has only contributed to show how far sculpture had declined when he, one of the most accomplished artists of any age, was in the full exercise of his profession, and enjoying the highest fame.

Rysbrach may be mentioned here, as he was much employed in England, and many of his compositions in monumental works are preserved in our churches. His productions have no particular qualities to recommend them to notice; and the *bravura* of art exhibited by Roubiliac, and the interest he commanded among influential persons in society, who exerted themselves to secure to him all the best employment in the country, drove Rysbrach altogether from the field.

It is not necessary to dwell longer on this phase of sculpture; and no advantage can be gained by enumerating the minute and laborious performances of the smaller race of sculptors who imitated the worst peculiarities of the school, if that name can be given it, which cast aside all the nobler objects of the art for the puerile and more mechanical imitation of trifling details. If, by accident, an artist of purer taste and of higher feeling appeared, he found no sphere of action for his abilities. He was neither seconded nor supported by any refinement or knowledge of art in the upper classes, nor by the sympathy of the public. At this time sculpture had reached the lowest step, in point of style, in its downward course. It was not in one country only that the decline of the art was obvious, and seemingly irreparable. In Italy, France, Germany, as well as in England (where foreigners only were employed), the same deterioration was visible. This was the more to be deplored because the degradation of sculpture was not attributable to ignorance or incapacity in the sculptors, as was the case in the rude ages of art; for it has been seen that in technical power the age was so far from deficient that it could boast artists of great accomplishment. It was owing to the utter disregard of true principles in art, to the insensibility of artists and the public to the nobler objects of sculpture, and, as it would seem, to the false impression that sculpture fulfilled its purpose if it servilely and closely copied whatever objects were offered for imitation. This led to sculpture being professed and easily practised by uneducated, and, of course, incompetent practitioners, who had neither the ambition nor the power to raise their art above mere mechanical figure-making. From such sculptors the public could learn but little to elevate or form their taste. No attempt was made to select or idealize. On the contrary, objects were continually being presented to them that could only have the effect of lowering the tone of public feeling. Mere hand-workmen, usually uneducated and ignorant of everything but the manual exercise of carving and modelling, they were utterly incapable of influencing society by their advocacy of art for its high purpose and as a language of beauty. Occupying a low position as mere artizans, they had no temptation or inducement to rise above it, or to claim a better recognition of their calling; and, unfortunately, it does not seem that the feeling of the age was of a character to raise the profession of art, by which sculpture might have gained a more worthy place in public esteem. If among the higher classes there existed any individual instance of more refined feeling and intelligence, it does not appear to have exhibited itself in a manner to produce any sensible improvement in taste, or to save sculpture from its condition of thorough debasement.

SECTION II.

THE honour of giving a new direction to taste, or rather of leading it back to a recognition of true principles, is eminently due to two sculptors, who lived in the present century; namely, Canova and Flaxman. To the former Italy owes her emancipation from those false perceptions which had, from the influence of the Bernini school, so long diverted the current of pure taste. To Flaxman the art owes equal if not greater obligation, though he had not the same favourable opportunity as Canova of making his merit known. But no modern sculptor has entered so deeply into the recesses of ancient art as Flaxman. His style was founded upon the principles of the noblest Greek practice, combined with the unaffected simplicity of the Pisani and other artists of the fourteenth century. But he did not servilely copy them. The sentiment which is so conspicuous and so attractive in his works, especially in his monumental designs and in his illustrations of Scripture, is the true reflection of a mind both earnest and original—

seeking, as was the case with the earlier Christian artists, to express itself in art-language in harmony with its own serious and religious impulses.

The purer taste of which some of the earlier works of Canova—as his "Theseus," his "Dædalus and Icarus," and others—gave promise, it must be admitted, is less conspicuous in some of the later productions of this eminent sculptor; and he appears gradually to have been seduced from the staid and somewhat severe simplicity which is one of the greatest charms of this art, by the fascination of highly-wrought execution and the elaboration of surface, in which, it is not too much to say, few, if any, have surpassed him. This success, however, was gained by the sacrifice of force and style; and the judicious critic will here lament that breadth and nobility of form seem to have been less the object of the sculptor's study, than the exquisite finish and *morbidezza* of the technical treatment.

Canova introduced colour in some of his works. A Venus and a sleeping Endymion had the cheeks and lips tinted with *red*. It was a meretricious and dangerous innovation, capable of doing great injury to art, from the temptation it would have offered for seeking a class of subjects for sculpture that should appeal especially to the sense. Happily it was not received with favour.

In Flaxman exceptions will be found of a directly

contrary character. In his works execution will be found a secondary object compared with design; though in one of the finest compositions of which modern sculpture can boast, "The contest of Michael with Satan," and also in his "Shield of Achilles," a work full of invention and beauty of every kind, Flaxman has shewn that this deficiency is not to be attributed to any want of knowledge or power.

Still, it is, unquestionably, a defect to be deplored in many of his productions which, in other qualities, may safely challenge comparison with any works produced in this art. This is not the place to enter upon a review of the performances of these deservedly renowned sculptors. Their works are well known, and the influence they exercised has been and is acknowledged on all sides; and though distinct schools have arisen out of those which they may be said to have formed, the merit is justly due to them of being the restorers of sculpture in an age of its greatest deterioration and degradation, and of having at least directed attention to the truly excellent, as it is seen in the best Greek sculpture; shewing it to be the only sure groundwork of the possible resuscitation of the art in modern times.

The short time, comparatively with other countries, during which sculpture, of a kind to be classed as fine art, has been practised in England, precludes it from taking a place in the early history of art with Italy, France, and Germany. English sculptors exercised no influence on the style of the art, as was the case with Michael Angelo, Bernini, and Roubiliac; whose genius, with all their peculiarities, made itself felt wherever sculpture was practised; and it is not till the eighteenth century that any formal or defined place can be claimed for native British artists. It may be observed, however, that although there is no record of names of sculptors, there is reason to believe the art was practised in England at a very early date. No reliance can be placed on the traditional account, quoted by Flaxman, respecting what he terms the "great and terrible" statue of Cadwallo, who died 677; but two extremely flat and now almost obliterated monumental effigies in the cloisters of Westminister Abbey, of two of its abbots, are of great historical interest, though the art exhibited in them is of the rudest kind. They are of the eleventh and beginning of the twelfth centuries. One represents Vitalis, who died in 1087; the other Crispinus, who died 1117. Whether two statues of Henry I. and his queen, in Rochester Cathedral, were of their date—namely, the middle of the twelfth century—is not determined; but there is evidence of the art having been extensively exercised in England within a hundred years of that time. It is a remarkable fact, that Wells Cathedral, which is copiously decorated with sculpture, was completed in the year 1242; and the importance of this is the more striking when it is remembered that Cimabue, one of the fathers, as he is called, of Italian art, was only born in 1240; and that Giotto did not appear till 1276. The building of this church was therefore going on while Niccolo Pisano was exercising his art in Italy; and, what is equally remarkable, it was finished between thirty and forty years before one of the most interesting monuments of the kind in Italy, the Duomo of Orvieto, was commenced.

The sculpture which decorates Wells Cathedral is, as might be expected, extremely rude in point of art; but it is of great interest, from the character of the designs, and from the date of its execution. It illustrates various subjects of Scripture history, and acts in the life of our Saviour; besides recording, in statues of heroic size, the memory of saints, kings, queens, and others, who were probably patrons and benefactors of the church. Another circumstance of interest is, that it seems to be the earliest example in this country of such sculptural enrichment exhibiting a connected series of Scripture illustrations; but its importance may be still greater if, as has been conjectured, it is the first specimen of the kind known to exist in Western Europe. Its origin, then, becomes a question of some importance.

It is probable that some of the earliest Italian practitioners may, in their wanderings, have penetrated as far as England; but as the style of the sculpture at Wells does not sufficiently resemble that of the Italian artists, who undoubtedly were employed on the tombs of Edward the Confessor and of Henry III., it is not so easily associated with the art known to have been derived from that source. Flaxman, admitting this, was disposed to think it was brought from the East; conceiving that, as it was not Italian, it might have been founded on examples seen by the Crusaders: a speculation which has little probability to recommend it. That the Crusaders influenced the civilization of Europe must be conceded, inasmuch as many of the ingenious eastern arts became known to, and were introduced by those who returned from those wars; but it scarcely can be likely that any light could be thrown on sculpture by the practice, at that period, of the eastern nations. There, as history has shewn, there could be no art, of this kind, worth appropriating. It will be more consistent to believe that, if it was derived at all from a foreign source, the earlier wanderers from the capital of Christendom, whether ecclesiastic or lay, brought the rude notions of figure-making then prevailing with them; and that these were introduced, with all the peculiarities consequent upon the want of practice, or any knowledge of form existing among ourselves, into the religious decoration of one of the most important edifices of the age. The only other supposition must be that native workmen of England were the originators of certain representative statues that were required to express the popular devotional feeling to the saints and holy personages who were the tutelary guardians of the church; or that were wanted to do especial honour to those among the rich and powerful who had contributed the lands to endow, and the funds to erect and ornament the edifice. There is nothing in these statues, remarkable as they undoubtedly are, to connect them especially with any contemporary school. They are ill-proportioned, their height compared with nature being most extravagant; the heads and extremities, where they can be seen, of the most rude design; the naked form, where it occurs, utterly without knowledge; and the dresses have no pretension to be called drapery. There is some reason, therefore, from the very fact of their rough execution and stiff design, to believe they may fairly be attributed to native workmen. At a not much later period there appears to be no doubt that English artificers were capable of executing extensive works of the kind.

The sculpture in various parts of Lincoln Cathedral exhibits the improved condition of this art in the fourteenth century; and the *motivi* and the sentiment of many of the compositions, in the spandrils of arches and in other portions of the architecture, are of a very high class. Unfortunately many of these works, of great interest in the history of the rise of Christian sculpture, as well as in their relation to one of the most beautiful of the ecclesiastical buildings of the time, are in a state of great dilapidation, so that it is almost impossible to discover the claims they have to respect and admiration. In these sculptures, executed in the same material as the cathedral, and no doubt worked on the spot, and not, as was sometimes done, brought for the purpose from any distant country, may be traced the influence of the art so ably developed by N. Pisano and his scholars. This admission will not by any means weaken the claim that may be made for the recognition of English art-workmen at this early period; but it may help to show that while native artists were capable of executing the works that were required, it was to the impulse derived from Italy that the improved character of the religious art of this country was owing.

Till after the death of Roubiliac, when he, Rysbrach, and Scheemacher, were chiefly known as the sculptors in England, there scarcely is mention of any native artist in sculpture. Of Evesham, a predecessor of Stone, little or nothing is known beyond his name, though it is stated he was an artist of considerable ability. Still no work by him is particularised except a monumental brass in St. Paul's Cathedral. It is said that before this time (James I.) it was not usual for sculptors to inscribe their names on their works; it is possible, therefore, many of the productions of the period may have been by this artist though there is no evidence of the fact. About the same time lived Colte, who held under the crown an appointment connected with his calling. He left a son who followed the same profession. Many of the family are buried in the church of St. Bartholomew Close, where there is a monument to their memory. The name of greatest note is that of Nicholas Stone, who was born in 1586 and died in 1647. He was appointed "master mason and architect," with a salary, in the reign of Charles II. His master was one Isaac James. There are many works in sculpture by Stone, by which his merit and the style of art of the day may be judged. It is not necessary to describe at any length characteristics that only exhibit decline; and the student may easily perceive for himself, from many existing productions of this artist, that the sculpture of the "architect and master mason of the court" was not calculated to restore the art to any degree of glory, nor to raise the fame of the country. One of his largest works is in Westminster Abbey—a monument in memory of Sir G. Villiers and his lady, created in 1616 Countess of Buckingham. There is also in the same church a large monument consisting of a recumbent statue of Dudley Carlton, Viscount Dorchester, who died in 1631. This sculptor also executed some of the statues of the English kings for niches in the area of the Royal Exchange in London. Stone left sons who were artists. One of these, Henry, acquired fame as a painter, and is still honourably known by his works. The younger son, also called Nicholas, followed his father's profession. He studied in Italy and became acquainted with Bernini, who was then in the zenith of his glory, and from whom the young artist appears to have received much kindness and advice. Cibber, an artist of some repute, resided in England, but was not a native of the country, having been born at Flensburg in Holstein. He is well known as the sculptor of two statues, remarkable for their expression and vigorous design, which formerly were in the entrance hall of the Bethlehem hospital for lunatics. They represent two phases of insanity: Frenzy and Melancholy. It scarcely would be just, considering the nature of the subject, to pronounce the contortions of the former figure exaggerated; but the violence of the action and the intense agony portrayed in the features are carried to the extreme limits which are admissible in fine art. The other figure is more simple. Grindling Gibbon was a distinguished artist in the reign of Charles II. Some accounts say he was born in Holland, of English parents, and, at the age of nineteen, came over to England, where he afterwards resided. Others that his father was a Dutchman, and that the artist was born in London. He became known, when a very young man, to Evelyn, by whom he was introduced to the notice and patronage of the king (Charles II.), and Gibbon's great ability soon procured him extensive employment as a sculptor, and more especially as a carver in wood. One of his larger works is still to be seen in the court of Whitehall. It is a bronze statue, life-size, of James I. This is a performance of great merit, and the execution of it is careful. The details, where the naked form is seen, shew knowledge of the figure, though there is a want of large and grand style. Like the sculpture of the time it fails in simplicity, and the costume exhibits the anomalous semi-classical taste of the period: the king being dressed as a Roman emperor. Another large work by Grindling Gibbon is a monument in Rutlandshire in memory of the Viscount Campden, consisting of two statues of the Viscount and his lady, and some children, in *rilievo.* There is also a monument by him to Mrs. Beaufoy, in Westminster Abbey; a work of no merit. The great reputation of Grindling Gibbon—and it is here well deserved—was as a carver in wood; and many very remarkable specimens of his great skill and taste in this art may be seen in various parts of England. The subjects he chiefly delighted in were birds—dead or alive—flowers, foliage, the elaborate imitation of lace, and similar representations. Some of the best examples of his accomplishment may be seen at Windsor Castle, where he was much employed by order of the king; at Hampton Court, also, are many beautiful specimens introduced as decorative frames to panels. In London he executed much of the ornamental carving for St. Paul's Cathedral, and St. James's Church in Piccadilly. Chatsworth also, the seat of the Devonshire family, possesses some exquisite wood-carving by Gibbon. He had no rival in this particular study, and his works may justly be referred to as the most perfect examples of the kind, and for their truthfulness of imitation, whatever may have been the object he proposed to copy. In *still life* this extreme fidelity in reproducing the original is quite legitimate, and Gibbon carried it to such perfection that it is sometimes difficult to believe that his dead birds, flowers, leaves, and lace, are only carvings in wood, and not the things themselves. Gibbon died in 1721.

Nothing could be lower than the state of sculpture in England during the reigns of the two first sovereigns of the house of Hanover. With the third George some slight reaction first appeared to give hope of improvement in the art-feeling of the country. It is, however, only during the last hundred years that the nation has awakened to the real value of such pursuits, and that English sculptors have shewn themselves fully capable of asserting the claim of this country to take its place as a member of the republic of art. The names of Banks and Bacon, especially, rank deservedly high among those who assisted, at that period, in making known the ability of English artists.

Monumental Sculpture.

Before dismissing the subject of sculpture in England, attention may be drawn to one exercise of the art which, though it scarcely can be connected with very high attempts, or associated with the beautiful of the best schools, has an interest of its own of a kind that may justify its introduction here. It refers, too, to an employment of sculpture greatly in accordance with the deep religious feeling which lies at the bottom of the English character. With this is intimately associated the respectful care of the dead, and the desire to preserve the memory of those who in life have deserved the affection and esteem of their relatives and friends. Formerly, when the ecclesiastical powers directed all the art, as well as the services and forms of the church, the particular treatment of memorial design was controlled by certain established rules; but long after it had ceased to be subject to the influence referred to, and even after it had departed from the most appropriate character of design, the impulse, originally derived from a true and natural feeling, has always exhibited itself strongly in the attachment of the English people to memorial sculpture of some kind.

It may be observed then that England is especially rich, perhaps beyond any other country, in its unbroken series of ecclesiastical, or, as it may be more correctly termed, monumental sculpture, which dates from the very earliest introduction of that class of art in this country. Reference has already been made to the effigies in low relief of two abbots of Westminster, which are of the eleventh and twelfth centuries. Others of the cathedrals of England possess works of very great interest of about the same time. At Salisbury is a monument of the above description to Roger, made bishop of that see in the reign of Henry I. This prelate was deprived of his honour at the accession of Stephen, and died in 1139. Peterborough and Gloucester Cathedrals also possess some valuable examples of such monumental sculpture of early date.

It appears that the earliest employment of sculpture for this class of memorial, where the effigy of the deceased was represented, was confined to ecclesiastics. This is easily accounted for by the control the clergy exercised over all matters connected with church services and decoration; and it may also be supposed that they would naturally seek to confine to the church such distinction as could be conferred by having the representation of members of their own body honourably placed within the walls of the sanctuary where they had exercised their ministry. There can be no doubt that the influence thus exercised was, so far, of the greatest possible advantage, inasmuch as it kept the art used for ecclesiastical and sacred purposes within the limits which should characterise such designs.

From the first flat reliefs above noticed works of a more ambitious character of art came by degrees to be executed, and admitted into churches; and after a time royal personages, knights, and ladies, are found to have their monuments, which were always or almost always surmounted by their effigies. Among the earliest and best of such representations is the monument in Salisbury Cathedral of William Longespee (or more correctly 'Long'espée) first Earl of Salisbury, the bastard son of Henry II. by the Fair Rosamond. He died in 1226. The warrior character of this figure is particularly striking, even in its simple recumbent attitude; while the turn of the head, and the graceful flow of lines in the right arm and hand, with the natural, heavy fall of the chain armour on one side, exhibit a feeling for truthful imitation unusual at so early a date.

The earliest monuments in England in which figures appear habited in armour are of the twelfth century. Those in the round ante-chapel of the Temple Church in London are probably among the oldest existing examples. Flaxman observes that in France coffin-lids were surmounted by figures, as early as the time of Charlemagne; that is in the ninth century; but he says there is no sepulchral statue known in England prior to William the Conqueror, when effigies began to be carved on grave-stones. The tombs referred to are of great interest. That of Magneville, Earl of Essex, and of two other knights similarly habited, may be attributed to the time of Richard I. It is generally thought the effigy called Geoffry de Magneville is correctly assigned to that knight, whose history affords some curious particulars of the habits of the time. His life was anything but exemplary, and it appears when he died he was under sentence of excommunication; although, probably with the desire to conciliate the clergy and make his peace with the church, he had, in his last moments, assumed the religious habit of the Order of the Temple. It was not, however, deemed right to grant him Christian burial till this dreadful sentence had been removed by the proper authorities; and, as this could not be obtained without considerable difficulty and delay, a singular mode was resorted to for preserving the remains of so distinguished a person, and yet avoiding the scandal of unconsecrated sepulture. The body was cased in lead, and was then suspended from a tree in the gardens of the old Temple, in Holborn, there to remain till the ecclesiastical decision should be known. The required absolution was after some time obtained from Rome, Alexander III. being Pope, and license granted for the usual funeral rites. The body was only then taken down and buried in the church. There is one rather remarkable circumstance in these three monuments; namely, that the swords of the recumbent knights are all worn on the right side. The repetition of this in all the figures is an argument against its being accidental. Some of the knights in monuments of the time are represented with one leg crossed over the other. It was formerly supposed by antiquaries that this was done to intimate either that the subject of the monument had served, or was bound by a vow to serve, in the wars of the Crusades. This explanation of the attitude is not now generally admitted.

The earliest example of a monumental effigy in a royal costume in England, is that of King John on his tomb in Worcester Cathedral. When this monument was opened and examined some years ago, there were sufficient remains of the original dress left to show that the costume of the effigy, lying on the tomb, corresponded with that in which the dead body of the king was dressed when it was buried.

The next royal effigies that occur in England are in bronze, of Henry III. 1272, and of Eleanor the queen of Edward I. 1290. They are in the chapel of Edward the Confessor in Westminster Abbey. They are entire figures, and are worthy of attention for the simplicity and elegance of the drapery. Three very interesting monuments of the fourteenth century represent sons of

King Edward III. That of the Black Prince in Canterbury Cathedral exhibits him lying at full length, completely armed, with a coronet round his helmet or basinet. In those of Prince William of Hatfield in York Minster, and of Prince William of Windsor in Westminster Abbey, the figures are also recumbent, but their dress is not military. The date of the monument at York is 1344; that of the Black Prince 1377 or 1378. In this century the monuments began to exhibit considerable accessorial enrichment; small sculptured and painted figures being introduced in the inferior parts of the work. Sometimes they were placed in small niches, and represented saints, or the priests of the church, and, it is supposed, mourning relatives. At this time tombs with richly decorated arches, and "testoons" or canopies, were introduced. From this date a more extended character of design appeared, and an exceedingly interesting class of ecclesiastical monuments became the fashion. Works of the most elaborate decoration, in memory of kings, queens, nobles, warriors—indeed of all persons of dignity and position, or others whose relatives could command the means of paying such monumental honours—enriched the churches of the land. Sometimes at the sides of the pillow on which the head of the effigy rests are small attending angels, like guardian spirits of the departed; sometimes they appear to be simply watching; sometimes they are represented administering the rites of the church, as throwing incense or praying. The elaborate treatment of such works, from the time of Edward III. to Henry VII., shews how such monuments may be highly decorated, and yet be in entire accordance with the true spirit of religious design.

From what has already been shewn of the condition of sculpture at the date referred to, the student will not expect to find here examples of high art; that is, of noble form and of what has been called *ideal* beauty. For other qualities, however, independent of technical recommendations—as repose and simplicity of treatment—he will find that many of these works offer valuable subject of reflection to the artist who desires to make his productions speak to the feelings and sympathies of the spectator.

It is a curious fact, and worthy to be noticed here in connection with the condition of sculpture, that when the architecture of the period is said to have reached its culminating point, in the perfection of the so-called Pointed and Decorated styles, the sculpture, associated with it accessorially, should, with respect to beauty of form and technical excellence, have been in a state of *quasi* barbarism and rudeness.

In the era of excellence of Greek art, architecture and sculpture went hand in hand, the latter the handmaid of the former. It is fair to assume—though architecture cannot be judged by the same test as sculpture, namely, truth to nature—that as this latter art was developed, step by step, among the Greeks, till it reached its highest perfection, the architecture with which it was so nobly and usefully associated was equally perfect. The condition of one would, it may be presumed, be a guarantee of the state of the other. It certainly was not so in the centuries under immediate consideration, and it leaves room for the supposition that, instead of having reached its maturity when it began its decline, Gothic architecture at the time referred to was only in a state of progress, and that its full development or climax was arrested by some cause or causes that have not been explained or ascertained. If, as has been declared, this phase of architecture had reached its perfection, as the crowning result of principles thoroughly carried out, and was not rather the rare and, it must be admitted, charming effect of mere fanciful combinations,* how can it be satisfactorily accounted

* This feeling is not unnaturally suggested by the character of some of the ornaments and accessories of Gothic architecture; in the unmeaning, however decorative, crockets and finials; in the squeezing of figures of saints and others represented standing, in horizontal and curved sunk mouldings; in the employment of the human head and face as brackets for supporting heavy weights, to say nothing of the irreverent use often made of monks and other ecclesiastical characters, mixed up with nondescript monsters, to act, with widely-opened mouths, as gurgoyles or draining pipes for throwing off the rain from the roofs of buildings.

for that the auxiliary arts of painting and sculpture of the same period were in so very imperfect a condition? But they not only did not partake of this assumed developed perfection in the architecture of the time, but, on the contrary, were even very far below what these two arts were, under ordinary intelligent direction, capable of achieving. Sculpture was no new, unknown art, and painting was not a recent discovery. Besides, these arts being imitative, and having their standard in nature, could easily be judged by a sure and unmistakeable cánon. If the age was incapable of seeing how far short of this standard these arts fell, it seems not unreasonable to doubt whether it was altogether capable of bringing to perfection a totally new style of architecture; or, without detracting at all from the great inventive powers in its designers, that there was the artistic ability existing to develope a perfect form of one art when its professors were unable to perceive that the *imitative* arts employed to assist its effects were in so defective a state.

It must be remembered that Gothic architecture was entirely unknown in the earlier and purer ages of Christianity. The first recognised monuments of the style, of an approved type, date as late as the twelfth and thirteenth centuries. It scarcely lasted above 180 or 200 years, and during that comparatively short period it was practised fitfully and, as is proved by the distinctive names given to the styles, with constant changes of one kind or other. In the fifteenth century it already began to show symptoms of decline; and it is considered by its historians and admirers to have sensibly degraded in the following century, and to have died out in what has been called the Perpendicular school. Its innate power must therefore have been either extremely weak, or, as is more probable—seeing how much that is noble, and beautiful, and picturesque, characterises the finest Gothic remains—its progress was arrested before it had attained its full development and the perfection of which, no doubt, it was capable.

It may still be possible to recover the broken link, and, with the ability and zeal that are now brought to bear upon the subject, to restore the successful study of this peculiar and original phase of art, with which the national feeling, it may be said, is so strongly associated. If this should be effected, the sister arts of painting and sculpture may then be made worthily to assist in giving additional splendour and interest, as decorative and illustrative accessories, to a style of architecture especially adapted to receive the best enrichment that these respective arts, in their present advanced condition, can give them.*

* One effect of this might be to suppress the pedantry and *affectation* of mediævalism in church building and decoration, which has been so striking and offensive in late years. To imitate, now, the stiff,

In referring to works of the particular class under consideration, it will be found that from its commencement till about the end of the sixteenth century, monumental sculpture exhibits the ecclesiastical or church influence of the earlier ages. It was of course modified in its forms and mode of representation, as may be seen in numerous examples of easy reference in cathedrals and older churches, but everywhere the prevailing sentiment was religious. Figures, whether they are lying recum-

attenuated figures of the sculptors and painters of the fourteenth century, and to reproduce the illegible inscriptions and confusing illuminations of that age, are, at best, *anachronisms*. The rudeness of the art of that time was the honest proof of the want of greater technical knowledge in the artists, and the lettering was, at least, that of the period. The fact of its being difficult to read was of less importance then, because this accomplishment was extremely rare, and almost confined to ecclesiastics. The painting and sculpture of the fourteenth and fifteenth centuries were neither *affected* imitations of earlier art, nor *intentionally* bad art. With all their faults they were the best that could be supplied, and their authors were too much in earnest to do less than their best. It is strange to find, in the present day, that a sham and counterfeit, in the imitation of mediævalism, can be considered by any class of persons an indication either of a knowledge of the true impulse of Christian art; or stranger still, as some seem to imagine, of devout religious feeling. It wants all that gives value to art—Truth. It will not be out of place to quote here the words of an eminent and thoughtful writer on one part of this subject. Speaking of the modern, fantastic, mediæval taste in inscriptions, he says—"It is an ill sacrifice to beauty to make that illegible whose only merit is its sense. . . . Write the commandments on the church wall, where they may be plainly seen; but do not put a dash and a tail to every letter, . . . and remember *you are an architect and not a writing-master*."

bent on their tombs or kneeling—a posture not so often met with in the principal subject in early monumental sculpture—are usually represented praying; or if not literally occupied in the act of prayer, they generally have accessories or accompaniments referring to religious exercises, or are attended by ministering angels, either supporting the cushion at the head or grouped at the feet of the person represented. There are exceptions to this rule, as in the effigies of the knights in the Temple church, and others that might be mentioned; but, generally, the sentiment described was the prevailing one in this class of works; and it is that which should pervade all designs of the kind, as the most appropriate to the place in which they are to be preserved, and as being more thoroughly in harmony with those feelings which it is the object of such monuments to excite.

In the sixteenth century a departure from this characteristic of church or monumental sculpture is observable. The first step towards its deterioration was in the desire to give more prominence to the *personal* character of the subject of the monument. It was no longer the humble, the dying, or the deceased Christian, with the hands in the attitude of prayer, or folded over the breast, or holding the Bible or a book of prayers; but the individual warrior, orator, statesman, or author, was to be distinctly portrayed. Not that the early element—

the devotional feeling—was even here entirely ignored. The knight or noble, and his dame and children, were still usually engaged in prayer, but this was rather apart and accessorial than, as it hitherto had been, the distinct purpose and sentiment of the design.

The taste exhibited in monumental design of the date of Elizabeth and James I. is exceedingly bad, as far as art is concerned; but in the monuments of that queen and of Mary Queen of Scots—both in Westminster Abbey—there still lingers the serious sentiment that required the effigy of the person commemorated to be represented as in repose, lying dead upon the couch or tomb, and not engaged in exercising any active function of life by which attention or honour should be invited only to the individual. Soon after this time this class of art still further deteriorated, and the monuments produced in the latter part of the seventeenth century are for the most part entirely wanting in the associations which seem to be so appropriate in works of this kind.

The total change in the character of sculpture required for monumental objects, and therefore to be placed in sacred edifices, is among the curious phenomena of the history of this art. There has been no employment of sculpture so likely to raise it to a lofty eminence, as a language of expression which should reach the universal sympathy of believers, as that of illustrating Scripture subjects, of commemorating the dead, and appropriately decorating the architecture of ecclesiastical buildings. Of course, in one important quality or element of which the ancients could avail themselves—the representation of the nude human figure—there necessarily has been great restraint placed upon the sculptors of modern times; and those who have understood and admired the perfection of Greek art might lament the impossibility of its introduction in contemporary religious designs. But, short of this, there was here every opportunity of making sculpture all that it had been in the best days of the art.

The most affecting episodes, the most sublime expression, whether of manly firmness or of feminine tenderness; grandeur in draped figures, as of the prophets, patriarchs, and saints; the noblest and most beautiful forms, even to the representation of the Saviour and the Virgin Mother—all presented themselves to the sculptor as legitimate and most appropriate subjects of art, and, by an almost incomprehensible fatality, were rejected. Had it been the factitious imagery of long-neglected or obsolete myths, this insensibility or disinclination of the age to their being made the subject of art might be accounted for; but it is not so easy to comprehend how a community of Christians should be insensible to the value of employing art in the representation of persons and events which had the devout belief of the whole population. The efforts of some few earnest and gifted men, exhibited in productions of touching beauty, so far as they went, in a period of little technical knowledge, had pointed out the possibility of carrying on a school of true art, and establishing sculpture on a sound and safe basis. But these failed to make a lasting impression, and the cold and affected *pseudo*-classical taste crushed out art that attempted to express real feeling; and gradually even the most affecting personal application of it, in memorials of the beloved dead, became mere heaps of academical and unmeaning statuary. This false and lifeless art was universal.

It has been asserted by prejudiced, and, upon this subject, very ill-informed writers, that the Reformation in England caused the degradation of sculpture applied to religious objects in this country. The reply to such an assumption is found in the fact—first, that at the period referred to England exercised no influence on art, and there was little or no native art to be so degraded; and, next, that it was not in England alone that this miserable decline in ecclesiastical sculpture was apparent. Throughout Christendom it underwent the same deterioration, and nowhere more strikingly than in Italy. This was especially the case in Rome, where it might be supposed the influence of the clergy would have been sufficiently powerful to preserve the traditions of the Church, and to prevent the artists from committing any very daring innovation on the established forms of Christian art, however bold and discursive they might be in their ordinary practice. In the Church of St. Peter, especially, in the monumental sculpture raised to do honour to sovereign pontiffs, cardinals, and other great Christian dignitaries, and where the utmost propriety and purity of design might naturally be expected to prevail, nothing can be worse in taste and inappropriate in sentiment, than the works erected about the period referred to. The same may be observed of the generality of monuments in other great churches of Rome, and indeed of Italy generally; of which sufficient examples have been pointed out in reviewing the succession of sculptors who flourished in the sixteenth and seventeenth centuries. This, as has been shewn, was not owing to any want of ability in the artists; so far from it, that there scarcely has been a time when there was greater technical power. The simple truth is, that the true spirit of religious art, as a language of sentiment, was a dead letter; and sculpture was only practised as an exercise which, while it contributed to form a striking feature in decoration, should gratify the ambition and love of display in the patron, or exhibit the artistic power of the sculptor.

The above remarks apply to memorial sculpture;

that is, to monuments to the dead, placed in churches where, especially, a certain character of sentiment should prevail. It is difficult to understand how another class of designs, found in the carved decorations of chancel seats and screens, in many of the religious edifices in England and elsewhere — of a date long prior to the Reformation—could have been acceptable to the people; and, what is more remarkable, permitted by the clergy, who of course had the care of the churches, and the direction and supervision of all works carried on in them. Many of these have been destroyed or removed, in later times (as may be seen in the scraped or cut away portions still left), the character of their subjects being too offensive to be allowed any longer to scandalize places of worship. The fact of their ever having been permitted, and of the prevalence of such inappropriate decoration for churches, affords a strange picture of the state of public morals, whether of the clergy or laity, at the time. It, at any rate, suggests grave doubts as to the quality of the religious feeling in the fourteenth and fifteenth centuries, when such subjects could have been admissible in a place of worship.

In England the falling off in the religious character of the design of monumental sculpture in the seventeenth and eighteenth centuries was not, as in Italy, compensated for by the merit of the technical art displayed in them. The larger class of such works were heavy, cumbersome erections, crowded with architectural members, upon which shields, lozenges, *pateras*, foliage, and every kind of enrichment, were lavished. In addition to the sculptured forms of this inappropriate ornamentation, gilding and painting, in every variety of colour, were resorted to; and the real subject of the work—the deceased—was all but lost in the confusion and multiplicity of accessories above, below, and around him. Of designs of the kind the student will find many curious instances in Westminster Abbey; and he cannot but be struck with the painful contrast they exhibit, in sentiment, to the more simple and affecting monumental erections that present themselves in the same building. In that church a study of the whole subject may advantageously be made. Examples occur, from the twelfth century down to the period now under consideration, in which may be clearly traced the changes that have so fatally acted on ecclesiastical sculpture of this class.

It has been observed that there was still the indication of the original impulse in many of the monuments of the declining period, however overlaid by details of bad taste and inconsistent accessories. A further deterioration was however possible, and this was effected by altogether omitting from such designs any reference whatever to religious hopes or feelings. Monuments were erected in which the deceased was no longer represented lying recumbent on his tomb or on his deathbed, or even kneeling in prayer. He appeared full dressed, and with a well-curled peruke on his head; either lolling negligently on a couch, resting on his elbow, and complacently looking around him; or sitting comfortably in his chair, holding a book or roll of paper; or perhaps mounted in a niche or pulpit, writing. Sometimes he is represented in action, making a speech, or brandishing a sword, or as if leading a charge or defying the enemy. But there is no accessory, nor any sentiment in the chief figure of the composition which has any reference to its being the monument of a deceased Christian, or to account in any way for its having a place in a church. It need scarcely be remarked that where there is such entire neglect of true and appropriate sentiment in the work, it is not to be wondered at that all other proprieties are disregarded. If the taste of either the artist or his employers inclined to the classical mode, modern heroes or worthies appear in the confused costumes of ancient Greeks and Romans; or, if they preferred the "natural" or the commonplace, in the ordinary dress of the day. Sometimes, indeed, a still more anomalous treatment is resorted to, where the modern dress is combined with ancient classical costume—the flowing wig of the eighteenth century with the naked legs and sandals of various Roman periods. This condition of sculpture is seen in almost all the monumental designs on the continent of that date; and that this false taste was imported into England from abroad, admits of no question, when the state of art at this period is considered. No stand could be made against the introduction of a prevailing fashion where there was so little interest in and patronage of art among the higher classes, and when its practice among native sculptors was almost, if not quite unknown. Foreign artists, who alone obtained favour among the wealthy and influential, found it easy to dictate to employers utterly ignorant of the true principles of art; and thus, dashing design and the curiosities of elaborate execution were supposed to be proofs of the highest powers in the sculptor. The effects of this may be seen in the works of the French and Flemish artists, and of their English imitators, which are distributed all over the country.

Affectation in sentiment and action, confusion of costume, far-fetched allegory, characterise the productions generally. Many of the works exhibit, it may be admitted, a considerable amount of technical skill; but this affords but little compensation for the absence of true artistic feeling in the subjects, and indeed makes its deficiency the more to be lamented. It is not necessary to do more than make a passing allusion to the evil influence exercised on all art in this country during the civil wars in the seventeenth century. Political divisions were rendered even more irreconcilable by the stern, uncompromising spirit of religious fanaticism which separated the two great parties then contending for power. The popular feeling had been so excited against the alleged abuses of the Romish Church, and the charge of idolatry brought against it, that the utmost horror was exhibited at finding objects of sculpture and painting in places of worship, and wherever they were met with they were ruthlessly and barbarously destroyed. This outburst of narrow Puritan prejudice against art in ecclesiastical buildings, and in connection with religion—one of its noblest applications—extinguished, for a long time, all hope and chance of its restoration to a healthy condition.

It was in this class of art especially that the great English sculptor Flaxman opened the road to a great revolution. That the example he set in the sentiment of art was not followed to the extent that would have restored ecclesiastical and monumental sculpture to something like consistent and appropriate character must be admitted, and is deeply to be deplored. But, unfortunately, although the number of sculptors was increasing, there was so little knowledge of art in England, among that class especially who might have assisted in giving it a wholesome impulse—the aristocracy and the better educated—that it scarcely can be a matter of surprise that the small minority of those who were at all capable of appreciating the value of a movement in a new direction were unable to give full effect to what, in the estimation of the general public, was an uncalled-for innovation.

It never has been thought worthy the consideration of the richest nation of modern times to educate either its higher classes or the people generally in the principles of fine art, or to teach them the value of the beautiful. It is but comparatively lately that government schools for the express purpose of elementary instruction in drawing and modelling have been established. Even this has been done under pressure from without, and avowedly only with the view of improving our manufactures and ornamental design; so that it is chiefly for utilitarian purposes that this tardy effort has been made to improve the universally felt inferiority of this country in this particular. The universities, the great seats of education for the upper classes, do not include in their scheme of study any provision for enabling those who desire the knowledge to acquire a competent acquaintance with the history and practice of those arts which, when properly exercised, more than anything attest the degree of refinement and the high civilization of a people; and, as is proved by the admiration still bestowed on the noble monuments of antiquity and the homage paid to the productions of the great artists of more modern times, give character and lasting glory to the nations in which the fine arts have been most successfully exercised.

The survey taken of sculpture through the long vista of years, from the age of Pericles in Greece to the present century, touches certain facts upon which the fortunes, the success, and the decline of this art have depended. The hope of restoring sculpture to a safe and healthy condition must depend upon the conclusions the sculptor, as well as the unprofessional promoter of art, may draw from the history of the great influential schools. It may be added that it is from the higher classes—the educated, the independent, and the influential portion of society—that the impulse for effecting this good must mainly be derived. There can be little fear, with the admitted executive power of the best sculptors of the present day, that the hand will fail to do its work, if those who desire its cunning will aid and support it in producing designs worthy of a refined and noble art. Such influence is quite distinct from meddling interference in matters in which the artist, from his practical experience, ought to be the best judge what is right; but it may be brought to bear most usefully and efficiently in sometimes controlling, at others in suggesting, the choice and the treatment of subjects fitted for art, and in elevating, by association and intercourse, the feeling and the aspirations of the artist, whose opportunities may have been limited, and whose occupations may allow him but little time for prosecuting studies not immediately connected with practice; but which, indirectly, are of the highest advantage, in their power of purifying the taste, enlarging the mind, and awakening his intelligence.

It might be expected that a much more careful review of sculpture in England than has been given should find a place in the history of the art, and would form a fitting conclusion to this treatise. But the difficulty of speaking of contemporary artists, with the freedom which alone would make an examination of the productions of the English school of any value, is sufficient reason for not carrying down the inquiry lower than the beginning of the present century. It has already been stated, that the object has not been to give an account of modern sculpture of any particular nation; but to survey the march of the art comprehensively, from its origin downwards, through various phases of its progress and practice in the most remarkable ancient schools, and among the nations where sculpture was almost a necessity, as a means of expressing ideas; and where, excepting painting, no other mode of addressing the popular feelings by palpable illustration was known. Sculpture had this character and mission in ancient Assyria, Egypt, and Greece; among the Romans partly so; but with the more modern nations it was adopted only, and used according to circumstances. In the early Christian time, with the artists of the so-called revival, it, in a measure, fulfilled the office of ancient art; but, technically, it was rude and of little value. It soon, however, as has been shewn, lost the hold it was taking on the public feeling as a handmaid to religious teaching, and sculpture drifted, with the current of *pseudo*-classicism, into a cold, senseless imitation of Greek and Roman figure-making. This has influenced, more or less, its condition in all the schools which have grown out of the impulse of the sixteenth and seventeenth centuries; and differences have only been perceptible in the modes of technical treatment.

It has been remarked, not without great apparent reason, that sculpture has essentially remained true to its old faith. The practice of modern artists has helped to perpetuate this tendency. It has appeared to be the object of sculptors again and again to return to the heathen mythology and classical poetry for their subjects, wherever they have desired to exhibit their talent in this art. If, as has been attempted—and it cannot be said always unsuccessfully—subjects have been sought that address themselves to modern sympathies, it must be allowed that one source of excellence in Greek sculpture is to a great extent proscribed. The habits of modern life are opposed to the free exhibition of the most beautiful forms that can be offered—the human;

and however successfully the subjects themselves that address modern sympathy may be presented, there must be, and ever will be, a striking inferiority to the art, as art, which could and did represent the human male and female form in its perfection. No doubt the foundation of excellence in all imitative art is *nature*, and wherever this excellence is sought in sculpture—and the sculptors themselves know and admit it—the highest eclectic standard is presented in the best Greek examples. In reviewing sculpture, reference is constantly and necessarily made to these; and it is no reflection on the ability, or the feeling, or the skill of the sculptor of the day, whether in Italy, France, England, or elsewhere, to say that, however accomplished he may be, the real judge of art in contemplating his performance, will intuitively, and almost without the power to control the impulse, compare the modern work with an *ideal* suggested by his knowledge of Greek sculpture. Indeed, the better the work, the more certainly will it be subjected to this trying comparison; and as the most ambitious productions are generally taken from classic authors, this comparison is the more absolutely and directly challenged. The modern sculptor, therefore, always prosecutes his art at a considerable disadvantage. Even if his work is founded on the highest Greek standard, and approaches very nearly the best ancient examples; nay, if, as may be the case, it be, in technical qualities, equal to them, it is felt it could not have been achieved at all independently of the ancient exemplars; and therefore it still is, after all, but an imitation, more or less, of Greek sculpture. If it bears no resemblance to it, the chance is that it will still more surely fail; that is, it never will be classed as a work of high art, to take its place by the side of the antique, to be admired by competent judges, or placed in schools and proposed to students of sculpture as a standard for their imitation. It may have great and various recommendation, in intention, and sentiment, and execution; but as an example of high sculpture, it will simply be pronounced unequal to what the Greeks could and did effect in the same direction. Another difficulty meets the historian in discussing modern sculpture. It is not now the original mind of the artist that seeks expression, so much as the desire to imitate the art of some particular age or phase of opinion. Thus one school professes to take all its inspiration from ancient classical Greek sculpture, adopting its subjects without always understanding them, and copying their forms and even extraneous accessories —as in introducing colour—because authority for it may be found among the Greeks; others, objecting to paganism in art, and justly alive to the want of power in the ancient forms to awaken modern sympathy, seek their examples in the mediæval and more modern standards;—the former of these quite out of date in its modes; and the other, the realistic, too often falling into vulgarity and commonplace. In neither of these forms of sculpture, nor in the varieties founded on them, is there any scope for discussing the art in a way that bears upon its general history; for all these have had due consideration in their proper place.

To review more particularly than has been done the modern practice of sculpture would not then be of any real service in illustrating the history of the art. It would only be, at best, the statement of the peculiarities that have crept into the practice of individual artists, whereby, in some instances, a kind of national character appears in the art produced in different countries. The task of commenting upon these, where the illustrations must be drawn from the works of contemporary and living artists, would be an invidious undertaking for any one, even if he should consider himself competent to enter upon so delicate an examination; but it would be one of especial difficulty to the present writer, who might feel some distrust of his own judgment, and whose motives might be misunderstood, however conscientiously he might desire and intend to fulfil the office of a critic and a judge.

Conclusion.

It only remains now to make a few remarks upon the technical operations of the sculptor.

The processes of sculpture are now so generally known that it scarcely seems necessary to describe them; but as a history of the art would not be complete without some little explanation of the mechanical and technical conduct of the work, a general notice of the sculptor's mode of proceeding is here added.

The artist having invented or conceived his subject, usually begins by making a small sketch of it in some soft and obedient substance, as clay or wax. He can change and alter this at his pleasure till he is satisfied with the lines and masses of the composition, and the proportions it will command of light and shadow. He then proceeds to copy this small but useful sketch, as his guide, in its general arrangement, for his full-sized model. Before commencing the larger model it is necessary to form a sort of skeleton or framework of iron and wood, with joints made of wire to support the great mass of clay in which the figure or group is now to be executed. This iron frame is firmly fixed upon a turning bench, or banker, so that the model may be constantly moved without difficulty, so as to be seen in different lights and in various points of view. As the clay is likely to shrink as it gets dry, it is necessary occasionally to wet it. This is done by sprinkling water over it with a brush, or from a large syringe, and by laying damp cloths upon it. This is the ordinary process for making a model in the "round."

In modelling in *rilievo* of either kind, *alto* or *basso*, a plane or ground is prepared upon which the design is, or should be, carefully drawn. This may be made of clay floated or laid upon a board, or the ground may be of slate or even of wood, though the latter is objectionable, in large works especially, from its liability to shrink and to be warped by the action of damp or moisture. The clay is then laid in small quantities upon this ground, the outline being bounded by the drawing, which should always be carefully preserved; and the bulk or projection of the figures is regulated by the degree of relief the sculptor desires to give to his design.

If the final work is to be in baked clay (*terra-cotta*) there must be no iron or wooden nucleus, as it would interfere with the model drying regularly and uniformly, and probably cause it to crack in shrinking. The model is therefore prepared for drying without such support. When perfectly free from moisture, the model is placed in an oven and slowly baked, by which it acquires great hardness and the peculiar brownish-red colour seen in these works. This art has been brought to great perfection in England within the last few years.

If the final work is to be in marble, or bronze, or only

in plaster, the next process after finishing the model is to mould it, in preparation for its being reproduced in a material that will bear moving about without risk of injury to the design. This is done by covering it with a mixture of plaster of Paris with water, which quickly sets or becomes consistent, forming a hard and thick coating over the whole. The clay is then carefully picked out, and an exact matrix or form remains. This is washed clean, and the interior is then brushed over with any greasy substance, usually a composition of soap and oil, to prevent the plaster with which it is next to be filled adhering too firmly to it. The fresh plaster is mixed to about the consistency of cream, and then poured into the mould, which is gently moved about till the inner surface is entirely filled or covered, so that all parts may be reached. The thickness or substance of the coating depends upon the size of the work, and the degree of strength required.

When the newly introduced plaster is set the mould is carefully knocked away with chisels, and a true cast appears beneath, giving an entire fac-simile of the original model. Some skill is required in making moulds, in order to provide for projecting parts and undercuttings; practice alone can teach the artist how to deal with those difficulties when they occur. The above general instructions sufficiently explain the ordinary processes of moulding and casting in plaster.

In metal-casting or founding great attention must be paid to the strengthening of the parts to bear the weight of the metal; but the principle described in plaster-moulding applies also to the preparation for metal-casting. The mixture of metals to form bronze, the proper heating of the furnace, burning and uniting parts, chasing, and other processes of founding, cannot be fully described in this place. They belong to a distinct practice, and to be well understood must be studied in the foundry.

If the model—now reproduced in plaster—is to be copied in marble or stone, the first step is to procure a block of the required size. Two stones, called *scale-stones*, are then prepared, upon one of which the model or plaster cast is placed, and upon the other the rough block of marble. The fronts of these stones have figured marks or "scales," to use the technical term, exactly corresponding. An instrument, capable of being easily moved and which is fitted up with socket-joints and movable arms, is then applied to the scale-stone of the model, and a projecting point or "needle" is made to touch a particular part of the model itself. This is carefully removed to the scale-stone of the rough block, and the marble is cut away till the "needle" reaches so far into the block as to correspond with the "point" taken on the model. A pencil-mark is then made to shew that the *point* is found and registered. This process is repeated all over the model and the block, alternately, till a rough copy or shape of the model is entirely made. These "pointing" machines are not always precisely alike in their forms, but the principle upon which they act is exactly similar in all. The statue being thus rudely shaped out, the block is placed in the hands of a superior workman, called a "carver," who, having the plastic model near at hand to refer to, copies the more minute portions of the work by means of chisels, rasps, and files; the pencil-marks made by the "pointer" shewing him the precise situation of the parts and the limits beyond which he is not to penetrate into the marble. When the carver has carried the work as far as the sculptor desires, he proceeds himself to give it the finishing touches, improving the details of form and expression, managing the different effects produced by two different materials—one, the plastic model, being opaque; the other, the marble, being considerably diaphanous: giving the proper varieties of texture in the flesh, hair, and drapery, and, more especially, harmonizing the whole.

The rich quality of surface that appears more or less in works in marble is produced by rubbing, with fine sand or pumice-stone and other substances, and the ancients appear to have completed this part of their work by a process which, as has been observed in speaking of "*circumlitio*," may probably mean not only rubbing or polishing, but applying some composition, such as hot wax, to give a soft glowing colour to the surface. Many of the ancient statues certainly exhibit the appearance of some foreign substance having slightly penetrated the surface of the work to about one-eighth of an inch, and its colour is of a warmer tint than the marble below it; a process, be it observed, quite distinct from and not to be confounded with *polychromy,* or what is usually understood by painting sculpture with various tints, in imitation of the *natural* colour of the complexion, hair, and eyes. Its object, probably, with the ancients as with modern sculptors, has been simply to get rid of the glare and freshness of appearance that is sometimes objected to in a recently finished work, by giving a general warmth to the colour of the marble.

INDEX.

obtained

2

9 783752 592092